Rhythm's Blues

Kimberly Brown

B. Love Publications

Author's Note

This work of fiction includes strong language and lewd sex scenes. If this is not your cup of tea, please choose something else from my catalog. Please leave a rating/review on Amazon/Goodreads if you like this book!

Chapter One

Rhythm Baker

I sat with my back against the headboard, listening to the *Talk of the Town* podcast on the radio that sat next to my bed. My boyfriend of three years was today's special guest. Raheem Cole, professionally known as Prince Cole, was a worldwide superstar to others, but to me, he was simply Raheem. We'd known each other since high school, back when he was making up beats on the cafeteria table with his homeboys or recording his rhymes in the closet turned studio in his childhood bedroom.

He always knew he'd make it big, and so did I. What began as a pipe dream, to some, soon became his reality. He got his big break right after graduation. Producers had been looking at him for the longest due to the popularity of his YouTube channel. He promised his mother that he would at least get his high school diploma before pursuing his music full time.

As soon as we graduated, he was on the first flight to L.A. that same day. Since then, his career had blown up, and so had he. I couldn't turn my head without seeing his face on a magazine cover or social media or hearing his songs on the airways. I was proud of him. Unlike some of our classmates, he'd accomplished everything he'd set out to do.

Three and a half years ago, we ran across each other when he performed at homecoming for my alma mater. I wasn't one of those girls who was star stuck by celebrities. While other girls in the crowd were screaming their heads off and showing their titties while he performed, I stood in the audience just vibing and rapping the lyrics.

I had front row seats, and his set was almost over when he stepped over to one of his security guards and pointed at me in the crowd. I thought nothing of it when he came back out and jumped into the last song of the night. His head of security approached me and told me to follow him. I was a little hesitant, but I followed him backstage to Raheem's dressing room.

After what seemed like forever, he came in, the sounds of screaming fans echoing behind him.

"Rhythm Baker. How the hell you doing, girl?"

While I could never forget him, I was surprised he'd remembered me. We hadn't seen each other in about eight years. He pulled me in for a hug, damn near lifting me from the ground.

"Damn, you look good," he said, placing me back on my feet. "I mean, you were always a beautiful girl, but shit, you filled out. What are you doing around these parts?"

"I graduated from SCSU. I had to come represent my alma mater for homecoming."

"I feel you. It's good to see you. You know, I've thought about you over the years."

"Have you?"

"Of course. I've never met another Rhythm. You know music is my life. Every time I made a beat when I first started, I thought of you."

I blushed. Truth be told, I'd always had a little crush on Raheem. I just never thought he'd be interested in a girl like me. We'd always kept it friendly, so to hear him say that was shocking.

*"Well, I'm glad to see you doing what you always said you would,"
I said, tucking my hair behind my ear. "I knew you'd be successful."*

"I appreciate that. What are you doing these days?"

"Occupational therapy. I work at Baptist back home."

*"I can see you doing that. You've always been a people person.
Listen, I have to get out of here, but I'd love to catch up with you. It's
always good seeing a familiar face. Maybe I could get your number?
I'm not sure how long you'll be in town, but I'd love to see you before I
head out."*

"Um... sure."

*He handed me his phone, and I programmed my number in before
giving it back.*

"I'ma call you when I get settled in tonight, okay?"

"Okay."

*He started for the door, but his hand lingered on the knob for a
moment. Turning back, he strolled over to me. He pushed a stray hair
out of my face and cupped my chin. His eyes met mine, and he licked
his lips.*

"There's something I've always wanted to do," he said softly.

"What's that?"

"This."

*Leaning in, he kissed me sweetly. I was slightly shocked that it was
happening. For a moment, I stood frozen, unable to believe that my
childhood crush was kissing me. When I finally snapped out of it, I
didn't hesitate to kiss him back.*

That was the beginning of it all.

I met him for lunch the next day, and it was like a fucking circus.
He was mauled by fans everywhere we went. They followed his car.
They waited outside of his hotel. Some of them even snuck up to the
floor he was staying on. While I enjoyed the little quiet time we got, I
quickly learned that I hated the spotlight.

I was a low-key type of woman.

Back then, I didn't rock the latest fashions. I didn't drive an
expensive car. I wasn't at every party, trying to be seen. I enjoyed my

simple life with my simple job. It brought me satisfaction. I would never fit in with his world. When I told him that, he said he understood, but that didn't stop him from pursuing me.

For six months, he randomly popped in to visit me, and he always wore a disguise so we could have some privacy. He completely toned down his image so that he was barely recognizable when we went out in public. It was nice to have a normal dinner or trip to the store with him. In those six months, I fell hard for him, and when he officially asked me to be his girl, I said yes. After a year, I moved out to L.A with him.

He took care of my every need and even footed the bill for me to open my own occupational therapy clinic, The Baker Method. Things had been good with us. I stayed out of the spotlight yet remained the super supportive girlfriend. It wasn't until fans started pushing him and his female labelmate together did a problem arise.

For too long, I'd been dealing with seeing the two of them in the blogs and listening to the rumors that they were dating. He assured me nothing was going on, yet he made no effort to let it be known he was in a whole ass relationship. He waved it off like it was no big deal, telling me that this was the music business.

Fuck that. I may not be seen but claim me.

As I sat planted next to my radio, I waited to see if it would come up today.

"Multi-platinum, multi-talented artist, Prince Cole is in the building, everybody. Thanks for being here, Prince!"

"Thanks so much for having me. It's great to be here! Y'all always show me so much love, so I had to slide through and pull up on you real quick."

"Fa'sho, fa'sho. Let's jump right into it. Your latest album Lyrical Warfare *is got some major buzz, and the single 'Street Scriptures' rode that number one spot on the charts for six weeks straight. What has this experience been like for you?"*

"It's been lit. Seriously, it's been beyond anything I could have imagined. Making that album was slight work, but the one I'm

4

working on is a tedious process. I hired a whole new team to make this shit what it is. This is my golden era, ya feel me? I needed the best of the best 'cause I'm a beast at what I do. I've been at this music thing for a long time. To see my lyrics still resonating with so many people is overwhelming in the best way."

"Right, right. The songs on the album seem personal to you. Is songwriting therapeutic for you? Where do you draw your inspiration?"

"Songwriting is therapeutic. It's how I process emotions and experiences. A lot of the songs were inspired by shit I went through and people around me. I didn't grow up with a silver spoon in my mouth. My mom worked two jobs to provide for me and my siblings 'cause these slack ass baby daddies ain't step up to the plate. But that's a story for another day. The music is a reflection of my life, growing up, and finding myself."

"I feel you on that, my brotha. Now, I'ma ask a question the fans are dying to know. What's going on with you and Lady Lingo? Y'all have been spotted everywhere together. You have a hit record with her, and I heard a new one is coming. I see the chemistry, so I'ma just ask. That's you?"

Raheem chuckled. "Come on now. That's just my labelmate. We vibe off each other in the studio. It's musical magic, nothing more."

The host chuckled. "A'ight, a'ight. So is there anybody special in your life? The ladies are listening."

Again, Raheem chuckled. "I'm just chillin' and doing me."

I frowned.

Just chillin' and doing him? What the fuck was that? He was out here acting like I wasn't here sitting in the home we shared. Like I wasn't making home-cooked meals and doing his laundry. Like I didn't fuck and suck him on the regular.

Tossing back the covers, I climbed to my feet and grabbed my phone off the charger. Before I could get to my call log to give my best friend, Monique, a call, she was calling me.

"Bitch!" she exclaimed.

"You heard that shit, right? I wasn't tripping?"

"Hell no, you ain't tripping."

"Why the fuck would he say that?"

"This industry shit is going to his head, boo. I know bitches love rappers and shit and it's all about his image, but what he ain't finna do is play with you like that."

"Nique, I'm so sick of this shit. Like, I get it. I'm not in the spotlight, but damn. He's been moving real funny lately, especially when it comes to that shit with Lady Lingo. Like, how many times is he gonna be photographed with that bitch sitting on his lap, whispering in his ear, and shit? He keeps telling me it's nothing, but he's not acting like it's nothing."

I flopped down on my bed and buried my face in the pillow. I willed myself not to cry, but this shit was really getting to me. I loved Raheem, but he was changing. To have been in the music industry for the last ten years, he was acting real brand new right now. I couldn't pretend that I wasn't unbothered. I could feel it happening in slow motion.

Part of me felt like it was my fault for keeping my identity under wraps. I didn't want my success to be based off his name. True, he footed the bill for the building, but I worked hard to grow my business to what it was. My clinic was one of the best in the city. We'd been featured in the news and magazines. We'd been nominated for awards. In a year and a half of its opening, we'd gained such notoriety, and I was proud of what I'd accomplished without his name being attached to it.

Of course, I supported him. I was his biggest cheerleader, next to his mother. There were countless nights where I stayed up with him in the studio until he got a track perfectly recorded. I listened to him spit his lyrics and gave him feedback. I looked over contracts before he signed them. I learned so much about the music industry so that I could support him on the back end.

I did it out of love, and for him to downplay our relationship like it was nothing hurt me. We didn't have to be the power couple, or *it* couple, but he didn't have to play like I didn't exist at all.

* * *

Later That Night

I jumped as the sound of music blaring woke me from my slumber.

After getting off the phone with Monique earlier, I'd consumed two bottles of wine and had myself a "Fuck That Nigga" party. Music was played. Tears were shed. I called Raheem and cursed out his voicemail because that muthafucka never answered my calls. He knew I listened to the bogus ass interview and that I was pissed, so I was sure he was trying to avoid the backlash as long as possible.

Looking over at the clock, I saw it was almost two a.m. Frowning, I tossed back the covers. The volume of the music had gone down, but it didn't matter. I was awake now, and once again, I was angry. Climbing out of bed, I shoved my feet into my slippers and stormed out of the room in nothing but my sports bra and boy shorts.

Furiously, I descended the stairs. I walked into the living room to find it filled with the potent smell of weed and cigarette smoke. Raheem and his flunkies sat around, passing about four blunts in rotation as they talked amongst themselves.

"Raheem!" I yelled over the music.

He was still smoking and vibing like he didn't hear me. I stormed over to the speaker and shut it off. Six sets of eyes looked up at me. Smiles broke out on the faces of his friends. Several of them licked their lips at me, but I paid them no mind.

"Did we wake you up, baby?" Raheem asked lazily. "Aye, where yo' clothes at? Y'all niggas, close your fucking eyes."

The one I knew as Rod smirked. "Too late. We've seen it all. I see why you keep her locked away. You bad as hell, lil mama."

I held up a hand dismissively. "Raheem, it's damn near two in the morning."

"I know, baby. We lost track of time in the studio. I had this fly ass track I wanted to add to the album—"

"I don't give a damn! They gotta go. I'm not trying to have it smell like weed in here and I'm trying to sleep."

"My bad, baby. We can turn the music down and take it outside—"

"No. They need to go, and you can go with them for all I care."

His friends looked at him and broke out in laughter.

"Damn, she mad at you, nigga," said another one I knew as Mikko.

Raheem waved me off. "She's always mad lately." He ashed his blunt and stood to his feet. "A'ight. Y'all heard the lady. Y'all gotta bounce."

They all groaned as they climbed to their feet. Raheem walked them to the door, and they said their goodbyes. Closing the door, he turned to me.

"Happy?"

"Don't do that. Why the hell would you bring them in here this time of morning?"

"Why would you come downstairs looking like this? Got niggas looking at your ass and shit."

"Fuck them niggas, and fuck you too, Raheem."

He shook his head. "Now it's fuck me? Come on. Let me have it. I got your voicemails and text messages. Go on and get it off your chest 'cause that's what it's really about."

I laughed. "I was gonna let you live until morning about that, but we can take it there. What the fuck did you mean you're just chillin' and doing you?"

"Rhythm... you know I love you. This is just industry shit. It's part of my image—"

"Is it part of your image to look like you're sleeping with your labelmate, Raheem?"

8

"You know I'm not sleeping with that girl."

"I don't know what you're doing. According to you, you're single."

"Look... I'ma be honest. The label thinks it would be a good idea for she and I to pretend to be a couple. It would be good for business. We're the highest grossing artists they have. A fake relationship could open up big shit for both of us. We'd be on some power couple shit and touching more money than we've ever seen—"

"Raheem, have you lost your mind? I'm not going for that shit."

"It wouldn't be real—"

"I don't give a fuck! What the hell do I look like allowing you to parade your fake girlfriend on your arm while I sit at home waiting for you?"

"You're the one that doesn't wanna be in the spotlight! You don't wanna walk the red carpet. You insist on being in the fucking background at my shows or events when you need to be out front being the loudest person in the room. You wanna be private and shit like you don't wanna be seen with me."

"Private does not equate to being kept a fucking secret. No, I don't like the spotlight. I'm sorry if I don't want to walk around with a camera or microphone being shoved in my face on the daily. I'm sorry that I don't want the world invading our private lives. I'm sorry I don't want gossip blogs spreading rumors and or putting together false narratives about us because somebody caught us having an argument, or I looked the least bit upset. You wanna talk about support?

"I'm at local every show when you perform. I manage your biggest fan pages across all platforms. I pray for you more than your black ass even knows! Background or foreground, I support you in every way, but I am not an accessory, Raheem. You understood that when you pursued me. Now it's a problem?"

He sighed heavily. "You know what the problem is, Rhythm? You wanna be with me, but you want me to choose between being Raheem and Prince. I give you everything. You don't want for shit. But you don't wanna do the work it takes to be a part of my brand—"

I scoffed. "Your brand?"

"Yes, my brand. I have an image to uphold."

I shook my head. "Well, I'm so sorry that I don't fit into your image anymore. Maybe I never did."

"What's that supposed to mean?"

"It means maybe this relationship has run its course."

"You serious right now?"

"You want me to be more than I am, and I want to mean more to you than I do. Where do we go from that?"

He looked at me but didn't say anything. He simply shook his head. Walking past me, he headed for the stairs.

"Where are you going?" I asked.

"To bed. I'm gonna pretend like you didn't say that dumb ass shit."

The next thing I heard was the sound of the bedroom door slamming shut. I took a seat on the couch and buried my face in my hands. I loved him, I really did. But I refused to be embarrassed because he wanted to portray a certain image to the media. The Raheem I knew was a man of his word. The Raheem I knew didn't give a fuck about what others thought of him. He was true to himself.

I didn't know who that man upstairs was, but it wasn't my Raheem.

Chapter Two

Channing Watson

I sat with my eyes closed, bobbing my head to the beat and lyrics as I played it back. Stella Solar was absolutely going to be the next big thing to hit the R&B scene. She had it all—the voice, the talent, the looks, the stage presence... all of it. I discovered her one night when I went to this open mic.

Every now and then, I liked to scout for new and undiscovered talents. I wasn't talking about people who made YouTube videos or posted themselves singing on social media. I was looking for the raw underground shit. Those were the types of people who one would never guess possessed the talent they did. They came to open mics or performed at little hole-in-the-wall spots just because they loved the vibe.

That was Stella Solar. The twenty-three-year-old waitress with vocals that sounded like a mixture of Jennifer Hudson and Fantasia had no idea she possessed a life-changing talent. Baby had lungs for days. She could silence the crowd with her vocals. The first time I heard her sing, there was dead silence when she finished.

It took a moment for people to digest what they heard, but after that, she got a standing ovation that was well deserved. From that point, she gave me goosebumps every time I heard her blow.

As the track came to an end, I opened my eyes. Stella was looking at me with hopeful eyes.

"What do you think?" she asked in a small voice.

Her speaking tone was so meek that one wouldn't think she could sing the way she did.

"You did an amazing job, Stella. I really like how smooth your vocals sounded on the last take, but let's see if we can add a bit more grit and passion this time."

"I'll channel some extra emotion into it this time."

"That would be great. Make it sound like you're really feeling the lyrics. And maybe we could slow down the phrasing a bit too... let it breathe in places."

"Okay, I got it."

She blew a breath and shook her hands like she was shaking away the nervousness. She really had nothing to worry about. She took direction extremely well, unlike some artists I worked with.

"Run that back," I told my assistant, Marco.

He ran the track back while Stella waited for her cue. When the beat dropped, she did exactly what I told her. A smile spread across my face. Subtle changes could strengthen the impact. I had to preach to my artists all the time. Erykah Badu already let us know. They were artists, and they had to be sensitive about their shit. For me, that meant taking criticism as love.

It wasn't just their names on a record or an album. My name was on that shit too, and I took great pride in what I did. I didn't care if the artist was the talent. What I wouldn't tolerate was my name being on some bullshit.

Stella finished up and looked at me for confirmation. I gave her a thumbs up.

"Love it. You gave the intensity while keeping control. I think we've got the lead vocal track. Let's layer up some harmonies in the next section. That should open up the chorus."

She smiled. "I'm ready when you are. I can't wait to hear how these layering tracks fill out the song."

"You the shit, Stella, baby. This is coming together nicely. Just a few more takes, and I think we'll have the vocals done for this single. By the end of the session, we'll be taking a shot to celebrate your first completed single."

She was all smiles as she put her headphones back on. I could tell she was going to be one of my favorite artists to work with. Her mother sat beside me, beaming with pride.

"I can't believe this is happening," she said, placing her hand over her heart. "My baby is going to be a star."

I smiled. "She really is. You should be proud."

"I'm very proud. I just wish her father was here to see it. She used to love singing with him. After he passed away when she was fifteen, she barely wanted to hum a tune, let alone sing a song. She's living his dream for her right now. Thank you for taking a chance on her, Mr. Watson."

"Call me Channing. And it's I that should be thanking her. You don't find raw, unfiltered talent like hers every day. She's got something special, and the world needs to hear it. That's what I'm here for."

She smiled and grabbed my hand as she turned her attention back to Stella in the booth. I tuned back in myself. After another hour in the studio and some fine tuning, the track was perfect. Stella and her mother both cried during the full playback. I smiled because I knew I'd done my job. This single alone was about to change their lives.

After saying goodbye to Stella and her mom, I killed time, waiting for my next artist to get to the studio. I wasn't sure how I felt about this one. He brought me in halfway through the process after firing his previous team.

Word on the street was he'd become a little difficult to work with lately. My sources said it was nothing more than an inflated ego. That wasn't uncommon. Many artists came into the industry humble and grew to be entitled. They wanted what they wanted, how they wanted it, and when they wanted it. I'd seen it time and time again. Artists sometimes got too big and forgot where they came from.

Fortunately for them, I could humble a muthafucka real quick.

Around two, the door opened, and Prince Cole walked in along with Lady Lingo at his side. I'd worked on her last album, so we were familiar with each other. She was the one who recommended me to him in the first place.

"Good evening," I said, standing to greet them.

Lady Lingo immediately came to me for a hug.

"Channing! It's good to see you again!"

"Likewise, baby."

"Channing, this is Raheem. Raheem, this is the infamous Channing Watson, producer extraordinaire. When I say you're going to love him, you're going to love him!"

I stuck out my hand. "Nice to meet you, man."

He dapped me up. "Nice to meet you. Imani has sung your praises."

I noticed he called her by her government name and wondered if there was something more between them than being on the same label. Everybody either called her Lady or Lady Lingo. That wasn't my business, though.

"All good things, I hope," I responded.

"You'd think she was obsessed."

She playfully slapped his chest. "Don't put me on blast like that! Channing, I was simply honest. You were amazing on my last album. I just want him to experience some of your magic."

I chuckled. "I appreciate it. Why don't y'all have a seat and we can get started. Prince, you can tell me about your vision for this album."

"Fa'sho."

They both took a seat, and he took off the backpack he was wearing. After digging through it, he pulled out a weathered notebook I assumed housed his lyrics. At least that was a good sign. He came prepared. My optimism was shifted when his phone chimed. He pulled it out, and a frown appeared on his face.

"Aye, excuse me a second. I need to make a phone call."

Lady Lingo gave a nervous smile. "Can it wait?" she asked through gritted teeth.

Something told me that whatever the problem was, it wasn't new.

"Nah, it can't," he answered, standing.

"Raheem, Channing is a busy man. He doesn't have time to waste."

Raheem looked between the two of us. "My apologies, man. I really need to handle this right quick. I can pay you for any extra time we take."

Since I didn't have another meeting after this, I decided to oblige him.

"Go on."

"Thanks, man."

He quickly left the room, leaving the two of us alone. Lady Lingo rolled her eyes as she sat back and crossed her legs.

"I'm sure it's his little girlfriend. Some people have no respect for your craft."

"Hmm," was all I gave her.

I didn't care what he had going on outside of this studio. When he came in, he needed to leave that extra shit behind. In here, we were on my time, and my time was nothing to be played with.

* * *

Several hours later, I was climbing into my Range Rover to head home for the night. My session with Prince Cole was interesting. For him to have a reputation for killing shit in the studio, he seemed awfully distracted. He left the room three additional times to take a phone call. Not only that, but he was also constantly texting, and his demeanor had completely changed.

Lady Lingo was visibly annoyed with him. I left the room once to use the bathroom, and when I came back, I could see them in the booth arguing. I wasn't sure what that was about, but once I entered the room, she left the booth and came to join me. I made it a point to shoot an email to his management to speak with him about his professionalism. What I wouldn't do was make this shit a habit. Once you let a muthafucka slide with disrespecting your time, they started ice skating.

After stopping to get food, I made my way to my house. As soon as I walked in, I was greeted by my two-year-old Rottie, Koda.

"Hey, pretty girl," I said, stooping down and scratching behind her ears. "Did you miss daddy?"

She whined as she rested her head on my shoulder. Koda was my big baby. It didn't help that she loved to be carried around like a toddler. She was always so content in my arms. If I ever got married or had a child of my own, I wasn't sure how she was going to react.

"Let's feed you, baby girl. Daddy is hungry too."

Standing to my feet, I walked into the kitchen. After washing my hands, I went to the mini fridge that housed food just for Koda. I fed her a diet of meat and vegetables. Tonight, I prepared a steak, seasoned with a beef flavored dog food topper, sweet potatoes, and a fried egg. I added a few supplements for joint, bone, and skin care that were essential for dogs.

Most people that knew me said I did too much for her, but Koda was my baby. If I ate good, why couldn't she? Nobody else had to foot the bill for her food consumption, so I really didn't give a fuck what they had to say. I placed the bowl on her mat then filled her bowl with water and two ice cubes.

Once I was done, I washed my hands and grabbed last night's leftover plate of chicken and rice. Tossing it in the microwave, I went to grab myself a cold beer. Once the timer dinged, I headed back into the living room and sat on my couch. After turning on the TV movie, I dug into my plate.

Maybe ten minutes later, my phone started ringing. Plucking it from my pocket, I saw it was Shavonn, the woman I dealt with from time to time. Smirking, I answered the phone.

"Hello?"

"Hey, handsome. Are you busy?"

"Nah. I just got home. Me and Koda are eating dinner. What's up?"

"Nothing much. Laying here all by my lonesome, wondering how I'm gonna entertain myself. Then I thought about you and realized I've been cumming by myself for two whole weeks."

I chuckled. "Now, ain't that a shame?"

"Isn't it? Imagine all of this good pussy juice going to waste."

I licked my lips. Shavonn definitely had some good ass pussy. My dick got hard just thinking about that tight, wet, fat muthafucka.

"What do you want me to do about that?" I asked, slouching in my seat.

"Invite me over, and you can do whatever you want."

"Is that right?"

"Mmm hmm..."

She started moaning in my ear, then I heard the sound of her vibrator buzzing.

"Oooo... I'm already so wet for you, Channing... shit!"

"Well, bring your ass on over here."

"Okay, daddy... mmm... We'll see you soon, baby."

"Bet. I'm gonna go hop in the shower, but I'ma leave the door unlocked for you."

"I'll be waiting for you."

We disconnected the call, and I finished eating. When I was done, I put the dishes in the dishwasher and let Koda out to use the bathroom. After she handled her business, I unlocked my door and headed upstairs to shower. I lived in a safe neighborhood, so I didn't worry about anybody coming in my shit.

I needed the stress reliever Shavonn was sure to provide me. As a single man of now four years, shit got a lil lonely every now and then. I wasn't opposed to a relationship. I didn't have an ex that did me dirty. I wasn't on some he-man woman hater's club type of shit.

I was simply cool with chilling by myself until my rib showed herself in my life. The next woman I entertained romantically had to be my wife. She needed to possess all the qualities I looked for in that special lady. I needed a woman that was independent, because fucking with me was a bonus and not a come up.

I needed a woman that was family oriented because I wanted children. She needed to be financially responsible. I couldn't have no female running through my hard-earned money as soon as I got it. Help me invest. Look for ways to multiply our income. Be fucking frugal at times. I made good money producing, but I lived a modest lifestyle for the most part.

My wife needed to be beautiful, inside and out. I didn't give a fuck if she was beautiful to anybody else. She could be a five to the world and a ten to me. As long as I was attracted to her mind, body, and soul, that was all that mattered. I wanted her to be kind-hearted, loving, respectful, and loyal. And she had to love Koda because my baby wasn't going anywhere.

I didn't think I was asking for much, but I hadn't run into a woman like that yet. Now, was I fucking and getting my dick sucked? Absolutely. A nigga had needs, and I was attractive. Women like Shavonn served their purpose. She knew what it was and what it wasn't. That was what I loved about her.

She didn't require commitment, and she didn't want it. I dicked her down, took her to a few industry parties, and broke her off a lil something when I felt like it. She understood that she wasn't my girl, and I wasn't her man. That was the way it'd always been.

Thirty minutes later, I shut off the shower and stepped out. Grabbing my towel, I dried myself off and brushed my teeth. As I reached for the knob on the bathroom door, Shavonn's signature scent drifted through the air, infiltrating my nostrils. She was here. I knew when I opened this door, she was going to be on the other side, assuming the muthafucking position.

I smirked as I twisted the handle and pulled it open. Sure enough, the five-foot-five, caramel complexion, thick ass beauty was on my bed, face down, ass up.

"Hey, daddy," she purred, making her ass jiggle. "We've been waiting on you two."

Crooking her finger, she motioned me to her. Slowly, I strolled across the room to where she was and smacked her ass. She moaned softly as she reached out to grab my dick.

"You missed me, baby?" she asked, stroking it.

I leaned over and grabbed a condom from my dresser. "Yeah... I missed you."

"How bad?"

"Open that pretty ass mouth and find out."

She smirked as she rolled over onto her back and hung her head off the bed. Opening her mouth, she stuck her tongue out and guided my dick down her throat.

If anything would relax and put me straight to sleep, it would be Shavonn's nasty ass. I'd say this was a perfect ending to a long ass day.

Chapter Three

Rhythm

I looked up from the food I was cooking on the stove when I heard the front door opening. A frown found its way to my face as I heard Raheem's footsteps approaching the kitchen. To my surprise, when he rounded the corner, he wasn't alone. Behind him was Lady Lingo with a smug look on her face.

"You can't be fucking serious," I said, placing my hand on my hip. "What is she doing here?"

"I have a name, you know."

"Oh, I have several names I can call you. Would you like the list to choose from?"

"All right!" Raheem yelled, holding up his hands. "Rhy, Imani is a guest. Chill out. We're going to the studio."

"You *just* left the studio, Raheem."

"And I barely got anything done because you kept calling and texting me, wanting to argue."

"Who was arguing? I said we needed to talk."

"And I told you I was busy. You blew up my phone the whole

time I was with my producer. That made me look unprofessional as hell."

"Oh, now you're worried about the way you look?"

Imani laughed. "This is why I told you not to date anybody outside of the industry. They have no respect for our craft."

"Bitch, who the fuck asked you!" I yelled, taking a step toward her.

Raheem grabbed me around my waist and walked me backward.

"Rhy, you need to calm your ass down. Damn."

I pushed him off me. "Don't tell me to calm down when you walk into our home with this bitch!"

Imani laughed. "You seem to love claiming ownership of things that don't fully belong to you."

I frowned. "The fuck is that supposed to mean?"

Raheem stepped into my space once again. "Imani, go on to the studio. I'll meet you there."

She smirked. "Sure thing."

She lightly touched his arm as she sashayed out of the kitchen and down the hall to the studio. Raheem took a seat at the table with a frustrated look on his face. I didn't care how upset he was. Shit, I was upset too. This wasn't the first time she'd been in our home.

A few months back, he had a bunch of people over in the studio. I'd just gotten home from work and arrived to find about five cars in our driveway. I'd silently prayed that they didn't stay too long because these muthafuckas never knew when to leave, and he didn't have sense enough to tell them to go.

I walked into the house and put my things down. After stopping in the kitchen to pour myself a much-needed glass of wine, I walked down the hall to the studio in the back. The potent smell of weed hit me before I even opened the door, and the sound of loud rap music engulfed my ears.

Opening the door, I was greeted by what looked like a whole ass kickback. Food, liquor, and ashtrays filled with cigarette butts and blunt roaches were all over the place. Raheem's friends were enter-

taining some random females. Then, there was him... sitting on the couch, with Imani blowing him a shotgun. She grinned and gave him a seductive look as she gazed down at him.

"You like that?" she asked.

"Hell yeah."

"Raheem!" I yelled over the music.

Lazily, he turned to look at me, and so did she. She turned up her lip as she backed away from him and took a seat in an empty chair.

"Hey, baby," he said, grinning as he climbed to his feet.

He made his way over to me and tried to kiss me, but I turned my head.

"What? No love for your man?"

"Can I talk to you?"

I didn't give him a chance to respond before I walked back down the hall. Behind me, I could hear his friends joking that he was in trouble. Closing the door, he followed behind me into the kitchen. I stood at the kitchen counter with a scowl on my face.

Raheem raised his hands. "I promise, I'ma clean the mess up when they leave."

"It's not even about the mess. It's you having a bitch in your face like that."

"Who, Imani? She's just my labelmate, baby."

"It looked like a whole lot more than music making going on. Did you see how she looked at me? Like I was interrupting some shit in my own damn house?"

He waved me off. "Don't start trippin', Rhy."

"Oh, baby, you haven't begun to see me trip. She needs to go."

"Hold up, now. That is my studio. We share every other part of this house, but that's my space. We're working."

"Raheem, ain't a lick of work getting done in there. Please don't act like I'm blind."

"Fuck, Rhythm! You blowing my high with your nagging!"

I scoffed. "Nagging?"

"Yes, nagging. That insecure shit ain't cute, ma. I'm your man.

You don't need to be worried about me with any other female if you trust me."

I laughed. "Okay, Raheem. Bye."

"Don't act like that." He tried to grab my hand, but I snatched away. "So, you mad?"

"Nope. I'm just starting to see a side of you that I don't like very much. You keep it up, and I'm gonna act accordingly."

"The fuck does that mean?"

"Whatever you want it to mean, baby. Have your fun, but you don't want me to start having mine."

I glared at him before walking out of the kitchen.

Here we were, months later, having yet another argument about the same bitch.

"What is it now, Rhythm?" he asked, glaring at me. "Now you wanna talk after you moved out of our bedroom."

I moved out of the bedroom after our argument that night. I could barely look at him, let alone sleep next to him. My feelings were hurt, and he didn't seem to give a damn.

"Well?" he asked.

"I don't like being in this space, Raheem. You already know how I feel about you and that girl, and you're gonna bring her into our home?"

"We're working, Rhythm."

"You've been at the studio for hours. You can't hold off for one night to talk to me about the state of our relationship?"

He threw his hands in the air. "What do you want me to do? You've already got it in your head that you don't mean to me what I mean to you. Then you tell me some shit about our relationship running its course. What am I supposed to say to that? Sounds like you've made up your mind to leave me."

"If I meant anything to you, you'd be trying to rectify the situation, not bringing the problem home."

"You sound so insecure right now, and I've never known that to be you until Imani came around."

23

I scoffed as I turned away from the stove. He couldn't be fucking serious.

"Insecure? Raheem, if I'm insecure about anything, it's because that's how you've made me! If the shoe were on the other foot, you'd be showing your ass! You think I don't have options? You think other men don't approach me or that there haven't been opportunities for me to act inappropriate with niggas close to you? I've always respected you as my man, and what do you do? You want me to be okay with you parading the next bitch around like she's your woman."

"I never even said I was going to do it!"

"You presented it like the opportunity of a lifetime! *It would be good for business. We'd be touching more money than we ever had.* That's what you said. What part of your fucked-up ass brain thought that was okay to bring to me? You wanna play house, go right ahead. But you can do it without me."

I grabbed the pot from the stove and tossed it in the sink before storming out of the kitchen. He called my name repeatedly, but I ignored him as I headed upstairs to the guest room. Stripping down, I headed into the bathroom and turned on the shower.

Once the water was just right, I stepped in and allowed the flow from the showerhead to mask my tears. I was mentally exhausted. I'd been able to pull myself together long enough to get through my workdays, but once I hit the front door, my emotions consumed me.

It was hard to come to the realization that my relationship wasn't as solid as I thought it was. I was beginning to feel out of place. Before I stayed where I wasn't wanted, I would leave. It wasn't like I couldn't afford to live without him. Sure, he took care of me, but I was more than capable of taking care of myself.

After my shower, I changed into a pair of sweats and a tank top. Going to the closet, I pulled out my duffel bag and suitcase and packed enough clothes to last a little minute wherever I ended up. I gathered my laptop and anything else I needed for work too. Thirty minutes later, I was walking downstairs. Music from the studio drifted from down the hall.

I shook my head as I headed out the front door. After tossing my things into my G-Wagon, I climbed in and pulled out of the driveway. The drive into town only took about twenty minutes. I headed straight for my favorite hotel chain and booked myself a room for a few days.

After getting settled in, I turned off my location and climbed into bed and pulled the covers up over my head. No sooner than I had gotten comfortable, my phone started ringing. I didn't have to look at the screen to know who it was because the ringtone was a dead giveaway.

I swiped the ignore button to reject Monique's call, only for it to ring right back. Again, I rejected the call. A few seconds later, a text came through.

Nique: Why is your location off?

Nique: I know you didn't just ignore me.

Nique: Stop playing with me, Rhythm. Answer the damn phone before I call your mama.

She really would call my mother if she couldn't reach me, and then my mother would call me fussing and asking a thousand questions. The last thing I wanted to do was discuss my relationship woes with her. She'd tell me it wasn't a good idea to come out here in the first place.

She'd preached to me repeatedly not to move all the way across the country for a man that wasn't my husband. Just because it had worked for my cousin didn't mean it was my path too.

I sighed heavily as I decided to call Nique back.

"What's going on with you?" she asked as soon as she answered.

"Nothing, Nique."

"Lie again. Did something happen with Raheem?"

I was quiet.

"Girl, if you don't start talking!"

I rolled my eyes and started from the beginning. I hadn't told her about the conversation he and I had the night I broke up his little smoke session with his boys. By the time I was finished, she was livid.

"I know you fuckin' lying! I'll beat his ass. The fuck you mean a fake relationship?"

"That's what he said." My voice was shaky as I began to cry. "What if he's already messing around with her, Nique? He brought that bitch in my house, and he could have already fucked her. She had this smug look on her face, like she knew some shit I didn't."

I began to cry harder, thinking about what could have been going on behind closed doors. What if this whole idea was a cover-up for an ongoing relationship? Did he really think I'd be stupid enough to go along with it?

"Where are you right now?" Nique asked.

"At a hotel. I told him if that's the life he wants to live, then he can do it without me."

"Wait, you plan to stay in a hotel until when?"

"I only packed for a few days. I just needed some space. I guess I can take this time to start looking for an apartment or something."

"Shit." Nique sighed heavily. "I was gonna surprise you, but I was coming to visit next week and stay for a couple days."

"Really? That would be great. I could really use my best friend right now."

"I can try to come earlier—"

"I don't wanna interfere with what you have going on, boo."

"Girl, fuck this job. Well, not really. I love my job, but I love you too. I'm due for a vacation, and my lil yea yea works in timekeeping. He'll make sure I'm straight."

"You're seeing somebody?"

"Not officially. He's something to do when there's nothing to do. But that's neither here nor there. I'll see when I can book my flight and hit you with the info. Maybe we can view a few places together."

"We can do that. You don't have to come early though. I could use a few days to process all of this so I'm not a crying mess when I see you. I appreciate you, Nique."

"You know how I feel about you, babes. You're my A-one since day one. Raheem is gonna see me when I get there."

"No. I don't wanna deal with any shit. I just wanna pack my things and leave quietly. He doesn't even know where I am, and he knows better than to come to my place of business, showing his ass."

"Okay, girl. I'll hold off on him for your sake... for now."

I sighed. "I just wanna sleep right now. It's been a long ass day, and I'm mentally exhausted."

"Okay, well get some rest. Call me if you need me."

"I will."

"I love you."

"I love you too."

We disconnected the call, and I put my phone on do not disturb. After plugging it into the charger, I turned out the lights and snuggled into the covers. For the longest time, I stared out the window at the night sky, wondering where the fuck I was going to go from here.

Chapter Four

Channing

"Run that back for me one more time," I said to the engineer.

I was in my zone working on this track for G.E.M. While I mostly worked with Hip-Hop artists, every now and then, I dabbled in the R&B shit. My ear for music was impeccable, and it made it easy to float through different genres. I had artists from all backgrounds in my arsenal. From rap to R&B, to country, to gospel, I did it all.

Part of me had been going back and forth for a while about opening my own label. I had connections in this industry that could make my own label highly sought after. I was on the fence about it. It was a lot of work, and I wasn't sure if I wanted that headache. Still, I'd been getting signs to go ahead and branch out. The perfect building was available. I'd already toured it and had a vision in my head. I just had to follow through.

I stopped the music about midway and called Emerald out of the booth. The one thing I loved about working with this man was his

28

work ethic. He took constructive criticism well and only had to be told once. He stepped out of the booth and came to have a seat on the couch behind us.

"You aren't feeling it?" he asked.

"It's not that I'm not feeling it. Something is missing. What vibe are you going for?"

"Well, I wrote this for my wife, so I guess I want it to resonate with the lovers and people who wanna be in love."

"You gotta sing it like that. You're singing a song you wrote for the love of your life. You gotta pack the emotion in there, man. Make whoever's listening feel like you're singing to them. Make them think about the person they love the most. Make a nigga wanna sing this to his ol' lady."

He chuckled. "I got you."

"We could add some lush harmonies and layered backing vocals to really make it soar. Maybe even bring in a subtle string arrangement to add to the romantic atmosphere."

Theo, the engineer, nodded. "I can do that."

"You go lay down the vocals, and we'll do the rest," I said confidently.

"Bet. You mind if I call my wife? She tends to put me in the right headspace."

"Whatever you need to do to make this next take hit like it needs to."

He nodded. Standing, he headed back into the booth, phone in his hand. While we waited for him to be ready, my phone vibrated in my pocket. Pulling it out, I saw that it was my mother. She never called me in the studio unless she needed something.

"I gotta take this," I said, standing.

I excused myself to the hallway to answer the phone.

"What's up, Ma?"

"Hey, baby. I'm sorry to bother you."

"You good. Ain't no bother. You need something?"

She sighed. "Somehow, I got a flat tire. I'm at Mama's therapy appointment, and she's getting irritable. I called roadside assistance, but they said it would be at least an hour before they could get here. We are only about five minutes from the studio. I'd appreciate it if you could come change the tire."

"I got you. Just let me holla at my client, and I'll be on my way."

"Thank you, baby. I love you."

"I love you too."

I hung up and headed back inside. I let Emerald and Theo know that I would be back. I left the room and headed down to my car, trying to make haste. My grandmother was in the early stages of dementia, and her moods could be unpredictable at times. It was already hard on my mother, accepting her condition. Anything I could do to lessen her load, I would.

I made it to The Baker Method in record time. On the way, I'd called my guy down at the auto shop and told him my mother needed a new tire and to charge my account. Since he knew of my gram's diagnosis, he told me he'd make a special trip to the house to change it for her. When I pulled into the parking lot, my mother was outside, looking like she was pleading with Grams to get back in the car.

I pulled in beside them and hopped out.

"Grams, whatchu doing?" I asked, walking over to her with my arms outstretched.

She came to me for a hug. "Your mama's got me out here in this hot ass sun. I wanna go home. You came to take me home?"

"I came to change the tire. Don't tell me you've been giving my mama a hard time, old woman?"

I smiled and she smiled back. "She was my daughter before she was your mama. I'll beat both y'all asses."

I raised my hands in mock surrender. "I don't want no smoke. How about you wait in my car? I got the AC on for you. I'll put on some gospel music and let you catch the holy spirit."

She smacked my arm and wagged her finger at me. "Don't play about God."

"I'm not playing, Grams. Come on and let me get you comfortable."

She reluctantly allowed me to lead her to my car and help her in. After pairing the Bluetooth with my phone, I went to the gospel playlist I had just for her. I closed the door and went to my trunk to get my tools. My mother stood behind her car, seemingly trying to hold it together.

Placing my tools on the ground, I pulled her in for a hug and kissed her forehead. She cried softly against me, and it broke my heart.

"You can't let her get to you, Ma."

"I know, Channing. It's so hard when she gets like this. She says things she wouldn't normally say... hurtful things."

"What did she say?"

"She told me I was useless and a horrible daughter. That she'd be better off in a nursing home than with me."

I sighed. "You know she didn't mean it. You take great care of her, Mama. It's just the illness. The doctors prepared us for this. This is just it coming to pass. It's sad. It's frustrating, but we got this. I'm right here with you. You know I've always got you."

"I know, baby." She pulled away from me and wiped her eyes. Cupping my face, she kissed my cheek. "You've always been a good boy."

I chuckled. "I'm a menace these days."

"Mmm hmm. Don't let me have to whip out my belt."

I grinned. "Let me get this spare on. I called my boy over at Martin's Auto Shop, and he's coming to the house with a new tire. It's already paid for."

"Thank you, baby."

"You don't have to thank me, Ma. You and Grams always made sure I was straight. I'm in a position to pay you back. If I got it, y'all got it."

She smiled softly. My mama was my heart, as was Grams. When my bitch ass father dipped out on us, the two of them came together and raised me. Shit had been hard. Sometimes my mother worked sixteen-hour days, six days a week to make ends meet.

She and Grams would trade off watching me so they could both get some rest. I tried my hardest not to get in too much trouble because that was all they asked of me. I wasn't out here fighting. I didn't become a teenage father. The most I did was drink and smoke, and even then, I hid it from them.

Now that I was an adult, I still tried to make them proud. I was a successful, award-winning producer, and all they wanted from me these days were grandbabies. Maybe one of these days, I would appease them.

My mother and I chatted while I changed the tire. It took me no time to get the busted tire off and the spare on. After saying goodbye to her and Grams, I headed into the building to see if they would let me use the bathroom to wash my hands.

"Good afternoon," I said to the receptionist.

She looked up at me, and her eyes widened. A smile spread across her face as she spoke to me.

"Good afternoon. How can I help you?"

"I'm sure your bathroom isn't open to the public, but my grandmother is a client here. She and my mother had a flat tire, and I had to change it. I just need to wash my hands."

"Go right ahead. I can't fault a man that takes care of his mama and grandma."

I offered her a smile. "Thank you, baby."

She giggled as I walked off to the bathroom. Inside, I washed and dried my hands. My phone vibrated in my pocket. Pulling it out, I saw that it was a video from Theo with a recording of Emerald. He'd successfully killed the track like I knew he would. I was so busy listening to him that when I opened the door, I ran smack into someone, damn near knocking them down.

Before she could hit the ground, I grabbed her around the waist. When my eyes landed on the beauty tightly gripping my shirt, I was slightly taken aback. I hadn't seen a woman this damn fine in a long time. Considering the industry I worked in, that was a big deal. I was surrounded by beautiful women, but none of them were quite like her.

She was thick, just the way I liked them. Baby had that Coke bottle figure; full titties, slim waist, round hips, and ass that went on for days. Her skin was smooth and free of blemishes. Beautiful brown eyes looked back at me with wonder.

"My apologies, love," I said, peering down at her.

"It's okay," she said softly. "At least you broke my fall."

I stood her upright and on her feet. A nigga was so captivated by her beauty that I didn't realize I was still holding her until she cleared her throat.

"Um... you can let go now."

"Oh, shit. My bad, beautiful." I released her and took a step back, reading her name tag. "Dr. Baker. It's nice to meet you. I'm Channing."

I extended my hand. She looked down at it momentarily, then gave me a firm shake.

"Nice to meet you."

"Any relation to the Baker on the building?"

"I *am* the Baker on the building."

"Boss lady, huh. I see you. Might I say that you are gorgeous."

She blushed. "Thank you. I really have to get going. It's my lunch break, and if I don't take it now, I won't eat."

"Maybe I can take you to lunch?" I said, like I didn't have to get back to the studio.

"Um... as nice as that sounds, I'm afraid I'm going to decline. I don't know you. You could be a serial killer."

I chuckled. "I'm pretty harmless unless provoked. But I get it. Maybe I'll see you around."

"Maybe you will."

"And maybe I'll get a yes next time."

She giggled, showing off a beautiful smile. "I wouldn't hold my breath."

I placed a hand over my heart, pretending to be wounded. "Damn... that hurt, Doc."

"Something tells me that even if one woman tells you no, there are ten others that will say yes. Your heart will be just fine."

I backed away from her with a grin. She smirked as she turned on her heels and made her way back down the hall. I watched the sway of her hips and the bounce of that ass until she disappeared.

"Damn," I muttered.

I might have to start bringing Grams to therapy if this was the caliber of doctors servicing her.

Chapter Five

Rhythm

Week Later

I sat outside of the airport, waiting for Nique's plane to arrive. I was too happy to have her here. I needed her good energy to keep me from becoming my own worst enemy. My grandmother always told me that an idle mind was the devil's playground. In my case, it was true. The more time I spent alone, the more time I had to think about Raheem. The more I thought about him, the more I searched his name on social media and hurt my own feelings.

While he'd been blowing my line up, asking where I was at, he wasn't so concerned that it kept him away from Imani. They were still seen out and about, or she was posting pictures of them in the studio, looking cozy and shit. Fans were suspecting them of being together at this point.

"They definitely fucking."

"When's the wedding?"

"Y'all need to stop capping."

"Hip Hop's power couple!"

Those were only a few of the comments. I read to the point of pissing myself off and calling him to curse him out. He was every son of a bitch in the book and could barely get a word in before I hung up on him. Last night, I'd cried my eyes out. I wasn't one of those females that went to social media to blast their ex. I didn't go crying to their parents, although I was sure Ms. Cole would lay into his ass on my behalf.

I could take my L's in silence. I was already embarrassed. There was no need to publicize that embarrassment. I prayed that Nique being here would lift my spirits. I hadn't seen my bestie in six months, and I desperately needed a hug from her.

When the doors opened and I saw Nique step out and look around, I hopped out of my car. My feet couldn't move fast enough to get to her. When she saw me, she abandoned her suitcase and ran to me, jumping in my arms. She shed tears of joy as we held each other tightly.

"I've missed you so much!" she declared.

"I've missed you too!"

For a solid five minutes, we shared an embrace. I just needed to soak up all the love and good energy radiating from her. Finally, we released each other, and she ran back to grab her suitcases before we headed to my car. After throwing her bags in the trunk, we climbed in and eased into traffic.

"It's so good to see you, boo," Nique said, grabbing my hand.

"It's good to see you too, Nique. You have no idea how bad I've needed to be around you. I almost booked a flight home."

"Well, I'm here now, and I'm determined to pull you out of this funk."

I smiled softly. "How long are you here for?"

"I'm not sure yet. I asked for a week and a half, but I can extend it. Are you still at the hotel?"

"I am. It had a king-sized bed, so you have plenty of room."

"We are long overdue for a sleepover. As a matter of fact, stop by the liquor store. We are getting tore up tonight by ourselves. It's a *fuck that nigga* kind of party."

I giggled as she twerked in her seat. Damn, I missed her.

After stopping by the liquor store, we headed back to the hotel. The moment we entered the room, Nique changed into her bathing suit and poured us up some drinks while I changed into my bikini. Every room on this floor had a private pool on the balcony. It was sunny out and the perfect day to lounge about and do nothing.

Nique grabbed the Bluetooth speaker from her bag, and we headed outside. She connected her phone, and soon, the sounds of Glorilla and Megan Thee Stallion's "Wanna Be" came through the speaker.

"That's my shit!" Nique declared, bending over to twerk her ass.

I didn't hesitate to join her. We danced through Megan's part before finally descending the steps of the pool and wading in up to our waist, liquor in hand.

"Why can't South Carolina ever have weather this perfect?" Nique complained.

"Because our weather is bi-polar as hell. I can't lie, I'm missing home right now. I would kill for my grandma's sweet potato pie or some fatback. I need to visit soon."

"Have you told anybody what's been going on?"

I shook my head. "No. My mama would just tell me to come home. It's not that easy. I have a whole business out here now, and it's doing great. I can't just up and leave."

"I get it, boo."

"Besides, I actually like L.A. It's more expensive than back home, but it's been a great experience... well, aside from the obvious."

"We can jump that bitch, you know. Raheem's ass too."

I shook my head. "I'm not fighting over no man, Nique."

"You wouldn't be fighting over him. From what you've told me, that bitch has gotten slick at the mouth with you before. And him... I just wanna deck him one good time and remind him of who he is. He needs to humble himself. Nigga came from the sticks of South Carolina and has let Hollywood boost his ego. We remember him when he wore secondhand clothes and dirty shoes. And that's not a dig at his struggle. That's the truth of the matter."

She was right about that. Raheem had his share of dusty days. Kids used to talk about him but never said it to his face, because he was known to fight. It wasn't until high school when he started hustling to help his mom did his wardrobe change.

He'd seemingly changed over the summer. When he came back to school our sophomore year, he dressed better. He took pride in his appearance. He always smelled good. Girls started looking at him, and the niggas that used to talk about him all of a sudden wanted to be his friend. I'd always thought he was cute. Even when he didn't have the means to look the part, he'd always had the potential.

I turned up my glass and downed my drink.

"I'm moving out," I announced.

"You decided?"

"Honestly, Nique, I think my mind was made up when I left. The man didn't even notice I was gone until the next day, Nique. Like, seriously. The bitch was only gone an hour, and Jodeci was in the fucking desert crying in leather about her ass."

Nique burst into the obnoxious laughter that only she could do.

"I'm sorry! I don't mean to laugh, but that was funny and completely accurate. But I get it. If you love me, I want you to be sick about my absence. You need to be on some 'Feenin' shit to get me back. Take my money, my house, and my cars, too, type of shit!"

It was my turn to laugh.

"Now don't be one of those bitches that moved out only to move right back in," Nique warned me.

"I'm not. I'm gonna stick to my guns... at least I'm gonna try."

"Don't try, just do it. Sweet nothings will always be sweet

nothings if ain't no action behind those words. If it's one thing I know, you can never trust a nigga's words. Show and prove, baby."

I sighed heavily. "I don't wanna talk about Raheem anymore," I said. "You're here. I wanna enjoy your company before you have to abandon me and go home."

She rolled her eyes. "Dramatic much?"

Turning up her own drink, she guzzled the contents.

"You know what? Fuck Raheem. We are going out tonight. We're gonna find a fine ass man to buy us drinks all night, and you are gonna forget that nigga ever existed. What did the song say? Fuck my ex, you can keep that nigga. That's our theme song tonight. Hey, Siri! Play 'Keep dat Nigga' by Icandy!"

"Now playing 'Keep Dat Nigga' by Icandy on Apple Music."

The beat dropped, and she raised her hands in the air and started twerking in the pool. I laughed as I fell into rhythm with her. Yeah, Nique being here was exactly what I needed.

* * *

Night had fallen.

Nique was absolutely what I needed. With her here, I couldn't be on my sad girl soapbox. She was just a ball of energy, and I missed having her around. Since she got here, we'd been sipping on drinks, lounging around in the pool, dancing, and having fun. Currently, we were sipping wine and failing horribly at copying Beyoncé's "Formation" dance.

"Bitch, my knees!" Nique screamed in laughter as she fell to the floor. "Damn, I'm getting old!"

"Nique, you at two years shy of thirty."

"Tell that to my back. But what can I expect, carrying all this ass around?"

She rolled over onto her knees and started twerking. I laughed as a hard knock came to the door.

"That's probably the people next door. We *were* kind of loud, Nique."

I turned the television down and walked over to the door. Without looking through the peephole, I opened it. My eyes widened as I stared into the face of Raheem, with two of his security team members behind him.

"Why are you here?" I asked, frowning. "How did you even find me?"

"For one, Nique left her location on in her Snapchat."

I looked back at my best friend. She'd posted a lot of our little turn-up session on her Snapchat story.

"My bad, girl," she said, getting up from the floor.

"That doesn't explain how you got my room number, Raheem. I hope whoever gave it to you knows they are getting fired."

"Ain't nobody getting fired. I know you love this hotel, and when I saw the pool, I knew what floor you'd be on. It was just a matter of knocking on doors until you opened it."

He pushed past me and into the room.

"Excuse you!" I exclaimed. "Get out!"

"So, this is where you been held up for the past week?" he asked, looking around. "You're really that mad, Rhythm?"

I ignored him.

"Get him out of here," I said to his security.

They remained on the other side of the door.

"Now!" I yelled.

"They don't work for you," Raheem reminded me. He leaned against the bed with his arms crossed.

Seeing that they weren't going to move, I slammed the door in their faces. Nique looked at me as though to say, *Bitch, what are you about to do?*

"You done with this hissy fit?" Raheem asked.

"Hissy fit? I packed my shit and left because you and that bitch disrespected me, and you think I'm throwing a hissy fit?"

"I think you're overreacting."

"And I think you are full of shit. You didn't even know I was gone until the next morning, Raheem. What? Were you too busy laid up in your studio to notice?"

He jumped to his feet. "See, that's the shit I'm talking about. You always jump to conclusions. You just think I'm out here doing you wrong."

"You've done a hell of a job in proving me right!"

"Where is the evidence? The cold, hard, factual evidence that me and Imani have something going on?"

"Look at the way you move with her! That bitch told me I seem to love claiming ownership of things that don't fully belong to me. The only thing she could be referring to is you."

"I'm not fucking with that girl, Rhythm!"

"Then you already have!"

He looked at me with angry eyes. He didn't confirm it, but he didn't deny it either. After an intense stare off, his face softened. He sighed heavily as he pushed off from the bed and came to me.

"Why are we doing this, Rhy? I love you. I don't wanna keep fighting with you. We been at war for weeks now, baby."

"We are exactly where you put us."

"We can fix this—"

"There is nothing for *me* to fix. You've made it perfectly clear where we stand."

"Look... just come home and let me fix this." He looked over at Nique. "We can talk in private."

Nique scoffed. "Now you wanna be private after flaunting around town with your whore?"

"Nique, mind your business! Damn. You always have to be in shit. Ever since we were kids, you just *had* to be involved."

"Fuck you, Raheem. Don't make me humble your ass."

"Why are you even here?"

"I'm here because my best friend needed me, and she couldn't depend on her so-called man."

"So-called? I'm every bit of a man. Been that."

"These days, you ain't been *much*."

"Coming from someone who doesn't even have a nigga, I can't take you seriously."

"Muthaf—"

"Enough!" I yelled, cutting into their banter. "Raheem, leave."

"Come home."

"No. I think you and I need to take a break."

"A break?" He shook his head. "A break until when exactly, Rhythm?"

"I don't know. I would say until you decide where you wanna be, but I'm not a consolation prize. Pick me the first time, or don't pick me at all."

I walked over to the door and opened it. Security stood on the other side, pretending they hadn't been listening.

"Leave."

Raheem looked at me in disbelief. Again, he shook his head. He made his way to the door, stopping briefly in front of me. He leaned down and kissed my cheek.

"This isn't over... *We* aren't over."

Without another word, he walked out of the room. I closed and locked the door behind him. I looked back at Nique, who stood shaking her head.

"Fucking asshole," she mumbled.

I pressed my back against the wall, fighting back tears. I didn't want to cry over him. I'd shed enough tears.

"Forget him, Rhythm," Nique said, coming over to hug me. "You did the right thing."

"Then why do I feel like this?"

She shrugged. "You love him. The feeling will pass."

I prayed that it did because, right now, I felt like my heart was in shambles. No matter the circumstances, I loved that man. Those feelings didn't just go away overnight.

Chapter Six

Channing

"I can't believe I let you drag me out of the house," I said to my best friend, Jeremy.

I looked around the overly packed club and shook my head. It was wall to wall in this bitch, and I was surprised the fire marshal hadn't shut shit down.

Jeremy kissed his teeth. "Come on, bruh. Don't act like that. I don't get leave very often, and I wanna enjoy it while I'm home. You ain't seen me in about a year, my nigga."

Jeremy had been my best friend since we were twelve years old. He had always been my ride or die. My boy had enlisted in the Air Force right after high school and had been active for the last twelve years. Every time he came home, linking up was a must. Me complaining was just to fuck with him. Whatever he wanted to do to get a taste of civilian life, I was down with it.

"I knew you wanted to be in the streets which is why I got us a section," I stated.

"My nigga!"

43

We headed over to the VIP section. Since I was a regular here and always got the same section, the bouncer let us in with no problem. We settled in and ordered a couple of bottles for the table. Our server was this bad ass, brown-skinned girl by the name of Patina.

Baby was thicker than cold grits. The club's attire for the servers consisted of a crop top and cut off shorts. She'd paired fishnet stockings and a pair of Doc Martens with hers. Those shorts did everything for those thick ass thighs.

"Damn she fine," Jeremy said, watching our server's ass as she walked away.

I shook my head. "How long has it been since you got some ass, man?"

"Too fucking long. I'm walking outta here with something tonight."

"You hell."

"Tell me you ain't on the same shit."

I chuckled. "Not tonight. I can always pull up the roster and tell one of my ladies to come through."

He playfully shoved me. "Not the roster."

"It's a small roster. Even though I stay strapped, I can't be sticking my dick in every bad bitch."

"I feel you on that. A few niggas in my brigade messed with this same female, and all of them got burned. I dodged that bullet 'cause shawty was heavy on my ass too. I might fuck on the first night, but I can't get with a bitch that's giving pussy to everybody on the team."

I shook my head. "Okay, man."

Patina returned with our drinks, and my man put on his best charm.

"I apologize for being rude earlier and not introducing myself. I'm Jeremy, and this is my friend, Channing."

She looked between the two of us and smiled. "You weren't rude at all. Most people don't introduce themselves."

"I mean, if you're serving me, I can at least be cordial. How you doin' tonight, beautiful?"

She blushed. "I can't complain. The night is really just getting started, so we'll see how it goes."

"Well, I hope you have a good night. Maybe if you aren't busy later, we can link up."

She smirked as she tucked the empty tray under her arm. Pulling out a pen and her notepad, she scribbled something on it and handed it to him.

"Hit me up," she said.

"Fa'sho."

She winked at him before walking away.

"And just like that, ya boy is in them guts tonight. Damn, I can't wait to see all that ass from the back."

I chuckled. "I hope you don't get none."

"Woooow! It really be the people closest to you praying on your downfall."

We shared a laugh as we poured up our drinks.

"How have you been, man?" he asked.

"Shit's been straight. Just going through it with Grams right now. She's in the early stages of dementia."

"Damn, man. I'm sorry to hear that. I gotta make my way over to see her and your mom before I ship back out. You know I love those two women. Your house was practically my second home."

"It was. Grams faithfully asked, *Is that silly ass boy coming over today?* when we were growing up."

He chuckled. "That lady loved me and my silly ass."

"She did. I'm sure she'd be happy to see you. I know my mom would. She asks about you."

"Awww, my baby missed me?"

I slapped the back of his head. "Don't start that shit."

He grinned. "You know yo' mama fine. Been fine. Always gon' be fine."

"Don't make me kick your ass, Jeremy."

He raised his hands in mock surrender but continued to laugh as he picked up his drink. As I took a sip from mine, I caught sight of two beautiful women coming into VIP. A smile spread across my face as I recognized one of them.

Dr. Baker.

She was bad in scrubs, but tonight, she looked so damn fuckable. Tonight, she wore this white, long-sleeved minidress that looked like a button up. The first couple of buttons were undone, giving a glimpse of her ample cleavage. Her nipple piercings shone through subtly. On her feet were a pair of strappy nude heels.

Toned legs and thick thighs glistened with a hint of some sort of shimmer. Her hair was pulled into a sleek top knot. Diamond studs twinkled in her ears along with a matching necklace and bracelet. Her face was free of makeup, but baby girl didn't need it.

I stood as they got closer to us and gently grabbed her arm.

"Dr. Baker."

She looked down at my hand and then back up at me, probably prepared to curse me out. When she recognized my face, hers softened.

"Hey," she said, stepping out of the way of foot traffic.

"Who is this?" her friend asked.

"I don't remember his name, but I do remember him almost knocking me on my ass the other week at work."

I chuckled. "It's Channing, and I apologized for that, beautiful."

"You did." She eyed me for a moment. "I never properly introduced myself. I'm Rhythm."

She extended her hand, and I shook it.

"Rhythm? That's your government name?"

"Yes."

"You lying."

"Why would I lie about my name?"

"I didn't mean any disrespect. I've just never met anyone with your name. It's dope."

"Thank you. My father loves music, and my mother allowed him to name me, so there you have it. This is my friend, Monique."

Her friend smiled and waved. "Hi."

"It's nice to meet you. This is my friend Jeremy."

Jeremy smiled his million-dollar smile, and her friend blushed.

"It's nice to meet you, ladies. Care to join us?"

"We actually have a section," Rhythm said. Her eyes trailed my frame. "Maybe I'll see you on the dance floor."

Jeremy laughed. "This nigga doesn't dance."

Both women giggled.

"I'm sure you can catch the beat," Rhythm said, pulling her dainty hand out of mine. "Have a good night."

She grabbed her friend's hand and pulled her away. Once again, I watched the bounce of her ass as she walked.

"That's a fine ass woman," Jeremy said, shaking his head. "She ain't trying to give you no play, my nigga."

"I ain't worried about that," I said, taking my seat.

"Where did you meet her?"

I ran him the story of me having to change my mom's tire the other week. I couldn't lie and say that her beautiful ass hadn't crossed my mind. I'd almost volunteered to take Grams to therapy this week, but her aide stepped in to give my mother a break.

I wasn't sure what it was about these short interactions with her, but she left a lasting impression. I'd never had a problem getting a woman. I wasn't pressed about her blowing me off a record two times now, but I couldn't say I wasn't intrigued with her beauty.

I looked over to where she was with her girl, already dancing at the railing that overlooked the dance floor. I really didn't dance, but should I find myself on the dance floor with her, I wouldn't be mad at that.

* * *

We'd been in the club for a good two hours or so. Jeremy and I ran into a few people we used to kick it with back in the day, and they joined us in our section to welcome him home. My boy was having the time of his life, popping bottles and entertaining women. His drunk ass had been on and off the dance floor half the night.

I sat back watching and shaking my head. I knew he needed to let loose. While we hadn't seen each other in about a year, we spoke pretty often. He'd told me about all the shit he'd seen while on active duty and how it had somewhat desensitized him to death.

I was proud of him for being in therapy, just in case his demons became a monkey on his back. Being back in his familiar stomping grounds was what he said he needed, so I was more than happy to oblige him by coming out tonight.

Every so often, I found myself looking over at Rhythm in her section. She seemed to be half here and half somewhere else from time to time. This time when I looked over at her, she was alone and scrolling through her phone. I looked over the railing and scanned the crowd for her friend, only to find her dancing with Jeremy.

I stood and excused myself from my people before walking down to where she sat. She looked up as I approached her and tucked her phone away.

"You mind if I have a seat?" I asked.

She waved her hand at the empty seat and crossed her legs.

"I see your girl and my boy hit it off," I noted, easing down next to her.

"Nique loves to dance, and your boy has been lit all night."

I chuckled. "That nigga is drunk. He can't be still."

"Let him enjoy himself."

"Are you enjoying yourself?"

She shrugged. "It's been decent. It has served its purpose for tonight."

"And what's that?"

"A distraction."

"What do you need to be distracted from?"

She giggled. "Aren't you nosy."

"I mean, you put it out there. I'm just making conversation, love. You don't have to tell me anything you don't want to."

She sighed. "Life... it's been kicking my ass, and I needed a break."

"Is it that bad?"

"It's not the end of the world... more like the end of an era. I'm okay though. At the end of the day, I know who and what I am. I can put on my big girl panties and carry on."

I didn't voice it, but it sounded like she was referring to a nigga. If that was the case, she was way too fine to be stressed over one nigga when there was probably a line of them dying to get at her beautiful ass.

To her, I replied, "My grams always said some things are meant to be a part of your history, but not your destiny."

She giggled. "Are you getting philosophical on me in the club, sir?"

I chuckled. "Nah, that's just some truth for your ass, love. Some things and people are meant for a season. Once they serve their purpose in your life, you gotta be okay with getting that shit up outta there."

She nodded. "You're right. It's just hard to let go of something you're so familiar with."

"I feel you on that."

She eyed me for a moment. "So... what brings you here? You can't dance. I haven't seen you entertain any women tonight. You haven't even left your section."

"Damn, you been watching me?" I jested.

She laughed. "I've been observing the place in general, thank you very much."

"On the real, my boy is on military leave. He just wanted a taste of civilian life, so I let him drag me out of my house."

"Aren't you a good friend."

"I'm an excellent friend. I always have room for another."

"So you wanna be my friend, Channing?"

My dick twitched at the sound of my name on her lips. *Fuck!*

"Maybe I do."

49

"And what kind of friend is that?"

"Whatever kind of friend you need, baby."

She smirked as she stood to her feet and tucked her phone into her pocket. "Dance with me."

"I—"

"Aht, aht. You wanna be a good friend, come dance with me. No sense in both of us sitting here all night."

I decided to oblige her. Standing to my feet, I grabbed her and pulled her behind me. We made our way to the dance floor just as the DJ dropped the beat to "Touchin'" by Honey Bxby. She must have been feeling the song because the moment we found a spot on the floor, she turned her back and started dancing on me.

There wasn't much space to move around, but I didn't mind her ass grinding on me. She raised her hands and swirled her hips to the beat in a manner that had me hypnotized. Now, just because I *didn't* dance didn't mean I *couldn't*. My hands found solace on her hips as I grinded back against her in perfect rhythm.

When she turned and snaked her arms around my waist, her eyes locked on mine. The smoky, intimate atmosphere of the club seemed to fade away as I got lost in the music and her beautiful brown orbs. I pulled her close, encircling her waist with my arms as we continued to grind against each other. She draped her arms around my neck, fingers softly playing with the hair.

Even as close as we were, she somehow managed to press even closer to me. Our bodies fit together like two puzzle pieces as we moved to the sensuous rhythm, hips swaying in perfect sync. My dick was straining against my slacks, and I knew she had to have felt that shit.

She smirked as she gave me the most innocent look. I just knew lil baby was a good time. She may have looked innocent, but she probably gave a muthafucka a run for their money.

"Why you looking at me like that, ma?" I asked in her ear.

"Looking at you like what?"

"You know what I'm talking about. Ask for it... I might let you have it."

Her eyes widened, and she blushed as she bit her lip.

"A closed mouth don't get fed," I reminded her.

Her breathing hitched in her throat. She swallowed hard as she backed away from me.

"I have to go to the bathroom."

Without another word, she disappeared into the crowd, leaving me standing there by myself. I started to go after her but thought better of it. Instead, I made my way back up to my section to join my boys. It was nearing one thirty in the morning, and the club would be shutting down at two.

Jeremy had found his drunken way back to the section and was ready to dip out. I didn't protest. Instead, we said goodbye to our people, I paid our tab, and we headed out to my car.

"I'm gon' sleep good tonight," he declared.

"You should with all the fucking dancing your ass was doing."

He laughed. "The ladies love your boy, man. I'm finna slide that big booty server my location and have her come through." He slapped my arm. "Yo, I saw your non-dancing ass with that fine ass girl from earlier. Did you get her number?"

"Nah. I didn't ask."

"Why not? She bad, man."

"As bad as she is, I don't think she's ready to put herself out there. She might talk big shit, but baby is timid."

He kissed his teeth. "It's plenty of fish in the sea, my nigga."

As we rounded the corner of the parking lot, I saw Rhythm and her girl coming out the back door. Our eyes met, and we briefly stared at each other before she headed down another row of parked cars.

I didn't get her this go 'round, but if I ran into her again, maybe the third time would be a charm.

Chapter Seven

Rhythm

When I looked up and saw Channing standing in front of me, I just knew my night was about to get interesting. His friend had already come to claim Nique, and my girl was living her best life with him on the dance floor. I'd opted to rest my feet for a moment. We'd been lit all by ourselves in our VIP section since we'd made it here, and I needed a break.

"You mind if I have a seat?" he asked.

My eyes slowly perused his tall, muscular frame. He had a fresh line up, and his beard was neatly trimmed. His striking brown eyes were slightly hooded, telling me that he was either a little intoxicated or he'd been smoking.

Tonight, he was dressed in all black from head to toe. He had to be the finest caramel coated man I'd ever laid eyes on. He easily towered over my shorter frame. His hair was cut low and so was the beard encasing those full, clit sucking lips of his. Both of his arms and hands were fully tatted as well as his neck. From what I could see, he seemed to have a chest piece too. Minimal gold jewelry added to his ensemble. He wasn't flashy or over the top. A man this fine didn't need to do much to still be fine and stand out.

I waved a hand at the empty seat and crossed my legs. I didn't miss his eyes traveling the length of my exposed thigh.

"I see your girl and my boy hit it off," he noted, easing down next to me.

"Nique loves to dance, and your boy has been lit all night."

He chuckled. "That nigga is drunk. He can't be still."

"Let him enjoy himself."

"Are you enjoying yourself?"

I shrugged. "It's been decent. It has served its purpose for tonight."

"And what's that?"

"A distraction."

"What do you need to be distracted from?"

I giggled. "Aren't you nosy."

"I mean, you put it out there. I'm just making conversation, love. You don't have to tell me anything you don't want to."

I sighed. "Life... it's been kicking my ass, and I needed a break."

"Is it that bad?"

"It's not the end of the world... more like the end of an era. I'm okay though. At the end of the day, I know who and what I am. I can put on my big girl panties and carry on."

That was the line I'd been telling myself for weeks now, *carry on*. I had to move like I wasn't hurting because, at the end of the day, what was crying all damn day going to do for me?

I continued to talk to Channing for a bit. When he started flirting with me, I kept a cool head, but inside, I was sweating bullets. My hormones were raging as his eyes trailed my frame. I needed something to distract me, so I asked him to dance. Music had a way of transporting me. I could be in my zone and block him out.

Mistake number one.

The dance floor was packed. We were damn near chest to chest with people. Still, we found a spot, and when the DJ dropped the beat to "Touchin'" by Honey Bxby—that was my shit—I immediately threw my hands up and started winding my hips. I felt his hands on my hips. For someone whose friend said he didn't dance, he was winding his hips like a pro, catching my rhythm.

I found myself turning to face him and wrapping my arms around his waist. He was solid. Beneath his clothes, I imagined he had the type of body I'd want pressed against mine without them.

That was mistake number two.

When our eyes locked, I couldn't force myself to look away from him. He pulled me in closer, and that was when I felt the hardness pressed against me, causing the corners of my mouth to lift. He leaned in and spoke into my ear.

"Why you looking at me like that, ma?"

I swallowed hard. "Looking at you like what?"

"You know what I'm talking about. Ask for it... I might let you have it."

My eyes widened, and I blushed as I bit my lip. Our movements had come to a halt, and now we were just standing there, looking at each other. I felt flustered. My temperature was rising, and suddenly, there were too many people around.

Channing waited for an answer. He'd arrogantly offered himself to me under the premise that he *might* let me have him. Any other time, it might have been a turn off. Tonight... with him... I almost wanted to give in and go against every moral I had.

"A closed mouth don't get fed," he reminded me.

My pussy was screaming, *Whatchu gon' do, sis?*

Before I did something I might regret in the morning, I backed away and hightailed it after telling him I needed to use the bathroom. I locked myself in the stall until I could gather my bearings. I sent Nique a text, telling her to meet me at the back door because we had to go.

She wasn't happy about leaving and met me with a frown on her face. I ignored it as we stepped outside. It was just my luck that as we hit the parking lot, there was Channing and his friend. Our eyes met momentarily before I ducked off down the row I was parked in, praying he didn't follow. We climbed into my car, and I hurriedly left the parking lot.

"Girl, why did you rush us out of there?" Nique complained as we drove back to the hotel.

"Bitch, I had to get away from that man," I said, fanning myself.

"What man? Did somebody touch you?"

"No, nobody touched me. I'm talking about Channing."

"The fine nigga with all the tattoos that stopped you when we walked in?"

"Yes."

"What did he do?"

"He had me hot and bothered, that's what he did."

She laughed obnoxiously. "You ran from the club because the man made you horny?"

"It ain't that funny, Nique. We were dancing, and I could be mistaken, but I was sure that wasn't a gun pressed against me."

She raised an eyebrow. "Was it big?"

I giggled. "It definitely was."

"You should have taken it for a test drive."

"I don't know that man! Besides, I'm newly single. The last thing I need is to be getting over one man by getting under another."

It had been a full two weeks since I left the home I shared with Raheem. After he showed up at my hotel last week, I ended up changing rooms for a double room. While I enjoyed having Nique with me, somewhere in between the last time I saw her and now, my girl developed a snore, and I couldn't take that shit in my ear. While I missed the private pool, the room we had now was just as beautiful.

With Nique here, I felt so much better. She never let me be a sad bitch for too long, if at all. I hadn't been on social media, and I'd blocked Raheem from contacting me. There was a slight sense of peace in that. The less I saw or heard from him, the less I would see or hear shit to further upset me.

The first few days of her being here, I'd taken off work. It was a much-needed mini staycation. All we did was eat, drink, and roam around the city. Even though we said we'd look at apartments, it hadn't happened yet. I was enjoying the amenities of the hotel anyway, although the restaurant downstairs was going to have me trying to unbig my back. The food was so good, and I sometimes overindulged in its goodness.

"Did you at least have fun tonight?" Nique asked.

"I did. This definitely took me back to our college days. You remember how wild those parties used to get?"

She laughed. "Chile, we used to be hell. Don't let them play our song and everybody got to strolling."

Nique and I entered Greek life our sophomore semester, and every chance we got to stroll with our line sisters or the bruhs, we were right there. It was a wonder that either of us could walk in heels at this point with all the hopping and jumping we used to do in them.

Nique grinned. "You know, Channing was giving those dawg vibes. I can see him hitting that nasty neck roll. Imagine if that man put you on his shoulders."

"Girl, please shut up!"

I laughed, but the truth was, in the short time I danced with that man, I imagined him having me *several* ways. The height difference between us as the hardness of his dick pressed right up against me caused thoughts of us in different positions to flood my mind. Not only was he fine as hell, but he smelled so damn good.

When he pulled me close, it took everything in me not to wrap a leg around his waist and off myself right there on the dance floor. Everybody would have borne witness to the dry humping I fought against. The way he looked at me told me he would fuck the shit outta me if I let him.

When I excused myself to the bathroom, I found the seat of my thong soaked. I had to take them off and trash them. That was when I knew I had to get the hell out of there. If I'd gone back to that man, there was no telling what might have happened, and I'd never been one to fuck on a stranger.

My attraction to him was absolutely insane to me. Maybe it was the fact that I hadn't been intimate with Raheem in months. He'd been pissing me off so bad that I just hadn't been in the mood to have sex with him.

Sex wouldn't fix what was wrong with us. I didn't trust him. I didn't trust that he wasn't out here sticking his dick in somebody else, especially a bitch he'd been parading around in my face. That was the curtain call on our relationship, and his little proposition was the benediction.

* * *

"Is that everything?" Nique asked as she looked around my bedroom.

I was teary eyed as I looked around as well. I couldn't believe I was moving out. I hadn't returned home since the night I left. Things between Raheem and me were done, and it was time for me to officially move out.

I chose today because I knew he'd be out of town for a show. I didn't have to worry about him being here or coming home while I was trying to move. It would only lead to yet another argument or him trying to convince me to stay.

Since I'd blocked him and changed hotel rooms, he'd been leaving messages on my voicemail at work, begging and begging. His words weren't lining up with his actions though. Against my better judgment, I went looking on the gossip blogs. There was still shit about him and Lady Lingo being put out, and he did nothing to alleviate the rumors. He seemed to be eating up the attention. Social media was flooded with pictures of them in the studio or the club appearances. They always looked real cozy and shit.

Before she joined his label, none of this shit had been an issue.

He worked with female artists before. He'd been photographed with them before, and they had never been inappropriate. Yet, there was something about him and this girl that just rubbed me the wrong way.

He told me I was seeing what I wanted to see. Why the fuck would I *want* to see the man I loved be all over another woman? Make it make sense. I was mentally and emotionally drained. My worst fear of moving out here was coming true. Before I got any deeper in my feelings, I felt it was best to just leave the relationship altogether.

All that was left to do was pack my belongings and gather the dignity I had left. If he wanted to fully submerge himself into this toxic lifestyle, he'd have to do it without me. By the time he returned from his gig, it would look like I was never here. Part of me wanted to be petty and fuck up his shit, but my heart wouldn't let me.

"That's it," I said softly. "At least I think it is. At this point, I don't care."

Nique came over and wrapped her arms around me. The moment they encased me, I broke.

"It's okay, boo," she said, squeezing me. "You're doing what's best for you."

"Then why do I feel like this?"

"Because you love him. It's gonna hurt for a while, but you'll bounce back."

"Was I wrong, Nique? Should I have just been the stereotypical rapper girlfriend and be his arm candy?"

She frowned as she pulled away from me.

"Hell no. You are your own woman, Rhythm. I haven't met a man yet that is worth wrapping your entire identity up in. It doesn't matter how much you love someone. You should never have to change who you are to fit in their life."

"I know. He wasn't always like this. Or maybe he was, and I didn't notice it because I wasn't there with him. When he used to come see me before we started dating, he did everything in his power to make sure that I was comfortable and not overwhelmed with the parameters of his success. He toned it down to get me, and now that I'm here, it's like I'm on his turf. Either play along or get left behind. I left a comfortable life to be here, Nique. I left my family and moved across the country for a fucking man that wants me to be okay with him being in a fake relationship with his coworker, all for likes, views, and money."

Monique shook her head. "I still can't believe he asked you that shit. The Raheem we grew up with was humble. I don't know who the fuck he is now."

"I know who he is. He's Prince Cole. He's trying to fully submerge himself into this lifestyle, Nique. It's not gonna happen at my expense. If I have to start over, then so be it."

"Well, at least I'll be there with you."

"Right, at least you'll be—wait, what?"

"I'm moving. I was planning to surprise you. That was one of the main reasons I was coming out here. I'd already scoped out a place and put a deposit down. I just wanted to see it in person. I got the keys the other day while you were at work, and my job has taken care of my transfer!"

"Oh my God! Nique!"

I pulled her in for a hug. If things had to be ending, I was happy to have her here with me.

Nique laughed as I rocked her back and forth. "I take it you're happy?"

"Happy isn't the word!"

She smiled as she pulled away from me. "And I have a two bedroom. You are more than welcome to stay. I miss you, Rhythm. It doesn't have to be permanent. I know we'll both want our space and privacy, eventually. It would be nice to have back some of the time I've missed with my bestie, though."

I nodded in agreement. "It would be. I'd love to stay. Only for a while though. You might meet a man, and I'm not trying to hear him clapping your cheeks."

"And you know this ass is gonna clap!"

Kimberly Brown

She bent over and started twerking, causing me to laugh. Of course, I had to hype my girl up and give her ass a playful smack. I really did miss her, and I knew it would be great having her here. She was just the person I needed to help me through this. I may have been smiling right now, but my heart was very much hurting.

Chapter Eight

Channing

"She won't come out of the bathroom. Every time I try to open the door, she screams at me to get out of her house."

I listened to Raven, my grandmother's aide, crying on the other end of my phone. I'd sent my mother on a much-needed spa day and told her aide to call me if there was a problem. She was under no circumstance to call my mother.

I ran my hand down my head. "All right, I'm coming. Just let her stay in there and don't bother her."

"Are you sure I shouldn't call the paramedics?"

"What did I say? I'm coming."

"Okay, Mr. Watson."

I hung up the phone and stepped back into the studio to grab my keys. I was working with Imani today on a new track for her third album. Prince Cole was with her since he was featured on the song.

I got an inkling that there was something going on between those two every time I saw them together, which was often. I'd heard the talk of their label trying to push them together. From the outside looking in, they definitely looked like a couple.

The chemistry was there. She was always affectionate with him, and he didn't seem to mind. Today, there seemed to be a little tension. Whatever was going on outside of the studio, they'd brought it inside, and it was fucking shit up.

She had an attitude, and he couldn't seem to catch the beat to save his life. Dipping out on this session had been heavy on my mind, and now I had an excuse.

"Aye, we gotta cut this short. I have to go check on my grand-mother. I don't know if or when I'll be back today."

Imani sat up straight. "Well maybe we can work in your studio tonight? I really wanna get this track done."

Prince came out of the booth as she finished speaking.

I shook my head. "Nah, not today. This is personal. Speaking of personal, I don't know what type of shit you two have going on, but fix that shit before you come back in my session. Y'all wasted a lot of my time today. All that outside shit... leave it outside. When you step in here, you come prepared to work."

Imani pouted. "I apologize," she said softly.

Prince extended his hand. "My bad, big dawg. I got some shit going on at home that I'm trying to fix—"

Imani scoffed as she threw him a glare.

"Whatever it is, handle it. I'll holla at y'all later."

Without another word, I grabbed my bag and left the studio. My mother only lived about twenty minutes away. Much to my surprise, traffic wasn't as bad as I thought it would be. When I pulled in the yard, I could see the aide looking out the window. Climbing out of the car, I headed up the front steps. She immediately opened the door to let me in.

"Is she still in there?" I asked.

"She is. She's quite irritable."

"What happened?"

"She was asleep when your mother left, and I didn't want to

bother her. I made lunch, and I went to check on her. She was in the bathroom already. When I asked if she was okay, she started yelling. I wasn't sure if it was because she couldn't see me or didn't recognize my voice, but she had a fit."

I shook my head. "This isn't your normal day. That might be it. Wait out here."

I should have known better than to interrupt the routine we had her on. I headed into Grams' room and knocked on the bathroom door.

"Grams... open up."

She sounded frantic as she asked, "Channing? Is that you?"

"It's me."

I heard the door unlock. When it opened, she rushed into my arms and hugged me. I opened my mouth to speak, but she began to cry. I wrapped my arms around her, hugging her tightly.

"I got you," I said, stroking her back.

"I was scared. I called for your mama, and she didn't answer."

"I sent Ma to the spa for the day, Grams. Raven is here with you."

"Raven?" She looked up and over at Raven who stood timidly in the bedroom doorway. "She... she didn't sound like herself. She's not supposed to be here today, Channing. It's on my calendar. She's supposed to be here tomorrow."

"I know, Grams. That's my fault. I should have talked to you about it first."

She pulled away from me and wrapped her arms around herself.

"I'm sorry," she said softly. "I must have scared you."

Raven shook her head. "No, ma'am. I just wanted to make sure you were okay."

Grams walked over to her bed and sat down. "I think you and Shey need to put me in a nursing home, Channing," she said.

"Absolutely not," I said firmly. "I'm not putting you in a nursing home, Grams. You want me to go to jail? 'Cause that's gonna happen if I have to break my foot off in somebody's ass for mistreating you.

63

You're staying here, and if Ma can't handle it, you can move in with me. I can always work from home."

She shook her head. "I don't want you putting your life on hold for me. This disease is only going to get worse. At some point, I won't know who you are, and I don't want you or Shey to have to deal with the heartbreak that brings. I already hear her crying. You've taken excellent care of your mother and I for years now. You should be dating... getting married and starting a family. You shouldn't burden yourself with taking care of an old woman."

I stepped in front of her and stooped so that I was at eye level with her.

"You helped carry the burden of raising me when your own child was grown. You pushed me to follow my dreams of producing music, and look where I'm at. Ain't no way in hell I'd ever push you or my mama off on somebody in a nursing home. I got you, both of you. That's for life."

I kissed her cheek and wrapped my arms around her in a hug. She cried softly against me. I could hear Raven sniffling at the door. This shit was hard, but I had to be mentally equipped to deal with it. I made a mental note to further dig into her diagnosis. I knew I'd never be fully prepared for everything, but the more I knew, the better I could handle it.

I ended up staying with Grams until well after my mama got home. She looked so relaxed that I couldn't bring myself to drop today's episode on her. I told Raven not to mention it and Grams that it would just be between us. Of course, she asked what I was doing at the house when I was supposed to be at work.

I simply told her it was on my spirit to spend time with Grams today. She eyed me skeptically but didn't question me further. I ended up cooking dinner for them and staying to clean the kitchen. Grams was tired and ready for bed, so Raven went to help her get situated in the shower.

As I washed the dishes, my mama dried them off. Our routine was quiet for a while before she nudged me.

"What's up?" I asked, looking down at her short frame.

"You're gonna make some lucky woman a very happy wife one day, Channing."

I chuckled. "You think so?"

"I know so. I'll be taking the credit for that."

"Yeah, woman. That's all you."

She giggled. "I don't know if I say it enough, but I'm very proud of you. You are every bit of the man I'd hoped you'd be."

She stood on her toes and kissed my cheek.

"Thank you, Ma."

"But..."

I rolled my eyes. "But what?"

"When are you gonna make me a grandma? I always wished I'd had more children. I feel like I should be swimming in grandkids by now."

"First of all, you got all you needed when you had me, okay? I'd hate to have to bust your other kids in their shit."

She slapped my arm. "Watch your mouth, boy."

I grinned. "Imagine how much you'd have to say that if I had siblings. And don't let us get to fighting."

"I'd be whupping ass, too."

We shared a laugh, but then her face turned serious.

"I wasn't joking about the grandkids. Now I'm not saying go out here and impregnate a bunch of women with your lil ding-a-ling. I want you to have a wife. Is there not anybody special in your life?"

"Not at the moment."

"So you mean to tell me that none of those women you entertain are wifey material?"

"I ain't say all that. I just wouldn't wife them."

"But you'd sleep with them?"

"I have needs, Ma."

She kissed her teeth. "Hell, I have needs too, Channing."

"Aht! I don't wanna think about that!

She laughed. "You realize I had to be doing the nasty for you to be here, right?"

"That was before my time and that ain't got nothing to do with me."

She shook her head. "Whatever. I'm serious. Don't make any woman a mother that you wouldn't make your wife."

"I strap up, so ain't no babies coming before I want them if I can help it."

She rolled her eyes.

"If it makes you feel better, there is somebody I'm interested in."

Her eyes twinkled. "Who?"

"Dr. Baker."

"Dr. Baker? Mama's Dr. Baker? As in Dr. Baker from The Baker Method?"

"Yes, woman."

She frowned. "When did you even meet her?"

"You in my business?"

She smacked my arm. "Channing Watson."

I laughed. "The day I changed your tire. I went inside to wash my hands and literally ran into her."

"Mmm hmm. Dr. Baker is nice. She's a smart girl with a good head on her shoulders. I like her, and I'd like her for you."

"I'ma work on that, then."

"Don't be out here playing with people's hearts, Channing. If you are gonna pursue that woman, go into it with good intentions, not just getting your dick wet."

I frowned as I handed her the last dish. "Please don't say that word again."

"Dick. Dick. Dick. You pissed on me enough for me to be able to say it around you."

I shook my head as I dried my hands. "I'm about to go. You've scorned me enough for one evening. I'm gonna bring Koda by in the morning. I think Grams would enjoy her company."

"That's fine. Thank you for the spa day and spending time with Mama. And, of course, thank you for dinner."

"It was nothing." I pulled her in for a hug and kissed her cheek. "I love you."

"I love you, too."

Before leaving the house, I went to say goodnight to Grams. Raven was just helping her into bed.

"Good night, old woman," I said, leaning in to kiss her temple.

"Good night, baby. I love you."

"I love you, too. Good night, Raven."

"Good night, Mr. Watson."

I left the room and headed out of the house. It was pushing nine, and a nigga was tired as hell. All I wanted to do was hop in my shower, climb in my bed, and watch TV until TV was watching me.

Chapter Nine

Rhythm

Monique had gone back to South Carolina three days ago to finish packing up her apartment for her move. We'd spent four days together in her new place, with her doing everything in her power to keep my mind off Raheem's ass. We'd gone shopping for the apartment, had a few movie nights, and I'd taken her around the city to show her more of the hot spots.

I was so happy that she'd soon be here on a permanent basis. Our goodbyes at the airport were bittersweet. I knew once we parted ways, I'd be knee deep in my feelings with a bottle of wine. Sure as shit, when I got back to the empty apartment, I broke down.

Raheem had been calling and texting her nonstop, trying to reach me. The day I left, he'd watched me on the camera taking my shit out. He was supposed to be away for a gig, yet he called her three times, telling her to tell me I'd better be at the house when he got back.

Fuck that and fuck him.

I knew he'd never leave his gig to come home and deal with me.

Rhythm's Blues

Monique and I worked quickly to pack my shit into my G-Wagon and dipped. For the last three days, I'd been lying in my new bed on my sad girl shit.

Since I took some personal time from work, my days consisted of junk food, sad ass music, chick flicks, and scrolling through social media. I knew I should have stayed off Raheem's page, and I did. It was the blogs that kept popping up on my timeline.

He and Lady Lingo were seen out and about all over the place. Rumors of them dating were hitting harder than ever, even though they both kept denying it. The shit pissed me off. Why deny it and still continue doing shit to feed the narrative?

Fuck Raheem.

If he could move the way he wanted to, then so could I.

Today, I decided I was done being sad. I got out of bed and cleaned my room. I did a load of laundry and ordered enough groceries to stock the fridge, freezer, and pantry for a few weeks. With all of that done, I decided to step out tonight and enjoy myself. I deserved to have a little fun.

Standing in front of my full-length mirror, I smoothed my hand over the form-fitting white knee-length dress I wore. It was strapless and had a split that exposed my entire right thigh. On my feet were a pair of chunky white heels. My hair was blown out and feather curled, framing my face with a middle part. I'd forgone a full face of makeup, opting for only mascara, a little eyeshadow, and some lip gloss.

I thought I looked great for someone who'd been crying for three days. Giving my hair a final fluff, I grabbed my clutch and ensured my essentials were inside. With everything I needed, I locked up the apartment and headed downstairs to where my driver for this evening was waiting.

L.A. traffic was horrible, and any time I didn't have to drive, I wouldn't. The driver greeted me with a smile.

"Good evening, Ms. Baker," he said with a bow.

"Good evening."

"My name is Charles. It's a pleasure to serve you."

He opened the door and extended his hand to help me in. I smiled and accepted. Seated comfortably in the back seat, we headed toward the downtown area. I had a VIP reservation at The Caviar Club, which was an upscale lounge. I planned to have a good meal, listen to good music, and just feel the vibe.

It had been a long time since I'd gone out by myself. That wasn't the smartest thing to do out here. I was putting myself in a vulnerable position by going out alone, but I desperately needed to get out of the apartment.

I sighed as we pulled up in front of the building. The driver got out and rounded the passenger side to let me out.

"Shoot me a text when you're ready to leave, Ms. Baker," he said, handing me a card.

"Sure thing. Thank you."

I stepped off the curb and walked up to the red rope separating me from the entrance. The security guard licked his lips as I approached.

"Good evening, beautiful," he said, his eyes shamelessly trailing me from head to toe.

"Good evening."

"Go on and hold your arms out for me, baby."

I did as he requested as he grabbed the handheld metal detector to check me for contraband. I could feel his eyes burning a hole in my ass, causing me to smirk. I knew I looked good as a muthafucka, and so did he.

"You're clear," he said with a smile as he removed the rope. "You wearing the fuck outta this white. Looking like a fucking angel, baby."

I giggled. "Thank you."

"Go on in."

I strutted past him and into the lounge. After giving my name to the hostess, she led me to my section. Eyes bore into me as I followed behind her. I was greeted with a plethora of reactions, ranging from lustful stares to eye rolls. I brushed them all off. I was never cocky, but I knew I was a beautiful woman, and a hating ass bitch could never make me feel otherwise.

The bottle of wine I requested was waiting on the table for me. After thanking the hostess, I took a seat and poured myself a glass. Crossing my legs, I sat back and enjoyed the relaxing vibe. My server eventually came over to take my food and drink order.

As she was walking away, my phone rang in my clutch. Pulling it out, I saw that it was Monique calling me via FaceTime.

"Hey, boo," I answered.

"Hey my—oooo, bitch! You look the fuck good! Let me see this 'fit."

I angled the camera so she could see my entire look.

"All right, now! You got the thigh meat out. Titties sitting up. The face card is super valid. Where are you, and who are you with?"

I giggled. "Thank you, Nique. I'm at The Caviar Club, and I'm by myself. I needed a little pick me up."

"Well, bitch, you look like somebody is gonna pick you up, all right."

I rolled my eyes. "I'm not trying to be on that type of time, girl. I just needed to step out and remind myself that I'm a bad bitch and a prize."

"Period. Point fucking blank. Shit on them L.A. hos. Damn, I can't wait to get back! We are painting the streets red when I pull up. Well, give me a few days. That drive is going to be murder on me. Something told me I should have just packed my clothes and essentials and started over. I didn't realize how much shit I had until it was time to pack up."

I laughed. "Don't I know it? I didn't even take everything I wanted to take from Raheem's. Is he still on your line?"

"No. I blocked him."

"Good. I'm just not in the mood to deal with him, Nique. He's still moving funny, and I don't have anything to say to him right now."

"I've seen the blogs. He's not helping his case at all."

I nodded as though she could see me. "It's cool, Nique. I now know what type of nigga I'm fucking with. I'm just gonna act accordingly."

She sighed. "Well, have some fun, girl. I'm not gonna hold you up. Send me your location. I can't get there, but I can at least keep track of you."

"I will. I love you, girl."

"I love you too."

We disconnected the call, and I took a long sip of my wine. Brushing all thoughts of Raheem Cole from my head, I focused back on the atmosphere. I was determined to have a good night.

* * *

I'd been in The Caviar Club for about an hour now. It was starting to get a little lit in here. I'd declined so many invitations to have random men join me. At least five drinks had been sent to my table, and I sent them all back. There was this one man that kept looking at me from across the room. He was beginning to make me uncomfortable. Just as the feeling set in, he made it worse by finally making his way over to me and inviting himself into my section.

"How you doing, beautiful?" he asked, sliding next to me.

I scooted away from him. "I'm fine."

"Damn right you are. What's a beautiful lady like yourself doing here alone?"

"Who said I was alone?"

He chuckled. "I don't see no nigga around. You been here for a minute, and I see you breaking hearts left and right."

"I didn't come here to entertain anybody."

"So, you got a man or nah?"

I frowned. "What's it to you?"

"I'm trying to get to know you, love..." He slid a hand across my thigh. "You so fucking sexy."

I slapped his hand away. "Thanks, but no thanks. I'm not interested."

"What I gotta do to make you interested?"

He reached into his pocket and pulled out a wad of cash as though it was supposed to impress me.

"Name your price."

I scoffed. "I don't have a price because I ain't one of those cheap ass hos."

He laughed. "Cheap ho. High class ho. All of you bitches have a price."

"Bitches? Who you calling a bitch?"

"I ain't mean no disrespect, ma—"

"You didn't mean any disrespect, yet you've been nothing but disrespectful since you sat your dusty ass down next to me, uninvited by the way. Why don't you and your hundred-dollar bill wrapped around a wad of ones go on about your business. Ain't shit poppin' over here tonight."

He grabbed my arm. "You think you better than me, bitch?"

"Get your fucking hands off of me!" I snapped.

"Let me tell you something—"

Before he could finish his sentence, he was being snatched up by a tall figure. I looked up to see Channing.

"Nigga, the fuck is wrong with you?" he asked, practically lifting ol' boy from the ground. "I know damn well I didn't see you put your hands on her."

"That's your bitch or something?" the guy asked, struggling to free himself.

"If it is or ain't, it don't make a fucking difference. It's niggas like you that give good niggas a bad name. The woman ain't interested, as she stated. Take your funky ass on somewhere. Let me catch you over here again and I'm breaking yo' fucking jaw."

"A'ight, nigga, damn!"

Channing glared at him before turning to me. "Apologize to the lady."

The guy frowned. "What?"

"Apologize, muthafucka. I didn't stutter."

"I ain't apologizing to that bi—"

Before he could finish the sentence, Channing had him in a death grip of a headlock. He struggled to breathe as he clawed at his arm.

"You not gon' do what?" Channing asked the man.

"I'm... I'm sorry!" he choked out.

"That's what the fuck I thought."

He released the man by tossing him aside. The guy gasped for air as he rubbed his neck. His gaze shifted from me to Channing as he struggled to his feet and walked away. Channing turned back to me.

"Are you okay?" he asked.

I nodded. "I'm fine. Thank you for stepping in."

"I wasn't trying to get in your business, but I saw that shit coming the minute he walked over here. I apologize."

"No need to apologize. You did more than enough."

He nodded. "You be safe. L.A. is too dangerous for beautiful women to be alone out here."

He turned to walk away. I was a little taken aback that he was just gonna leave after saving me from that creep. The times I'd seen him before, he flirted and whatnot, but tonight, he seemed to be over it.

"Can I at least buy you a drink to say thank you?" I asked, causing him to stop in his tracks.

He turned back, eyeing me skeptically. "Nah. I'll buy you one though."

I motioned for him to sit and called our server over.

"Let me get Hennessy on the rocks," Channing said. "And whatever the lady wants."

"I'll have a Lemon Drop."

"Coming right up."

She left us alone, and my eyes settled on the handsome specimen. I hadn't been remotely attracted to another man since Raheem and I had been together. Tunnel vision was real. I felt foolish now for putting my all into one man. Now that I was *single*, single, maybe it was time to have a little fun.

"Are you here alone?" I asked, crossing my legs.

His eyes drifted briefly to the thickness of my thighs before finding my face.

"Yes, ma'am."

"Isn't that dangerous for you too?"

He chuckled as he leaned forward on his elbows. "I'm more than capable of protecting myself. I'm an army of one, baby."

Baby.

The word sent chills up my spine. I wasn't sure if it was the deepness of his voice or the confidence laced in his tone. Maybe it was because he was just so damn fine. Every time I saw this man, he made my body heat up. I didn't know what the fuck was wrong with me. My nipples hardened as he licked his lips and smiled. God, what a smile!

"I hear you," I said as the waitress brought over our drinks.

We both took a sip before placing them on the table.

"You aren't from here, are you?" he asked. "You have a little southern twang. I heard it the last time I saw you, but I can't place it."

I giggled. "I'm not. I'm from South Carolina."

"What the hell are you doing all the way in Cali?"

I rolled my eyes. "Following a damn man. Before you judge me, I knew him way before."

He raised his hands in mock surrender. "No judgment. Love makes you do crazy shit."

"Stupid shit." I sighed. "Cheers to that being over."

He tipped his glass at me. "Is that what you're celebrating tonight?"

"I guess you could say that. He's moving funny, so it's fuck him. You single?"

He smirked. "Very."

"Lucky me."

"Why's that?"

"I don't know. I guess by the end of the night, we'll see."

I grabbed my drink and took a sip of it. Tonight, I was throwing caution to the wind. I was a single woman. I'd allowed Raheem to play in my face for far too long. I was young, beautiful, and I had options too. If he didn't know what he had when he had me, he'd just have to learn to miss his water when his well ran dry.

Chapter Ten

Channing

Ms. Rhythm was fucking me up.

I'd been chilling with her in VIP for a good lil minute now. We'd been drinking and chatting it up. She avoided telling me anything too personal about her, but still, I liked her vibe. We'd migrated from the VIP to the dance floor. Once again, she was grinding that thick ass up on me.

"DFMU" by Ella Mai crooned through the speakers of the lounge. I could tell she was feeling the music with the way she was winding her hips and touching all over me. The lust in her eyes told me she was looking for trouble. I wasn't the least bit opposed to being the trouble she got into.

"You keep looking at me like that and you gon' know something," I said, wrapping my arm around her waist.

"I'm down to learn a lesson. Take me out of here and teach me something."

I chuckled. "The last time I told you to ask for it, you ran from me."

"Why are you bringing up old shit?"

I had to laugh. "You been drinking, ma. I don't need you waking up in the morning with regret."

"I've been drinking, but trust me, I'm sober. I know exactly what I'm saying."

I eyed her curiously. I knew she was probably on some get back shit with her nigga. I didn't care about that. This wasn't some immediate love connection I was trying to make with her, and I was positive it wasn't that for her either. I could give her a taste of what she was looking for.

I leaned in and spoke into her ear. "Listen, baby. If I take you outta here, I'm not being gentle about shit. You'll be thoroughly fucked."

"Is that a promise?"

She smirked as she slipped out of my arms and grabbed my hand. I led her through the crowd and out of the lounge. After I handed the valet the ticket for my car, we patiently waited for it to be pulled around. My eyes trailed her thick ass frame from head to toe.

Shit, she was fine.

She was brown skinned with a killer set of hazel eyes and a plump set of lips. Baby had that Coke bottle figure, full breasts, slim waist, round hips, and ass for days. Unlike a lot of these L.A. broads, her shit was homegrown. I was talking collard greens, cornbread, neckbones, and fatback fed. Everything matched.

The tattoo etched into her thick brown thigh was on full display with that split in her dress. I wondered where else she had ink, and if it was somewhere I could see while I was hitting her from the back. Whoever her nigga was had to be a damn fool for having her out here like fresh meat. If a woman this fine was my lady, she would never be out like this without me.

The valet pulled my car around, and I opened the door for her. She climbed in, and I closed the door before heading to the driver's side. When I climbed in, she pulled out her phone and snapped a picture of me.

"Whatchu doing?" I asked.

"Sending your picture and my location to my girl. If anything happens to me in your care, my daddy is the black Brian Mills, and he will hunt your ass down."

I chuckled. "You're safe," I assured her. "I'd never die over some pussy... no offense."

"None taken."

She strapped herself in and relaxed into the seat. I shook my head as I pulled off from the curb. A short drive later, I pulled up to a luxury hotel. Once again, the valet handled my car while Rhythm and I headed inside. She copped a seat in the lobby while I took care of our room situation.

Once that was done, we headed up to the eighth floor. The entire elevator ride, she stood with her ass planted against me, even though there was ample space in the empty elevator. I didn't mind, though. That muthafucka was just as soft as I liked it. She had no idea the type of back shots I was about to deliver to her pretty ass tonight.

The elevator chimed, and we stepped off, making our way to room 869. Scanning the keycard, we entered the room. It was fitted with a king-size bed, kitchen, and a massive bathroom with a huge walk-in shower. She tossed her things on the counter, took off her heels, and strutted over to the bed. I kicked off my shoes as I watched her climb on.

She crooked her finger, beckoning me to her seductively. When I was in her space, she rose to her knees and wrapped her arms around my neck. Her lips pressed softly against mine before she sucked on my bottom lip. The sexiest moan escaped her as she opened her mouth to give me her tongue. Remnants of the Lemon Drops she'd been consuming all night lingered behind.

My hands had a mind of their own as they slid down her back to her ample ass. I gave it a hefty squeeze before giving it a firm slap.

"Shit," I mumbled.

As we kissed, I inched the dress up over her ass. Pulling her thong aside, I dipped a finger into her wetness from behind. She gasped as I breached her tight, wet walls.

She moaned my name. "Channing..."

"Kissing makes your pussy wet like this, ma?" I asked, stroking her hole.

She bit her lip as she nodded.

"Take this shit off."

I pulled her dress up over her head and tossed it aside. Before me, she wore nothing but a tiny black thong. Pierced nipples stared back at me as I licked my lips. Lil mama was stacked like a brick house, and I was ready to knock her walls down.

I stepped back and disrobed as she watched me. Various emotions played in her face. On one hand, she squirmed with excitement as I removed layer after layer of clothing. On the other, she looked a little nervous and unsure. I paused with my boxers on, closing the space between us.

"Where's your head?" I asked, cupping her chin.

"What do you mean?"

"You look a little hesitant. I'm not pressed to slide between these thick ass thighs. We don't have to do shit."

"I'm fine," she said, though her words weren't convincing.

"Nah, baby. I don't like your energy right now." I picked up her dress and tossed it back to her. "The room is paid for. You can chill here for the night, but I'm gonna head out."

I grabbed my clothes to redress, but she stopped me.

"It's just... I haven't been with another man in years, okay? I'm used to one. I know what he likes, and I do it well. I don't know—"

I held up a hand to stop her. "I'm not a selfish lover. I know how to get me off. My job is to make sure *you* leave satisfied. This ain't my first rodeo, baby. I handle pussy, very well, I might add. You don't have to do shit but take this dick."

I grabbed my dick for emphasis. Her hesitancy made him deflate just a little, but he was still a sight to be seen.

"Tell me what you want," I said.

Rhythm's Blues

"Something new... even if it's for a night."

Rhythm pulled my clothes from my hands and dropped them on the floor along with hers. Sitting back on the bed, she maneuvered her thong off and tossed it at me. The seat of the thin fabric was soaked in her juices, and the aroma made my mouth water. She spread her legs, and nothing but clean shaven, dripping wet pussy greeted me.

She reached between her thighs and circled her clit with her fingers before dipping them into her wet center. Her back touched the bed, and her nipples peaked as she slowly stroked herself. My dick strained against my boxers as I watched her writhe against her hand and moan in pleasure.

Pushing my boxers down, I stepped out of them and grabbed the condom from my wallet. As I rolled it on, I closed the space between us. Grabbing her ankles, I pulled her to the edge of the bed. She pulled her fingers from her wetness and spread her essence on her nipples.

Sitting up, Rhythm beckoned my lips to it. I stuck out my tongue and licked the hardened buds, causing her to shudder. The taste of her on my palate was so fucking sensational that I had to close my eyes. Her hand went to the back of my head as I alternated between breasts, devouring her sensitive buds.

"Oooo..." She moaned loudly and arched her back.

I pulled back and wrapped my fingers around her throat. Her teeth sank into her bottom lip as she looked up at me and smirked. I kissed her lips, and she opened her mouth to welcome the essence of herself on my tongue. She moaned as she sucked on it.

Dick in hand, I ran it between her slick lips as I kissed her. She was already so fucking wet that the muthafucka was talking back at me. I positioned myself at her entrance and slid into her with one swift stroke. Her breathing hitched as her pussy stretched to accommodate taking me all at once.

She cried out. "Shit! Ooo fuck!"

I hit her with those long, deep strokes as I slightly gripped her neck.

"Good girl," I praised her. "You taking this dick so well. Play with this pussy for me."

She reached between us and began strumming a rhythm on her clit. The more she stroked it, the wetter her pussy became. I watched myself sliding in and out of the mess we were making. Her nigga had to be crazy. As wet as her shit was, I'd be in this muthafucka every night. She was leaking so bad that it was dripping in between her ass cheeks.

What an ass this was, too. I just had to see it from the back. Pulling out of her, I flipped her onto her stomach and climbed onto the bed with her. She tried to get into position to arch her back, but I pushed her down flat.

"Nah, baby. I need you where you can't run from me," I said.

"I'm not a runner," Rhythm tossed over her shoulder.

"Fucking with me, you will be."

I pushed her legs apart with my knees and slid back into her. This time, I hit her with steady strokes that had her ass slapping against my thighs. With one hand wrapped around her throat, and the other gripping her hair, I pounded her sweet pussy with no mercy.

"Oh fuck... oh shit!"

She braced herself on her elbows, attempting to throw her ass back at me, but I pushed her back down.

"Stay," I commanded. "This is my pussy tonight. Let me take care of her. You just enjoy it."

"It's so good... fuck! It's so good!"

I chuckled. "I know, baby."

"You're so deep... Oh my... fuck!"

Against her word, she pushed back against me. I grabbed her hands and gripped her wrists.

"I thought you weren't a runner?" I said, pounding her. "You can take this dick, right?"

"Y-yes!"

"You should see the way this pussy is creaming on my shit. So fucking beautiful."

"Oh, God! Please... make me cum! I wanna cum!"

"You tappin' out on me already, ma?"

I slowed my strokes but made sure to keep tapping her G-spot. Her pleasured whimpers were music to my ears. She panted heavily. I felt her tucking her feet around my legs. Her hips wound in a circular motion as she used me for leverage to ride my shit. I freed her arms and watched for a moment as she fucked herself.

"That's it, baby," I said, giving her ass a firm slap. "Take what you need."

Rhythm lifted herself up on her elbows and bounced her ass on my lap. Her hand disappeared between her thighs as she feverishly stroked her clit. I gave her about ten seconds to please herself before I gripped her neck and pulled her back against me. I gave her short thrusts, assaulting her G-spot. Reaching around, I replaced her fingers with my own on her clit.

"You ready to cum for me, Rhythm?" I whispered in her ear.

"Y-yes!"

"Make this pussy sing for me."

As if all she needed was my permission, her pussy contracted around my dick, and she coated me to the point where I could feel her juices leaking down to my balls. With an exasperated breath, her body stiffened as I erupted into the condom.

For a while, Rhythm just stayed put while my dick throbbed within her walls. When I released her, she slumped forward and looked back at me.

"That... is some fucking... demon dick..." she declared.

I chuckled as I pulled the cum filled condom off and headed to the bathroom to flush it.

"You done, or you trying to go another round with a demon?" I asked.

"Just let me catch my breath," she said, rolling over onto her back.

I smirked. This might be a long night.

Chapter Eleven

Rhythm

The rays from the morning sun beat down on my face, forcing me to open my eyes.

Pain registered throughout my loins. My body was sore as hell. I looked over at Channing, knocked out beside me, and shook my head. I didn't know what I was thinking, having a one-night stand. I had no idea that I was going to run into Mr. Good Dick with the stamina of a fucking stallion.

When that man told me I'd be thoroughly fucked, he didn't lie. Last night, he had his way with me on every surface of the room. When we ran out of the three condoms in his wallet, he'd shamelessly gone down to the vending machine in the lobby and bought a whole box. By the time we tapped out, it was well after four in the morning.

The minute my head hit the pillow, I was off to Lala Land. Now it was morning, and I needed to get the hell out of here. I slipped out of bed and tiptoed around to grab my clothes. I was quiet as a mouse as I slipped my dress over my head.

I looked down at the thong in my hand, and a smirk appeared on my face. I walked over to the desk area and grabbed the pen and notepad from it. After scribbling a note on it, I place it and the underwear on the pillow next to Channing. Grabbing my shoes and my clutch, I quietly opened the door and slipped out.

On the elevator, I put my heels back on and finger combed my hair, so I at least looked somewhat presentable as I did my morning walk of shame. As I stepped off, I was the picture of grace. No one would ever know I was throwing it back for a stranger last night.

I stepped out of the building just as a cab was pulling up to let someone out. Hopping in, I gave the cabbie my address and settled into the back seat. Pulling my phone from my clutch, I saw that I had several texts from Nique.

Nique: Bitch, is that Channing's fine ass?

Nique: Why are you at a hotel?

Nique: You bout to get some dick?

Nique: Oooo you nasty slut! I need details!

Nique: Bitch, I know you saw me call you.

Nique: Are you alive, Rhythm? Please don't make me call the police. Call me back!

Nique: You have until ten to call me before I'm on your ass.

I laughed to myself as I read her ongoing rants. Just as I was about to text her back, she called me again.

"Good morning, Nique."

"Good morning, whore."

I giggled. "Why do I have to be all that?"

"Because I've been over here dying to know about your night while you were probably getting dicked to go."

I laughed harder. "I literally just left the hotel."

"See! You did get some morning dick!"

"No, I didn't. I left him asleep."

"Oh, well you're a dumb whore then. I would have gotten something to hold me over."

"Trust me, I'm more than held over. I can't tell you about it right now. I'm in a cab."

"Just tell me... was it worth it?"

"Hell yeah."

"Was it big?"

"Absolutely. And pretty."

I salivated, thinking about the ways that big pretty monster assaulted my walls last night. Channing was blessed. He had length and girth, with a mean ass curve and killer stroke game.

"Rhythm!" Nique yelled in my ear.

"Huh?"

"Look at your ass over there fantasizing."

I giggled. "My bad, boo."

"Are you gonna see him again?"

"No. It was a one-time thing. I was tripping off Raheem. I can't be out here being reckless like that. I just needed something to take my mind off of him. That probably wasn't the best thing, but shit, it worked."

"Don't go back to the apartment and be on no sad girl shit, Rhythm. I know you feel exhilarated right now, but once that shit wears off, you're gonna feel everything you were trying to avoid."

I sighed. "I know."

"I'm here if you need me. If push comes to shove, I'll just get my people to pack up my place and I can come back early."

"I don't want to inconvenience you, Nique. You're making a big move, and I won't cloud your needs with my relationship drama. Eventually, I'll have to deal with Raheem. I can't avoid him forever."

"You can't."

I pouted as I sank into the back seat. It would have been much easier to avoid him if I was back home in South Carolina, but I wasn't. My life was in Cali now. I couldn't let him and his ego run me out of the place I called home. I'd just have to suck it up and face the music at some point.

Nique and I caught up the duration of the fifteen-minute ride to our apartment. I paid the cabbie and climbed out of the car with her still yapping in my ear. Entering the parking garage, I took the elevator up to the floor where my car was parked. There were a few documents I needed to get out for work. I might as well busy myself with paperwork.

As I rounded the corner to where my car was parked, I stopped in my tracks. Parked behind my G-Wagon was Raheem's Audi. The door opened, and he stepped out. Walking around the front, he leaned against it and crossed his arms.

"Nique, let me call you back," I said.

"Something wrong?"

"I don't know yet. I'll call you when I get inside."

"Rhy—"

I disconnected the call and slowly made my way over to where he stood.

"How did you find me?" I asked.

"There's a tracker on your car. I can always find you, Rhythm."

I rolled my eyes. "What do you want?"

"I gave you time to calm your nerves, but you need to come home."

"This is my home now, Raheem."

"Your home is with me." He looked me over curiously. "Where are you coming from?"

"I went out last night."

He frowned. "With who?"

"Friends from work. Why does it matter!"

"Why are you coming home this time of morning? Where did you sleep?"

"In the fucking guest room at my friend's house!"

I didn't know why I was lying to him. I mean, I couldn't exactly say I went to a hotel with a strange man and let him fuck me to oblivion, could I?

Raheem kissed his teeth. "I miss you, Rhythm."

"Really? Because you and your labelmate seemed awfully chummy. It didn't look like you were thinking about me at all."

"Come on, baby. We run in the same circles—"

"Same circles my ass, Raheem. You're doing exactly what the label wants, or should I say what you want? I mean, you're a free agent now, right? It's fuck me and my feelings, right?"

"I'm sorry, okay! You know I love you, Rhythm. You know that."

"A man that loves me would never ask me to do what you did! I don't know who you are anymore, Raheem. No, I take that back. I know exactly who you are. You're Prince Cole. Mr. Hollywood. Mr. I Can Do Whatever The Fuck I Want. Your ego has gotten so big that you would shit on the people who knew you when you had nothing and still fucked with you. All you care about these days are your image and making money.

"What happened to the Raheem that was humble? The Raheem that just wanted to make music and get his mama and sisters out of the hood? The Raheem I knew was never this selfish. How would you feel if the shoe was on the other foot and I had you watching me all hugged up on another nigga? What if I had your mind wandering with thoughts of whether or not another nigga has tasted me? You'd be pissed, and if you say you wouldn't be, you're a fucking liar."

He stared at me, muted. What the hell could he say when I was right? Finally, he pushed off from the car and closed the space between us.

"I'm sorry," he said softly. "I know that probably doesn't mean shit to you right now, but I mean it. I love you, Rhythm. I just want you to give me another chance. Please, come home. The house doesn't feel right without you there. I miss you. I miss your cooking. I miss that loud ass music you play every Sunday morning. I miss walking into a room and it smell like you."

He stepped closer to me and wrapped his arms around my waist.

"I miss holding you and making love to you. I fucked up. You know you're my heart, Rhythm. My high school crush turned into my lady. I'm sorry I was selfish and careless with your feelings. I'm sorry I took advantage of the love you have for me. And I'm sorry that I didn't realize all you've done for me. Please... let me make it right."

He pecked my lips several times before moving to the sensitive spot on my neck.

"Tell me you'll come home, baby."

I closed my eyes, trying to muster up the will to not fall victim to his tender words. I loved him. That hadn't changed just because I was mad at him. Yet, just because I loved him didn't mean I had to accept any old thing from him. He had a lot of work to do to prove that he deserved another chance.

Gently, I pushed away from him.

"I can't do this, Raheem," I said softly.

"Baby—"

"No! It's not that simple. I think we need to chill. I'm not coming back, and you don't need to pop up here uninvited or unannounced. If you really want to be with me, you'll move differently."

He raised his hands in mock surrender. "I can do that." He took a step back, shoving his hands into his pockets. "Can you at least come to my listening party? I finished the album."

"I don't know, Raheem—"

"Please? I won't bother you. I won't even say anything to you. I just... I need you to be there, Rhythm. We put in a lot of late nights with this one. I just want you to hear how it all turned out. Please, baby."

I sighed, knowing I was possibly going to regret my decision.

"Fine. When is it?"

"The fifteenth at Cartier Lounge. I'll get you a section. You can bring Nique."

"I'll see if she wants to come."

"Okay." He stared at me for a moment before leaning in and kissing my cheek. "I love you, Rhythm."

"Goodbye, Raheem."

He looked like he wanted to say something, but instead, he nodded and backed away. He climbed into his car, and I stepped aside as he made his way out of the parking garage. I sighed as I unlocked my car and grabbed my work bag. I then made my way to the elevator and up to my floor.

Inside the apartment, I stripped down and gave my body a good scrubbing. After taking care of my hygiene, I changed into a pair of boy shorts, an oversized T-shirt, and my favorite fuzzy socks. I made myself a nice cup of coffee and got comfortable on the huge bean bag chair next to the big open window with a beautiful view of the city.

For a while, I just sat there, contemplating life. I was supposed to call Nique back, but Raheem had me feeling vulnerable. If I spoke to her right now, I would end up crying, and I didn't want to cry.

I thought about all the months leading up to this moment. Honestly, I didn't know what he was doing with lady Lingo. All I knew was what I saw. Yet and still, as a man in a relationship, being inappropriate was being inappropriate. I'd never play in his face or disrespect him like that.

Bitch, you fucked a whole nigga last night, I thought to myself.

I *had* crossed a line with Channing. I knew I shouldn't have been with him, but I was single. It happened, and I couldn't take it back. He was a random encounter, we didn't exchange contact information, and the chances of me seeing him again were slim to none.

What harm had really been done?

Chapter Twelve

Channing

A week had passed since my impromptu one-night stand with the beautiful Ms. Rhythm. When I woke up the morning after and found her thong and a simple thank you note, I couldn't help but laugh. She definitely played my ass with that nigga move.

That night lived rent free in my head. She gave me some of the best pussy I'd ever sampled, and I hadn't seen her since. Thinking about the way she rode my dick that night had my shit bricking up. It was the way her thick ass had rippled as she rode me reverse cowgirl. It was the way her swollen clit had peeked at me as she rode me on her tiptoes. Her pussy had creamed and coated me thoroughly. Baby had a fucking super soaker.

I was almost disappointed that she ghosted me. We hadn't exchanged numbers. Sure, I knew where she worked, but I wouldn't be a creep and just show up unannounced or without Grams. What I *did* know was if I ever crossed paths with her again, I was down to run it back.

The sound of the studio door opening broke my thoughts. I looked up to see Raheem coming through the door. I was waiting to see if Lady Lingo would be with him since she'd been to every other session we had. Much to my surprise, he was solo.

"What up, man?" he asked, slapping my hand as he sat down.

"What's good witchu?"

"Ain't shit. Ready for this listening party. I low-key wanna drop this album a little early."

"You're just excited. You worked hard on this one. Honestly, it might be your best work yet."

"I appreciate that, big dawg. Shit been rough lately. Me and my lady ain't been seeing eye to eye. The label is trying to push me and Imani together. Just a lot of shit been on my head."

"Shit, the way you two were moving, I thought she *was* your lady."

He chuckled. "Nah. It ain't like that. I mean... it was something like that, but it wasn't serious, you know what I mean?"

"Hmmm."

Just from his vague statement, I gathered that he'd either fucked her or they shared some sort of intimacy. It definitely wasn't innocent, but that wasn't my business. I wouldn't involve myself in his relationship drama. If his girl was willing to stick around while he dipped and dabbled in another woman, that was her business.

"Anyway," he said, slapping his hands together, "whatchu got for me today?"

"We're working on the last of the masters. The tracks have been equalized, and the frequencies are balanced. The levels and dynamics have been adjusted. Right now, I'm going through each one to see if I need to reduce the noise. I just need you to decide what order you want the songs in for the album so I can format it."

"I got you. Will we have time for a full playback?"

"This is my only project for the day, so I don't see why not."

"Bet. I'ma get a few of my people in here for a lil turn up session to celebrate. I appreciate you for real, Channing. Imani spoke highly of you. I know you're the big dawg of producers around these parts, a fucking legend. It's an honor to work with you."

He extended his hand, and I shook it.

"We're helping each other. Black man to black man, I got you on this music shit. You just need to be focused. That shit you've got going on with Imani needs to take a back seat for more than one reason. I've listened to your music. I've heard your story. You came out here hungry and ready to put in work so you could take care of your people. I respect the hustle. I come from humble beginnings. This shit was my way out too."

He nodded. "It was hard watching my moms working two and three jobs to make ends meet. The niggas that called themselves our fathers ain't even been shit but a figment of our imagination. It was always on me to get us out."

"I know it was hard, but you did it. Ten years in the game and you are a household name. Are you bringing your mother out for the album release?"

He grinned. "Yeah, man. She hasn't missed one yet. I gotta fix shit with my lady by then. I don't need my mama in my ear telling me to be a better man. Rhy is a good girl. She ain't out here in these streets or putting on shows for niggas. She's all about her business and her people."

He looked down at his feet for a moment, shaking his head.

"Fuck! I gotta get right."

"I can see the stress on you. Let me tell you something about this business, Raheem. Everybody is for themselves. Whatever is going to make them the most money or gain the most attention, that's what they are gonna do. You have to have your own mind and some integrity. Imani is beautiful and talented, but there's a shit ton of beautiful, talented women out there. They might look good on your arm. The pussy might be fire, but does she feed your soul? I would think you aren't with this girl just for the sake of being with somebody."

"Nah. I love her. One of these days, that's gonna be my wife and the mother of my kids."

"If you want that girl, get your shit together. Time doesn't wait on anybody. Don't be surprised if somebody else steps in and takes what's yours while you're out here being reckless. That ain't my business, though. I'm not here to get in yours."

I didn't say shit else after that. I jumped into working on his tracks. He sat there for a moment, seemingly in deep thought, before he pulled out his notebook and started writing.

* * *

It was Saturday, my free day.

I made it a habit of turning off my work phone and not answering emails on Saturdays. Dealing with muthafuckas all day long, five days a week, was tiring. I believed that everybody should follow their dreams, but they also needed to know their limits. Some of the artists these labels were putting out were trash. There wasn't enough tweaking or auto tune in the world to fix that shit. I'd wrecked my brain on many occasions trying to figure out what the fuck they had me listening to.

Since it was my free day, I decided to take Koda to the groomers for a pamper day. She loved her baths and getting treated like the queen she thought she was.

"She always does so good!" the groomer said, stroking Koda's coat.

Her name was Tanya. She was a white girl with a fat ass that flirted with me every time I came in here.

"You take such good care of her," she complimented.

"Thank you."

"I always see you in here alone. I take it there's not a Mrs. Watson or that Koda has a mom?"

My brows furrowed. "You in my business."

She giggled. "I'm just curious. You're a very handsome man, and

I'm a very single woman who would love to show you a good time." She gently touched my arm, tracing my tattoos. "I have a few of these I'd love to show you."

"Is that right? Like what?"

I was gonna shoot her down regardless, but I decided to let her amuse me.

"A butterfly that I can make flap her wings. Of course... you'd have to be in the right position to get the full effect."

She winked at me. I chuckled.

"As flattered as I am, Ms. Tanya, thanks but no thanks. You're a beautiful woman, but I prefer my women more on the melanated side."

"Oh..." She looked slightly disappointed before she smiled. "Chocolate can be white too."

"Unhand my damn dog, woman."

I snatched the leash from her and headed back toward the front door. I was gonna have to start bringing Koda on the days she didn't work. If she decided to fuck with my dog because I turned her down, I was gon' raise all types of hell in this bitch.

As usual, after her beauty appointment, I took her to the pet store to grab treats and a new toy. I allowed her to lead the way while I trailed behind her and her habit of sniffing everything. As we wandered aimlessly, I heard a familiar voice that caused me to stop.

"Well, Nique, you don't come back for another week, and I'm lonely. Why can't I get a puppy? Look how cute this one is!"

I rounded the corner, and there she stood. Today she was dressed in a white tube top, jean shorts that stopped mid-thigh, and a pair of all-white Forces. Her hair was pulled into a sleek ponytail, and her face was free of makeup. Gold jewelry and a brown crossbody completed her outfit.

She looked too damn good.

"Girl, I don't know about no damn dog," said the girl on her Face-Time call.

"How can you say no to this face? I'm gonna ask to hold him."

95

She turned to get an associate's attention, and her eyes landed on me. "Oh, shit."

"What's wrong?" her friend asked.

"Nique, I'm gonna call you back."

"Girl—"

She disconnected the call as I made my way over to her.

"Ms. Rhythm," I said with a smile.

"Channing. Fancy seeing you here." She looked down at Koda and smiled. "Hi, pretty girl."

Koda's tail wagged, but she remained seated. The sweeter you talked to her, the happier she was. She loved people but wouldn't go to them unless I gave the command.

"Is she friendly?" she asked.

"She is. Hold out your hand." She held out her hand without hesitating. "Koda, give her paw."

Koda lifted her paw and placed it in hers. Rhythm smiled as she stooped and shook it.

"You are just beautiful," she said, scratching behind Koda's ears. "How old is she?"

"Two."

"She looks really well taken care of."

"Of course she does. That's daddy's baby."

She looked up at me and smirked as she stood. "All right, daddy. See you around, Channing."

She tried to walk past me, but I gently took her arm.

"Don't try to slide past me the same way you slid out of our room that morning," I said, peering down at her. "You left your panties behind, but I would have rather had a taste of you before you left."

She blushed. "We both knew what that night was, Channing."

"I'm aware. But who said I was done with you when you dipped?"

Her top teeth sank into her bottom lip as she gazed up at me.

"You think about it?" I asked, cupping her chin. I ran my thumb across her bottom lip. "I've thought about that sweet little pussy all week long."

Leaning in, I pressed my lips to hers. My hand dropped from her chin to her neck where I gave a gentle squeeze. A moan escaped her throat as she placed her hand to my chest and pushed me back.

"You can't be doing that in public," she said, her chest heaving.

I chuckled. "You did say kissing gets you wet, didn't you?"

I grabbed the phone in her hand and went to her contacts to put my number in.

"Call me if you ever need me to take care of that."

I tugged Koda's leash for her to follow me. Just as I turned my back, Rhythm spoke up.

"You don't want my number?"

I looked back at her. "I'm not the one that's semi-attached to my ex. You know what you want, and you also know the type of dick I'm swinging. If you want me, you know how to contact me. Just drop me a location."

She looked as though she were thinking hard about it. I'd let her have that. Again, I tugged Koda's leash for her to follow, and we left her standing there while we headed to checkout.

Chapter Thirteen

Rhythm

T*he Listening Party*

"I can't believe I let you drag me here," Nique said as we walked through the doors of the venue where Raheem was having his listening party. "Furthermore, I can't believe you agreed to come."

She gave me a hard side eye as security waved the metal detector over us and pointed us to the elevator.

I sighed as we stepped on. "I only came to show my face."

After Raheem pulled up on me, he seemed to be on his get back game strong. Since that day, I'd received flowers daily. It wasn't just one bouquet. He sent five at a time. When Nique came back, she said it looked like a florist threw up in our apartment. Not only was he sending flowers, but he was sending gifts.

So far, I'd received diamond jewelry pieces, new handbags, shoes, entire perfume collections, and he'd wired six figures into my account. Earlier today, I'd received a delivery from my favorite boutique. He'd sent me a beautiful, sexy dress and heels for tonight. I couldn't resist putting it on. Nique had rolled her eyes too hard when she saw me in it, but even she had to admit I looked damn good.

It was a metallic red dress labeled The She Devil. It was strapless, form-fitting, and stopped below my knees. It laced up in the front and if somebody took scissors to it, I was done for. The metallic red heels were the perfect compliment. I'd accessorized it with white gold jewelry and a little studded bag for my essentials. For my hair, I'd done a curly updo to accent my neckline.

"Mmm hmm..." Nique said as we stepped off the elevator. "Just know you aren't leaving with big money grip tonight. You could have been getting dicked down by Mr. One Night Stand."

I'd told her about my run in with Channing at the pet store. That man had me so flustered after he left that I didn't even get the damn puppy. I had to sit in my car for a minute, to get myself together. His lips on mine caused flashbacks of the night we shared. My nipples hardened, my clit throbbed, and my pussy ached like she missed him. I hadn't even had the nerve to use his number.

"I'm not thinking about that man, Nique," I said.

"Lie again. I know you thought about it, and if you didn't, you dreamed about him. I heard you in there moaning in your sleep the other night."

I didn't acknowledge her accusation. I had, in fact, dreamt of him... vivid dreams at that. Instead of confirming or denying her claims, I led her over to the bar for a drink.

"Two amaretto sours, please," I said.

While they were being made, I turned around to survey the space. It was already packed in here. People were standing around laughing and talking. Bitches were dressed in their nigga snatching outfits. They wore dresses so short that it left nothing to the imagination. We got our drinks and headed to find a seat. As we made our way through the crowd, someone grabbed my arm.

"Rhy!"

I looked back to see my cousin, Rhyon.

I squealed as I hugged her. "Hey, boo!"

Rhyon was my cousin on my mom's side. She moved out here to L.A. with her husband, Emerald, a few years ago. When I first moved here, I hung out with her all the time while I was settling in. She showed me the city and what not. These days, we mostly talked through text or FaceTime since she was busy with her law firm and family life, and I was busy with my clinic.

"I miss you," she said, kissing my cheek. "Honey, you are wearing the fuck outta that dress. Hey, Monique."

They shared an embrace as well.

"How have you been?" I asked.

"I'm living, girl. Between the firm, my babies, and my husband, I barely have time to breathe. We have to do lunch soon or you come by the house. The kids would love to see you in person."

"We can make that happen. Where is Emerald?"

She looked around. "Girl, he's here somewhere. You know he did a feature on the album, so he had to come support. I see you came to support your man. You finally okay with the spotlight?"

"Raheem and I aren't together."

Her eyes widened. "Since when?"

"A few weeks now. It's a long story, girl."

"Damn. I'm sorry, boo. It's nice you came to support him still."

"'Cause I would have said fuck him," Nique said, rolling her eyes.

Rhyon laughed. "You're still feisty."

"Always, girl. And now my feisty ass is here on a permanent basis."

"What! You finally left little ass Columbia, too?"

Nique linked her arm through mine. "I missed my boo, and I needed a change of scenery. It just so happens that my company had an opening for a higher position with better pay. They paid for me to move and covered my first six months of rent. No way I could pass that up."

"I know that's right. The three of us really have to get together. We have to show these L.A. girls how we do it in the south."

"Period!" Nique said, raising her glass.

"I know that ain't loudmouth Monique Talbert!"

We looked behind us to see Emerald aka G.E.M walking over to us with a grin on his face. Nique rolled her eyes. Emerald was actually her cousin on her mom's side.

"Hey, Nique Nique," he said, pinching her cheeks.

She slapped his hand away. "Don't start that shit, Em."

He pulled her in for a hug and kissed her forehead. "I've missed you, lil bit."

"I bet you did. You miss bullying me."

He laughed. "I've never bullied you. Hey, Rhythm."

"Hey, Em."

"Yo, your man is about to break records with this album."

"He's not my man," I corrected.

"Oh... I thought—"

"It's a long story, babe," Rhyon interjected. "We aren't gonna talk about it tonight. Go on and mingle with your friends. My girls got me."

"Did you just dismiss me, woman?"

She giggled, and she leaned in and kissed him. "I love you. Now go."

He slapped her ass as he walked off into the crowd. I'd always loved how much they loved each other. When he came back home to get her, I thought it was the sweetest thing. I had to respect a man that put in work to get back the woman he loved. I thought about Raheem. He was trying now, but would it matter? Nique said he was trying to buy my love back, and I could see where she got that idea. He was sending all these gifts, and while they were lovely, they didn't make up for the disrespect. He had to *do* more... *show* more... *be* more.

The girls and I finally found an empty section and claimed it for ourselves. While we waited for the show to start, we caught up with

Rhyon and made plans to have lunch this week. About thirty minutes later, the DJ got everyone's attention to let us know that Raheem was in the building.

He made his grand entrance, smiling and waving at fans. He stopped for a few pictures or to sign autographs. I had to admit, he looked good tonight. He was decked out in all black from head to toe. Gold chains hung around his neck. A diamond encrusted watch glistened on his wrist. He just looked like money.

My eyes followed him up to the DJ booth where he grabbed the mic.

"How y'all doing tonight!"

The crowd went wild with cheers.

"I just wanna thank y'all for coming out to celebrate withcha boy. I'm ten years in the game, and y'all have always shown me mad love. Tonight ain't no different. I'm excited to share my newest album with you guys. A lot of late nights, blood, sweat, and tears went into *Savage Symphony*. I do this shit for my mom, my little sister, the kids on the block, and the niggas that look like me. We all have a story to tell, and this album is mine. I'm not gonna hold y'all on my soapbox though. DJ... drop my shit."

The DJ dropped the track.

Almost immediately, the whole space started vibing. I couldn't help but bob my head and rap along. He'd played the tracks so much that I knew them word for word. As we listened, Raheem made his way through the crowd, speaking to various people. The closer he got to us, the more nervous I became. I didn't know what to say to him. I wasn't sure if I should hug him or shake his hand or what.

The choice was taken out of my hands when he approached us with a smile.

"Ladies."

He stooped down to hug and kiss Rhyon's cheek. He did the same with Nique, though she gave him the stank eye. When he came to me, he grabbed my hands and pulled me to my feet. His arms came around me in a tight hug.

"You came," he said, pulling back and kissing my forehead.

"I told you I would. Congratulations."

"Thank you." He stepped back, still holding my hands. His eyes trailed me from head to toe. "Damn you look good. I knew this dress would be perfect for you."

"You did good."

He bit his lip as he looked me over again. "Can I holla at you for a second?"

I looked back at Rhyon and Nique. Rhyon avoided my eyes as she sipped her drink, while Nique gave me a look that said, *Bitch, you bet not.*

"Please, Rhy?"

I looked at him and those pitiful eyes. I sighed.

"You have five minutes," I said.

"That's all I need."

With his hand on the small of my back, he led me over to an unpopulated corner. I leaned against the wall with my arms crossed, waiting to hear what he had to say.

"I take it you've gotten my gifts?"

"I have. You're doing too much, Raheem. Buying me gifts won't get me back."

"I'm just trying to show you I'm sorry."

"The best apology is changed behavior."

"I can change, Rhythm. I can't show you that if you won't even talk to me, baby."

"I beg to differ."

He sighed. "I told the label no to fake dating Lady Lingo."

"That's good. I would be more impressed if you had shut that shit down from the jump. You considered it and brought it to me, Raheem. That's my problem. Additionally, you haven't been moving like the rumors aren't true."

"Whatchu want me to do? Make a public statement? You gon' come out as my girl?"

"No, because I'm not your girl. I gotta go. I don't wanna talk about this here. I just came to support you tonight. Congratulations. I know this album will be a success."

I started to walk off, but he gently grabbed my arm. "Rhythm."

I turned back with a frown. "What?"

"Can you just come by the house later so we can talk?"

"Raheem, I don't think that's a good—"

"Prince Cole!"

The sound of a familiar voice interrupted us. Raheem looked over my head, causing me to turn around. When I did, I could have shitted a brick. It was him. Mr. One Night Stand. Our eyes met, and while I stood frozen, he played it cool.

"Channing, what's up, man?"

Raheem slapped hands with him. His familiar scent infiltrated my nose, and immediately, images of us fucking like rabbits filled my mind. I closed my eyes, willing them away. I felt Raheem's hand on my waist as he pulled me into his side.

"Rhythm, this is Channing Watson. He's the producer on this album. Channing, this is the woman I was telling you about."

Shit! Shit! Shit!

My guilty eyes met Channing's, and he smiled as he extended his hand.

"Ms. Rhythm... it's very nice to meet you."

Chapter Fourteen

Channing

Son of a bitch!

God had a sense of humor. Wasn't no way the woman I'd dicked down a few weeks ago was the same woman I'd given this nigga advice about. Wasn't no fuckin' way. Here I was, just coming to speak, and found myself in a messy ass situation. The look on her face was going to give us away. I wasn't afraid of this lil nigga, but I'd rather not have to beat his ass about fucking his girl that really wasn't his girl.

"Ms. Rhythm... it's very nice to meet you."

She looked down at my hand before hesitantly giving me hers.

"It's nice to meet you too." She turned back to him. "Raheem, I really have to go."

"Can't you stay just a little while longer?"

Her eyes shifted to me. "I really can't."

"Five minutes. Let me go speak to some people, and I'll walk you out."

She rolled her eyes and sighed heavily. "Fine. I'm going to the bathroom. If you aren't done by the time I come out, I'm gone."

She brushed past both of us and headed to the back. Raheem shook his head.

"Still trouble in paradise?" I asked.

"She's stubborn, as you can see. I'll wear her down though."

"Good luck with that. I just wanted to congratulate you on a job well done."

"I appreciate that. You the GOAT. We definitely have to get together for the next one."

That shit wasn't happening. I'd already fucked this man's girl. Nine times outta ten, I was gon' fuck her again. I couldn't be in his face, knowing I took his girl down. I wouldn't tell him that, though.

Instead, I said, "No doubt."

"Bet. I'ma holla at you, man."

"Be easy."

We slapped hands before he disappeared into the crowd. I stood there looking around for a moment before heading in the direction Rhythm had gone. It was a single stall bathroom, so I tapped on the door.

"Just a minute!" she called.

I tapped again.

"I'll be right out!"

I tapped a final time before the door swung open.

"I said—"

She didn't have time to say anything before I pushed my way in and locked the door behind me.

"Are you crazy! What are you doing! Get out!"

"You worried about your lil boyfriend catching us?"

"He's not my boyfriend."

"That ain't how he's telling it."

"It's complicated, okay?"

"Doesn't seem that complicated to me. I mean, what's to think about with a nigga playing in your face?"

She frowned. "I never said he was playing in my face."

I chuckled. "Knowing who he is and who he's associated with, it's not hard to put two and two together."

"Have you seen something? Is that what you're alluding to?"

"I'm not alluding to shit. As far as I'm concerned, if you're Ray Charles, then I'm Stevie Wonder. I don't know shit about him, and he doesn't know about us. At least not yet."

"You can't say anything to him, Channing."

"Why would I do some dumb shit like that? You, on the other hand, are gonna give yourself away looking guilty and shit. Your paranoid as gon' fuck around and tell on yourself."

"I was shocked! You think I was expecting to see you here? Why would I knowingly show up to the place I knew my man's producer would be, knowing I fucked him?"

I smirked. "I thought he wasn't your man?"

She glared at me. "I liked you much better with my pussy in your mouth."

I pushed her up against the counter, causing her breath to hitch in her throat.

"Don't make it my mission to have you again, Rhythm."

My eyes trailed her frame in this dress that made my mind wander. She was so fucking sexy, and this shit hugged her in all the right places. The sliver of exposed skin from the lace up reminded me of all the places my mouth had been on her. I could see her nipples hardening beneath the fabric.

"You look so damn good tonight," I said, sliding an arm around her waist.

"Th-thank you..." she whispered. "I-I need to go."

I traced the tops of her breasts with my finger. "You never answered my question."

"Wh-what question?"

I pulled her right breast from the confines of the dress and licked her nipple. She whimpered as I sucked it into my mouth and released it with an audible plop.

"Do you think about it?"

Rhythm swallowed hard. "Yes... Channing... please. You have to stop—shit!"

I tugged her nipple harder as I inched her dress up and over her ass. The feeling of her soft, supple skin beneath my fingertips caused my dick to brick in my pants. My hand slipped between her thighs where I found the seat of her panties wet with desire. Pulling them aside, I parted her slick lower lips and strummed her clit. She gasped and tossed her head back as she arched against my hand.

"Oooo shit... fuck!"

Her chest heaved as her nails dug into my arm. I slipped my fingers into her wet tunnel, slowly moving them in and out for a few minutes before I located her G-spot. When I stimulated her clit as I stroked her, her walls clamped around my messy digits.

"Wh-why are you doing this to me?" she whispered.

"'Cause I love the way you cum for me. Don't you think you deserve to cum like this?"

"Yes... I'm almost there..."

"Look at me, mama."

Her head dropped back down, and her eyes met mine. I licked my lips as I watched the pleasure dancing in her beautiful orbs.

"There you go... That's my good girl. Cum for me. Make that fucking mess."

The walls of her pussy gripped my fingers, and her body trembled against mine. Her mouth opened, and I covered it with mine, swallowing her cries of pleasure. She slumped against me, panting heavily. She moaned softly as I pulled my fingers away. I lifted her from the counter and placed her on her feet.

"Now you can leave."

Moving past her, I grabbed some soap, then washed and dried my hands. Without another word, I opened the bathroom door and left out. I sauntered my way back into the party, cool as a cucumber. My eyes scanned the crowd for Raheem. I found him in a corner talking to Imani and looking around suspiciously like he wasn't trying to get caught by Rhythm.

Imani didn't look happy at all. He seemed like he was trying to calm her down to avoid making a scene. I watched as he leaned in and whispered something in her ear. Her face seemed to soften. She nodded, and the next thing I knew, she was leaving. I shook my head as I made my way to the bar. That nigga was gonna get caught up yet.

After ordering my drink, I copped a seat on a barstool to survey the crowd. Rhythm finally emerged from the bathroom. I chuckled to myself as I watched her pull it together. She walked over to the woman I knew as Emerald's wife and her friend I remembered as Monique. They spoke for a moment then shared an embrace with Rhyon before she left them be.

Her lips were moving a mile a minute, and I could only guess that she was telling her about what transpired. Her friend wore a wide grin as she looked around the room. When her eyes landed on me, she pointed, but Rhythm slapped her hand down. I raised my glass in their direction and smiled.

While her friend waved, Rhythm folded her arms and glared at me. By this time, Raheem had made his way back across the room to her. They spoke briefly before making their way toward the exit. I gulped down the rest of my drink and followed. We met at the elevator, and I could feel her tense up.

"You leaving?" Raheem asked.

"Yeah, I have an early day tomorrow."

"Word."

The elevator door opened, and we stepped on.

"Channing, I don't think you met Monique," Raheem said, pointing to the brown-skinned beauty standing next to Rhythm. "She's my lady's best friend and an old classmate of mine."

I extended my hand. "It's nice to meet you, Monique."

"Mmm hmm," she mumbled with a smirk. "Nice to meet you."

"Nique, since you're moving out here, maybe you two can hang out," Raheem suggested.

"Mmm, maybe not. No offense, I just don't think Channing and I are for each other. You know how you Hollywood niggas can be. I didn't come out here to catch a case."

I chuckled. "I'd hate to be the reason you end up in jail."

Raheem shook his head. "Channing is good people."

Rhythm snapped at him. "Raheem, she said no. Leave those grown ass people alone."

I bit back a smirk. Was she being territorial?

Raheem pursed his lips the rest of the ride down. We stepped off the elevator and headed out into the cool night air. Rhythm handed the valet her ticket and so did I. While we waited, Raheem pulled her off to the side to talk in private, leaving me alone with her friend. She looked up at me with a smirk.

"I hope you enjoyed tonight's festivities," she said coyly.

"I most certainly did."

"Mmm hmm. Word of advice." She turned to face me fully. "Don't get too invested. I'm sure that..." she nodded her head at Rhythm and Raheem, "it's going to be a thing again. Even good dick can't compete with a woman in love."

I smirked. "So, she said it was good dick?"

She laughed as my car pulled up to the curb. "Good night, Channing."

"Good night."

I nodded my head at Raheem as I rounded the vehicle to the driver's side. My eyes met Rhythm's briefly before she shyly averted her gaze. I chuckled to myself. This wasn't over... not by a long shot.

Chapter Fifteen

Rhythm

My eyes locked with Channing as he climbed into his car. Quickly, I averted my gaze. Staring at that man too long would have me reliving what went down with us just moments ago. I needed him out of my sight and out of my mind. I didn't even know this nigga well enough to let him have me acting like this.

I mean, he wasn't a total stranger. That night at The Caviar Club, we'd had a decent conversation before we headed out onto the dance floor. How could I not want to know a little something about the man that saved me from an aggressive asshole who couldn't take no for an answer?

We didn't get too personal that night. We didn't talk about work. We mainly discussed L.A. and how I liked living out here. We talked about food and drink spots and the nightlife. It was crazy that he never brought up that he was a producer since we had a lengthy conversation about music.

If he had, I would have asked him about the artists he'd worked with. Had Raheem's name came up, I would have never let that man beat my back out that night. Even worse, tonight wouldn't have happened either.

"You hear me talking to you, Rhythm?" Raheem asked, breaking my thoughts.

I snapped back to reality. "Hmm?"

"I asked if you would come to my album release party."

"Raheem... tonight was a lot."

"Baby, I'm trying. You gotta give me something to work with. You gotta meet me halfway. I can change, but you gotta change too. I want you by my side during my big moments. Not just in the building. Not in the background. Right by me."

I pointed a finger at him. "Don't. Do not do that. I've always supported you. Why does it matter if I'm in pictures or if you can flaunt me around? I'm not a trophy, and I've told you that."

"You are a trophy. You're a fucking prize, baby. What's wrong with me wanting to show you off?"

"A relationship isn't supposed to be a spectacle, that's why. You want a spectacle, you can be with Lady Lingo. I'm surprised I didn't see her here tonight. What? She willingly missed an opportunity to be all over you?"

He kissed his teeth. "I don't wanna talk about that girl, Rhy." He pulled me into his arms and pecked my lips. "I wanna talk about you and me."

"There is no you and me," I said as my car pulled up to the curb. "Not right now." I pulled away from him and took a step back. "I love you... I'm proud of you, but I'm not ready to get back together, and I don't know if I ever will be..."

I walked off to my car with Nique following behind me.

"This ain't over, Rhythm!" Raheem called. "*We* ain't over by a long shot."

I ignored him as I climbed into my G-Wagon and pulled into traffic.

"Same shit?" Nique asked.

"Same shit."

"You know he's gonna try to wear you down, right?"

"He's wearing my last nerve. Between him and Channing, it's a wonder I have any nerves left tonight."

She laughed. "Channing, Channing. Mmm, mmm, mmm. That nigga was fine as hell too. He just walks like that dick is something serious. I see why you let him hit."

I shook my head. His dick was something serious.

The dick.

The mouth.

Those fingers.

The man was a walking orgasm, and he seemed like he was making it his mission to give me as many as possible. After he left the bathroom, I had to take off my thong because it was ruined. It was currently sitting balled up in a bunch of paper towels in the trash while I was out here freeballing it. I couldn't be around him, especially not around Raheem. Every time he looked at me, I thought about the night we shared. Now I had tonight to add to the list of forbidden memories.

"Bitch, I can't believe I let that man finger fuck me in the bathroom!" I exclaimed, beating my fist against the steering wheel. "How old am I!"

Nique snickered. "I mean, if it had been me, I would have bet money he followed me. What do you have going on, girl?"

"I don't even know, Nique. This isn't like me. If Raheem would have kept his shit together, I would have never fucked Channing to begin with. This is what I get for acting off pure emotion. I should have stayed my ass in the house that night."

Nique was quiet. It was rare that she didn't have something to say or a comeback. I looked over at her.

"What?"

She shook her head. "Nothing, nothing."

"Say it, Monique."

She sighed. "What are you doing with Raheem, Rhythm? Are

you getting back at him? Are you going back to him? What? Let me know what's up."

I was quiet, causing her to slap my arm.

"Don't bullshit me. You're my girl, and I love you. I'm with whatever makes you happy, but don't let that nigga play in your face."

"I love him, Nique. I can't just turn it off."

"I know that, baby, but you also can't just let him come back with open arms. At least make him work for it. And by work for it, I mean longer than a few weeks. He's gotta do more than send you gifts and money."

"I know that, Nique. I told him that tonight." I sighed heavily as we pulled up to a red light. "I don't wanna be that girl. I already uprooted my life to move out here and be with him. The man I moved for isn't the same man I've seen the last year. I hate that. I guess... I keep waiting around for him to show me that the man I fell in love with is still in there."

"I get it. You've invested a lot of time into him. I can imagine you don't wanna see another bitch reap the benefits of all the work you put in."

"I don't. But that isn't a reason to be with him."

"Neither is love. Love... it makes you do stupid shit. It makes you tolerate shit no sane bitch would. I'm not saying the old Raheem isn't still in there, but don't play the fool."

I heard what she was saying. I didn't want to be Raheem's fool, which was why I hadn't taken him back. I wanted more, and if he wanted me, he had to do more. I could withstand him begging and pleading. I had more willpower than that... at least when it came to him. Clearly, I didn't have it when it came to Mr. Producer. Good sex had a way of clouding judgment, just like love.

The last thing I needed was to lose all sense of my morals.

* * *

The weekend was over just like that.

It was Monday morning and time to get back to work. I woke up bright and early to get in my daily workout before I had to shower and get ready for work. Dressed in my signature black scrubs and sneakers, I put my coffee on to brew while I packed my work bag. When it was done, I poured the coffee into my favorite to-go mug and headed for the door.

"See you tonight, Nique!" I called over my shoulder.

"Have a good day!"

"You, too!"

Ensuring the front door was locked, I closed it behind me and made my way to the elevator. I took the short trip down to the parking garage to my car. The first thing I noticed was the rose and an envelope attached to my windshield. Looking around, I didn't see anybody. Pulling a tissue from my bag, I grabbed the envelope and opened it. Inside was a note and what looked like a receipt.

Dear Rhythm,

I know you may not feel like I'm worth a second chance, but I know you are it for me. I won't stop until you come home. Have a great day at work. Breakfast is on me. I know how much you love those breakfast sandwiches from Sunny Side Up. Just show them the receipt and my name and they will get your order. I love you.

Raheem

I looked down at the receipt to see my usual order comprising of a steak, egg, and cheese croissant, potato bites, fresh fruit, and orange juice. I smiled softly as I tucked the receipt into my bag. Of course, he couldn't win me back with food, but food would forever make me happy. Plucking the rose from the windshield, I climbed into my car and cranked up.

I put on my morning gospel playlist to get myself in the right mind frame and pulled out of the parking space. The ride to work was only about twenty minutes with stopping to get my food. I walked into The Baker Method with a smile on my face as I greeted my staff. I made my way to my office to look over my client list for the day while I ate my breakfast.

"Good morning, Ms. Baker," my secretary, Evie, greeted me.

"Good morning, Evie. What are we looking at today?"

She grabbed her clipboard and followed me into my office. "You have a ten o'clock with Mr. Owens, an eleven with Mrs. James, then consultations at one thirty, two, and two thirty. Your last appointment is at four."

"Sounds good. Could you pull those consultation forms for me?"

"Already done." She pulled a folder from her clipboard and handed it to me. "I also included the last meeting notes in case you need a reference."

I smiled. "That's why I like you. You're always ahead of me."

"Just trying to make things easier for you."

She smiled and left my office, closing my door behind me. I spread out my breakfast items and got to eating while I looked over everything. Ten rolled around quick, and before I knew it, I was walking into my first appointment. Oscar Owens. He was a forty-two-year-old man that got hurt on his construction site. An accident that should have killed him left him with a traumatic brain injury and several broken bones.

His road to recovery had been long and hard. He was just getting to where he could move around on his own. His wife said he was stubborn at home, but whenever he came here, he had no problem putting in the effort. I wasn't sure what the problem was, but I suspected she wasn't as patient or as kind to him as I was. She never seemed to acknowledge the progress he was making. She didn't participate in his therapy or encourage him.

Anytime she came in, she kind of lingered in the background until we were done, and that was if she stayed at all. Today, she spent the entire session on her phone. I decided that today would be the day I said something. When our session was complete, I had my assistant help with Mr. Owens while I called his wife back to my office. She sighed heavily as she put her phone away.

"You can have a seat," I said, motioning for her to sit down.

We got comfortable, and I leaned across my desk with my hands clasped.

"Mrs. Owens, thanks for taking the time to meet with me today. I wanted to discuss your husband's care and see how you're managing. How have things been going?"

She seemed shocked that I asked her that. Almost immediately, tears formed in her eyes. I reached for a tissue and handed it to her.

"Take your time," I said softly.

She took a few deep breaths before she spoke. "Honestly, it's been tough. I'm constantly exhausted and overwhelmed with all the responsibilities. I knew he needed a lot of care, but it's all on me. It's too much."

I nodded. "That's completely understandable. Being a caregiver can be very demanding. You acknowledge the challenges you're facing as well. Can you tell me what is most difficult for you?"

She scoffed. "It's everything; feeding, dressing, bathing, using the bathroom, it's physically and emotionally draining, Dr. Baker. I have to manage his medications, appointments, and meals. We also have custody of our granddaughter, so I'm being a parent again after raising my own. I have to take care of the household on top of all of this. I feel like I don't have any time for myself anymore."

I reached for her hands, and she gave them to me.

"You're taking on a lot, and it's natural to feel overwhelmed. Caregiver burnout is a real concern, and it's vital that we find ways to support you. Would you be able to get help from other family members? Have you been looking into care services?"

She shook her head. "I've been hesitant to ask for help. I feel like it's my responsibility to take care of him. He took care of this family since the day we got married. He's never asked for anything, and I feel so bad that sometimes I just want to throw in the towel."

"First, your dedication is admirable. It's important to remember that you can't pour from an empty cup, Mrs. Owens. Taking care of yourself is not selfish; it's necessary so that you can continue to provide the best care for your husband. I have great resources that are available to you. We can explore some options that could help lighten your load."

She sniffled. "I'm open to suggestions. I know I can't keep going on like this. It's not fair to Oscar."

I smiled. "The first step to getting help is always admitting you need it. First, let's identify tasks that you need help with, like grocery shopping or laundry. We can also look into home health aides who could provide assistance a few times a week. This would give you some much-needed time to yourself. There are also resources available to help cover the costs of these services. I can connect you with a social worker who can assist you in exploring your options. Additionally, I'd like to teach you some techniques to make daily care tasks easier on both you and your husband."

She began to cry audibly. "I would appreciate that so much. Thank you for your help and understanding."

"You're welcome, Mrs. Owens. Remember, you're not alone in this journey. We're here to support you and your husband every step of the way."

For a good thirty minutes, she and I spoke about her needs. I gave her the contact information for every resource she could possibly need, and I made a note to have Evie reach out on my behalf as well. By the time she left, she was in good spirits. She'd even kissed her husband and told him what a good job he'd been doing. The light that entered him when she said that was the reason I did what I did.

The extra time with Mrs. Owens didn't leave room for me to take a break in between clients. Before I knew it, it was time for Mrs. James to come in. Luckily, I loved this little old lady. At seventy years old, she was feisty and said whatever was on her mind, rude or not. She suffered from the early stages of dementia. While there was nothing I could do to combat the disease, there was plenty I could do to assist in improving her quality of life.

She usually came in with her daughter, and our sessions were outside or somewhere that stimulated Mrs. James. I usually let her tell me what she was up for and tailor my therapy to her. Her sessions usually took longer because we weren't always on site. For that reason, I let it run over into my lunch hour. One thing about Mrs. James, she was going to want to eat.

Walking into the waiting room, I found her sitting in a chair, tightly holding her purse. When she saw me, she smiled.

"Hey, baby," she said sweetly as I approached her.

"Hey, Mrs. James." I took a seat beside her and crossed my legs. "How are you feeling today?"

"I feel just fine. I really could have skipped today."

I pretended to be offended. "And make me miss my favorite client? How dare you?"

She waved me off. "Don't blow gust up under my skirt, gal."

I giggled. "Where's your daughter?"

"The heifer had a doctor's appointment, and my aide is out sick this week. My grandson brought me today. He's parking the car." She looked at me and smiled. "He's quite handsome, you know. He might be a little loose, but a pretty girl like you can tie him down, no problem. I can tell you now, he's gonna be looking at all that ass in those scrub pants. He likes 'em thick too, chile."

I laughed. "Mrs. James! Are you trying to be my grandmother-in-law?"

She giggled as the bell above the door chimed.

Looking back, she said, "There's that bighead ass boy now. Come on over here, baby."

She reached for my hand, and I helped her to her feet as heavy footsteps approached.

"Dr. Baker, meet my grandson Channing."

My eyes widened as I looked up into the face of the very man I said I was going to avoid. He smirked as he realized who I was.

Fuck. Me.

Chapter Sixteen

Channing

"Slow your ass down, Channing!" my grandmother yelled at me.

"Grams, chill out. I'm going the speed limit."

"Well, it feels like you are speeding. I'd like to get to therapy in one piece."

I shook my head. My grandmother was dramatic as hell, even before the dementia diagnosis. Since then, her moments of irritability kicked it up a notch. I wasn't sure if she was irritable right now or if she was just being herself. I'd been in the studio working with a familiar client when I got the call from my mother asking me to take her to therapy this morning.

Part of me was a little annoyed that she waited until the day of to ask, but I couldn't say no to Grams. She was gon' give me hell today, but knowing that there would be a time when she didn't know who I was gave me all the reason I needed to take her. I'd deal with her slick mouth and cherish the moments while I could. She and my mama sacrificed so I could live better than they did. While it wasn't all sunshine and rainbows, I found significance in every moment with them.

I pulled into the parking lot and up to the door. She tried to get out, but I had the child locks on, causing her to shoot me a glare.

"Don't look at me like that, woman. I'm just keeping you safe."

"I'm not a child, Channing. I raised your black ass. I don't need raising."

"I hear you."

I got out and rounded the car to her side. Opening the door, I helped her out and into the building.

"You wait right here," I said, easing her into a seat. I'm gonna park, and I'll be right back."

"Mmm hmm."

I jogged back out to my car and found a parking space. After a quick check of my email about a session later tonight, I went back inside. As I came through the doors, Grams looked back at me with a smile, letting me know she was up to no good. On the ride over, she'd talked about how pretty her therapist was and how she was gonna hook us up so I could leave these loose ass women alone.

I had to laugh at her.

One, she didn't know that I had already taken her therapist down. And two, she thought she knew what I needed better than I did. In all honesty, she could have been right. On one hand, I was getting too old to just be fucking with nothing meaningful in mind. On the other hand, I thoroughly enjoyed single life. I didn't have to answer to anybody. While I didn't have a bunch of women in rotation, my small little roster hit heavy for me every time.

I would entertain her today, though.

I walked over to where a woman in scrubs was helping her to her feet.

"Dr. Baker, meet my grandson Channing."

The woman looked up, and her eyes widened as she recognized who I was.

"Ms. Rhythm," I said, wrapping an arm around Gram's shoulder. "Had I known you were the therapist she's been talking about, I would have started bringing her here long ago."

"You two know each other?" Grams asked.

"We are quite acquainted," I answered.

I could see Rhythm reeling in her feelings. She swallowed hard and put on a pleasant smile.

"Mr. Watson. It's nice to see you again." She turned to Grams. "Are you ready, Mrs. James?"

"As ready as I'm gonna get. How about music today? Channing had me listening to the god-awful rap music he likes on the way over here."

Rhythm chuckled. "I think I have something you might like. Follow me."

She walked up ahead of us, and my eyes zeroed in on her ass in those scrubs. If that shit didn't look fat before, it was looking right and sitting up now. Grams slapped my arm.

"I see you."

"You're the one who raved about how pretty she is, Grams. I'm just admiring her—"

"Ass. You're admiring her ass."

"It's a nice ass, Grams."

"I can hear you," Rhythm said over her shoulder as we turned the corner.

We entered a room filled with musical instruments. The first thing Grams went to was the old, classic jukebox. She ran her fingers over it and smiled.

"I haven't listened to one of these in forever," she said.

Rhythm smiled. "My b—"

She paused for a moment and looked at me. I could tell she almost slipped and said boyfriend but thought better of it.

She cleared her throat and continued. "A friend bought this for me when we first opened. I told them how music helps people stay mentally active and promotes memory recall."

Grams scanned the music selection before choosing a song. A few seconds later, the sounds of "Ain't Too Proud To Beg" by The Temptations came through the speakers.

"This was one of my favorite songs," she said, turning around. "I was fourteen years old when this song came out. I begged my mama and daddy to let me go to their concert. I'd saved all my babysitting money to buy a ticket."

"Did they let you go?" I asked.

"Papa said no. He didn't think a fourteen-year-old girl should be at a concert like that alone. Mama had your uncle John and auntie Mary to look after, and he had to work, so neither of them could take me."

She giggled as she danced around me and Rhythm.

"I couldn't let them keep me away though. Honey, I used to love me some David Ruffin. In my mind, that was my husband, and I had to see my man. I snuck out and went to the concert anyway. I had the time of my life. It was worth being on punishment when I got caught sneaking back in."

I shook my head. "Not you out here being a menace, Grams."

She laughed as she grabbed Rhythm's hands, pulling her in to dance with her. She didn't hesitate to fall in step along with her. I leaned against the wall, watching them. It made my heart smile to see her in a good space. Pulling out my phone, I shot a quick video and sent it to my mother.

When we first learned of her condition, Mom took it the hardest. It had been her and Grams for the longest, and she couldn't fathom going to check on her one day and Grams not know who she was. She cried in my arms for the longest time that day.

The more it progressed, the more she called me in tears. I'd hired one of the best aides I could find, to come help her at the house a few days a week to lighten her load. I dedicated every Sunday to spending time with them. Koda and I would go over early that morning and just chill the entire day.

Rhythm's Blues

She and my grams had a special relationship. Grams would sneak her shit she wasn't supposed to have, and in turn, Koda laid up on her like a big ass baby, showing her love. I prayed that even when her memory faded, she would still be able to sense the love she had for the people that loved her most.

* * *

I could see why my mother loved having Rhythm as Gram's therapist. She sang her praises all the time. Watching her with my grandmother did something to me. It showed a softer side to her. Well, maybe not a softer side, because I didn't know much about her. I guess I was just learning something new, and it intrigued me. She was soft, gentle, and extremely caring. She had patience and was so encouraging. Grams didn't give her any shit either.

Currently, we were out at lunch at a little bistro not too far from the therapy center. I thought it was weird until she revealed that it had become a common part of Gram's therapy. With her condition worsening, we avoided public dining as much as possible as not to overwhelm her. If too much was going on around us, Grams got irritable and distracted, sometimes refusing to eat. There had been plenty of times she demanded we take her home.

"How do you get her to stay so calm?" I asked quietly as we ate.

Rhythm grabbed a napkin and wiped her mouth. She turned to me with a pleasant smile.

"Well, it's helpful to choose restaurants that have a quiet, calming atmosphere with very little distractions. This can help her stay focused on eating. You see how quiet this place is? Not too much noise, not too many people. It's a great place to have a nice meal and a nice conversation to keep her engaged."

I nodded. "That makes sense. Any other tips?"

"Consider going out during off-peak hours. You can also ask for a table in a quieter area, away from the high-traffic zones."

"What about helping her with eating? They told us it might get difficult over time."

"Unfortunately, that is a downside. You can always help her by cutting her food into smaller, more manageable pieces. If she has trouble using utensils, consider bringing adaptive utensils from home that she's more comfortable with. Whenever we have lunch, I bring some just in case she has trouble."

I smiled. "That's thoughtful of you. I never thought about that. I mean, I don't know many people that carry around utensils for the hell of it, but that makes sense."

"It's all about making sure she's comfortable. She may have dementia, but she can still have meaningful experiences. Everybody loves a good meal. Take her out. Engage her in conversation about the meal, reminisce about past dining experiences, or talk about the different flavors and textures of the food. It'll keep her focused and make the outing more pleasant. Just because she's sick doesn't mean you have to treat her like she's sick."

I nodded. I looked over at Grams who was eating and humming a tune to herself with a pleasant smile on her face. It was almost like she was in her own little world right now. It saddened me. I guess it showed on my face. Rhythm reached out and grabbed my hand.

"I'm sure you all are doing your best," she said softly. "If you ever need anything, if it ever gets overwhelming... we have plenty of resources to help families. You aren't in this alone."

I squeezed her hand. Pulling it to my lips, I kissed it.

"Thank you."

"No problem."

We stared at each other for a moment. For a second, she wasn't just the woman I'd dicked down a few weeks ago or had cumming against my fingers at her nigga's listening party. She smiled softly at me, and I smiled back. It wasn't until Grams interrupted us did we release hands.

"Don't you two look cute," she said, finally acknowledging us again. "Are you single, Dr. Baker?"

Rhythm tucked a stray hair behind her ear. "Um... technically, yes."

"My Channing here could use a wife."

"Grams," I said firmly.

"Oh, hush!" She waved me off. "I'm doing you a favor."

"I don't need help finding a woman, woman."

"I don't see you with one."

Rhythm snickered and covered her mouth. "My bad."

"Don't apologize, honey," Grams said. "He needs to let go of them lil fast tailed girls I know he has in his bed. He's just like his grandfather. I know because I was the fast tailed girl. He talked me right out of my panties, chile."

I rubbed my temples. "Grams, I didn't need to know that."

She scoffed. "How do you think your mama got here? It sure as hell wasn't no stork. As my only grandchild, it's your duty to make me a great grandma before I leave this earth."

"Do you want children?" Rhythm asked.

"I do."

"Do you wanna get married?"

I looked at Grams, and she snapped her fingers.

"I didn't ask you the question, boy," she sassed.

I rolled my eyes. "One of these days," I answered. "If I found the right woman, I'd settle down, get married, and give this lady the great grands she deserves."

Rhythm's facial expression was one of surprise. I was sure that, given our history, she wasn't expecting that as a response. I leaned in and whispered in her ear.

"There's more to me than good dick, love."

She blushed as I pulled away with a grin on my face.

"Duly noted."

We went back to eating. This time, Grams dominated the conversation by telling Rhythm embarrassing stories about me as a kid. She thought the shit was funny. She kept slapping and touching my arm as she laughed, and that shit made my dick twitch. My attraction to her had only heightened by watching her with my grandmother. If she knew like I knew, she'd stop while she was ahead.

We made it back to the center around twelve thirty. While Grams waited in the car, I walked Rhythm to the door. Shoving my hands in my pockets, I peered down at her.

"I um... I just wanna thank you for all you do here. This shit has been rough, you know."

She nodded. "I know."

"Grams seems to adore you, though. She doesn't raise hell like she tends to do."

Rhythm giggled. "I adore her too. She's one of my favorite clients. She reminds me a lot of my grandmother back home."

"So she's sassy as a muthafucka too?"

She laughed. "Very." She looked up at me, the smile still on her face. "You should bring her again. Give your mom a break."

"What? You like seeing my face?"

She playfully rolled her eyes. "Boy, bye."

I chuckled. "Nah, for real. I can do that. It was nice spending time with you and getting to know you a little."

She smirked. "You mean you enjoyed my company without having me cumming all over myself?"

"Make no mistake, love. It can always be that. You won't always be at work. You have my number. Tell me you need to cum, and I'll make that happen."

The smile slowly dropped from her face. Her eyes perused my frame like she was thinking about it.

"Don't think too hard," I said, stepping closer to her. Cupping her chin, I pecked her lips. "I'll see you around, love."

She simply nodded as she backed away from me and headed into the building. I watched until she disappeared. The sound of my horn blaring broke my concentration. I turned to see Grams rolling down the window.

"Come on here before you make me miss my stories, boy!"

I shook my head as I headed back to the car and climbed in. She gave me a heavy side-eye as I pulled out of the parking lot.

"What, lady?"

"Mmm hmm... I see you. You are trying to get in that girl's drawers."

I chuckled. Little did she know, I'd already gotten the drawers.

We drove back to my mother's with her listening to some old school music and singing along. When we walked into the house, my mother came around the corner with a basket of laundry in her hands. She set it down and came to hug me.

"Hey, baby. Hey, Ma. How was therapy?"

"He's trying to sleep with my therapist," Grams answered, bypassing us and going down the hall to her room.

"You're messy as hell, Grams!" I called after her.

I turned back to my mother who was looking at me with her arms crossed.

"What?"

"Are you trying to sleep with the therapist, Channing?"

I kissed my teeth and chuckled. "Follow your mama up if you want to."

She shook her head. "Seriously, how was therapy?"

"It was great. She sang. She danced. She ate good. She had a good day."

She covered her heart and heaved a sigh of relief. "Thank God."

I pulled her into my arms and hugged her tightly.

"Grams is gonna be good, Ma. Even when she isn't, she's got us, so she'll *still* be good."

"I know, baby. It's just hard."

"I can take her anytime you need me to."

"No, no. I love having her here. She keeps me company most days. I wanna enjoy the time we have with her while we can."

I nodded, though she couldn't see me. Kissing the top of her forehead, I gave her a squeeze. Shey Watson was one of the strongest women I knew, but even the strong had weaknesses and breaking points.

That made me think about Rhythm. I wondered what her breaking point would be with Raheem's ass. The man was a talented artist with the potential to be one of the greats. He was fucking up royally with her, though. He could keep at it though. The more he fucked up, the easier it would be to take his woman right from under him.

Chapter Seventeen

Rhythm

"Honey, I'm home!" I called, walking into the apartment.

Nique came from the back with a smile on her face.

"Somebody is in a good mood," she noted, taking a seat on the couch.

"I had a great day."

I put my things down and went into the kitchen. Grabbing two glasses, I poured up some wine then took it and the bottle into the living room to join her.

"Tea?" she asked, taking a glass from my hand.

"Not really tea. Guess whose grandmother happens to be my client?"

"Who?"

"Channing."

"You lying!"

"Hand to God. When that man walked in to accompany her, I could have fallen the fuck out, Nique."

She laughed. "So, were you two horn dogs able to keep your hormones under control in front of granny?"

I rolled my eyes. "Yes, although he was looking good as hell in those gray sweats and white tee. Tattoos and dick just all out for the world to see, girl."

"Oh, so he was in typical slut attire?"

"Slut with a capital S.L.U.T."

We shared a laugh.

"He was different today, though. I learned a little about him, thanks to his grandmother. Sis was trying to hook us up before she even got to the place. That lady told him she deserved great grand-children, and he had to give them to her before she left this earth."

"Is she sick?"

"She's in the early stages of dementia," I said sadly.

"Oh no! Damn. How's he handling that?"

"Well, he had a little moment today when we had lunch with her. I could tell it was weighing heavily on him that she's going to get worse. Apparently, she and his mother raised him, and they are pretty close."

Nique poked out her lip. "My heart hurts for him."

"Yeah, mine too. She's a sweet old lady, at least with me. Now, she can be sassy and rude, but she's funny as hell."

"You said you three had lunch?"

"Yes, and before you get started, it's a regular part of her therapy."

She giggled. "I'm just saying. Lunch dates with granny... getting to know him..."

"I'm not invested, girl. Not in him."

"Better not be in Raheem." She gave me a side eye. "I see I didn't have to accept any deliveries today."

I rolled my eyes. "He left a note and rose on my windshield this morning."

"Stalker much? What did he have to say?"

"Basically, he loves me and he's not gonna stop proving he can change until I come home."

She shook her head. "I have to ask again... do you want him back?"

I sat quietly for a moment, dwelling on my thoughts. I loved Raheem... it was Prince Cole I'd grown a disdain for. If the man I loved would show up and stay around, I'd give him another chance. I could admit that he hadn't been photo'd with Lady Lingo in a while. Anytime he posted a video or picture of himself, he was either in an empty studio, with his boys, or at the house.

Now, that wasn't to say it wasn't planned. I was fully aware that a nigga would do what he wanted, when he wanted, and with who he wanted *if* he wanted to. I wasn't naive to that. All I was saying was he seemed to be on some solo dolo type of shit for the most part.

"I don't know, Nique," I finally said, taking a sip of my wine. "Eventually, I'll have to make that decision. Right now, it is what it is."

"Hmm."

She sipped her wine as she grabbed the remote and turned on the TV. I knew she wanted to say something, but right now, I was grateful that she kept it to herself. I didn't want to think too much about that man and get in my feelings.

We sat in the living room for a few hours, watching TV. We ended up ordering takeout for dinner and chilling until at least ten before retreating to our spaces. I stripped out of my clothes and went into the bathroom for a nice, relaxing soak in my tub.

To set the ambiance, I lit a few candles, dimmed the lights, and turned on some soft music. Easing into the tub, I gave a satisfied breath as I relaxed into the water to soak away the day's events.

My thoughts drifted to Channing as I thought of his grandmother. There was something about that man. I couldn't quite put my finger on it, but I liked him a little more after today. Since sex wasn't on the table, it left the room to have a real conversation.

I kept thinking to myself, it would be messy as hell to get involved with my ex's producer. Then I realized it was too late because I was already involved. Maybe I didn't know it at first, but now that I did, I would definitely be labeled a trifling bitch in these streets.

Still, there was something about him that kept drawing me in. I found myself swiping at his contact to call him. Panic set in as the phone started ringing. Before I could hang up, I heard his voice on the other end.

"Hello?"

Shit!

"Hello?"

"Uh... hey... Channing."

"Rhythm?"

"It's me."

I could hear the smile in his voice. "Well, isn't this a pleasant surprise. To what do I owe the pleasure of this call?"

"Well... I um... I was just thinking about you."

"Were you now? Why don't you let me see your beautiful face?"

Before I had a chance to protest, he sent a FaceTime request. I hesitated for a moment before I answered it. His video populated, and there he was, shirtless, lying on his couch. He smiled when he saw me.

"Looks like you're relaxing."

"Trying to. What did you and Grams do after therapy?"

"Man, that woman rushed me to get home so she could watch her stories. You know the first thing she said when my mama asked how things went was, I was trying to get some ass."

I couldn't help but laugh because I could see her saying that.

"Grams is a trip. I love working with her. Every time I see her, I have to call my grandma and check on her."

"How's it been being out here without family?"

"Well, I'm not completely without family. Emerald's wife, Rhyon, is my first cousin."

"Word?"

"Yes. Her mom and my mom are sisters."

"It's a small world. Em is cool people. He's about business in the studio. In and out is his motto."

"Trust me, after all he went through to get Rhyon back, he makes it his mission to spend all his free time with his family."

"As he should. A man that doesn't prioritize taking care of his family ain't a man at all."

"So that means I expect you to be a good husband when you get married. Don't let us revisit this conversation."

He chuckled. "I'll be a great husband, both active and attentive. I told you, there's more to me than just good dick."

I rolled my eyes. "Anyway! What are you doing?"

"Watching a ball game."

"Is that what you do in your spare time? Watch sports?"

"Sometimes. Occasionally, I'll go to a home game since I have a season pass. Either that or I'll hit up a lounge or club, scouting new talent. I'm real chill for the most part. It's just me and my baby girl."

He angled the camera to where I could see Koda lying on his chest.

"She's just so adorable! Hi, beautiful!"

She looked up at me then back at Channing.

"She's a big ass baby. She's basically my second shadow at home."

"Oh, hush. I bet you have her spoiled."

He chuckled. "I can't lie, I do. She's the closest thing I have to a child, so it's only right."

"Are you as bad as the dog moms?"

He laughed. "I think I might be worse. If I ever get you over here, you'll see for yourself."

"I don't know if I trust myself being alone with you."

He smirked. "Why is that?"

"Because I tend to lose all inhibitions when we're alone."

"What's wrong with that?"

"You're Raheem's producer, Channing. It was bad enough that we had sex when we didn't know the link between us. Getting entangled when we know the truth... it's messy."

"Listen, Rhythm. I'm a grown ass man. I don't need permission from anyone to entertain a woman on any level."

"That may be true, but if he finds out—"

"Why do you care so much about him finding out? I'm sure that nigga does what he wants when you aren't around."

"That's the second time you've made reference to that. Do you know something I don't?"

"I know what I see, which is probably the same shit you see in the media. What about him makes you wanna be with a nigga that disrespects you like that?"

I looked away from the camera. It seemed like everybody wanted to question me about Raheem today. When I looked back at him, he was still waiting for an answer.

"I know it sounds like excuses..." I said softly. "You met him as Prince Cole, the rapper... the international superstar. I met him as Raheem Javon Cole, the guy who used to make beats on the lunchroom table with his friends. The guy who was all about making sure he got his mama and sisters out of the hood. The guy that bent over backwards to make sure I was comfortable being with him when we first linked back up. I don't know this version of him that's come about in the last year. It's hard to accept that he's let his image consume him this much."

"You realize that you don't have to accept the versions of people who no longer align with who you are, right? People change and grow at different paces. Sometimes you outgrow them, even if you love them. Don't get so comfortable having people in your life that you don't know when it's time to remove them."

He spoke with sincerity, and it made me tear up. I swiped at the tears in the corner of my eye.

"Don't cry," he said softly.

"I feel so stupid," I said as the tears continued to fall.

"We've all been there."

"You've held on to someone you should have let go of?"

"Fuck no. I'll cut your ass off with a quickness."

I giggled. "Just like that?"

"Straight like that."

"You realize you're contradicting yourself?"

His brows furrowed. "How?"

"This whole thing between us... It was supposed to be a fuck and done type of deal."

He smirked. "True."

"So, what is it about me?"

"I don't know. Maybe I'm not used to having women ghost me the morning after."

"Oh, so you do the ghosting?"

"Nah. It's a mutual goodbye. I don't know what it is about you. You seem like a good girl. Seeing you with my grams today... I guess I kinda see you in a different light, one that doesn't involve you face down, ass up, or on top of a counter cumming for me... though I rather enjoy that."

"I bet you do."

He chuckled. "I like your vibe."

"But?"

"You're stuck on ol' boy. Do I give a fuck about him? No. Once this album is out, my ties to him can be severed. I'm not the type of nigga that waits for somebody to tell me I can have something. If I want it, I get it. So yo' nigga is just gon' have to take his L in good stride 'cause I want you."

That shit had me hot and bothered. I shifted in the tub, willing my hands not to find their way between my legs.

"Wh-what would you do with me?" I asked curiously.

"Everything he can't. I'ma let you sit on that though."

I was quiet for a moment. In plain English, he told me I was going to be his, even if he had to snatch me from another man.

"Are you coming to this album release?" he asked.

"I don't know. I'm on the fence about it."

"What if I asked you to come and leave with me?"

I blushed. "That's a pretty bold move."

"I'm a pretty bold nigga."

I giggled. "You are."

"The club we're gonna be at has private VIP rooms. You can look out, but nobody can look in. I'll get you a space, and you won't even have to see that nigga. I wanna see you."

"You can't see me outside of the party?"

"I can and I will. But I wanna see you then, too."

I thought for a moment. My ego was slightly inflated. How trifling would I be if I showed up to my ex's album release to please the man that I was fucking? Nique wasn't going, so there was no doubt that it would just be Channing and me in that VIP section. My mind raced with all the things that could happen behind closed doors with him. I was intrigued to say the least.

"Fine," I said. "You get the section, and I'll come."

"Bet. I'll put you on the list so you don't have to wait in line."

We stared at each other for a moment. The way he was looking at me had me blushing like a damn schoolgirl with a crush. Maybe I did have a little bit of a crush on him. He was so damn fine, but more than that, I liked his energy. Part of me wanted to get to know him, even though it meant being messy as fuck.

"I should go..." I said quietly. "I need to finish up in here and get ready for bed."

"That's fine. You have my number, and now I have yours. Will you respond if I reach out?"

I hesitated. "Yes."

He smiled, and it made me smile.

"A'ight then. Sleep good. I'ma holla at you."

"Okay."

We disconnected the call, and I placed the phone on the counter. Something told me that I was about to open a whole can of worms fucking with this man. The sad part was... part of me didn't even care.

Chapter Eighteen

Channing

The Album Release Party

I looked myself over in the mirror in my mama's bedroom. I'd come to bring Koda to spend a little time with Grams and figured I might as well get dressed here to head to the party.

Tonight, I kept it casual and dressed myself in a black Armani polo shirt, black jeans, and my favorite black boots. Around my neck was a white-gold Cuban link. I wore the matching bracelet on one wrist and my white-gold Rolex on the other. A diamond stud adorned my ear.

As I looked myself over, I thought I looked good. After spraying on my favorite cologne, I packed up my belongings and headed out front to where my mama, Grams, and Koda were sitting watching a movie.

"Don't you look handsome!" Mama said, smiling.

She never failed to make me feel like a chap again when she complimented me.

"Thank you kindly," I said, striking a pose for her. "You think this will get me laid?"

She slapped my arm. "Boy, stop it!"

I chuckled. "I'm joking."

"I bet you are," Grams said.

"I'll be by to get Koda sometime tomorrow." I went over and scratched behind her ears. "You be a girl for daddy. Grams, don't be feeding her all kinds of stuff. I packed her meals and her snacks."

She gave me a side-eye but didn't say anything, letting me know that she was gonna do whatever the fuck she wanted. I kissed her cheek and then my mama's.

"I love y'all."

"We love you too," Mama said. "Have a good night."

"Oh, I will."

She shook her head as I walked out the door. I hopped in my car and made my way out of the driveway. The ride to the venue was only about twenty minutes. The line was already wrapped around the building. It seemed like all of L.A. was here to celebrate Raheem.

I had to give it to him. He may have been a shitty boyfriend, but he was a great artist. The people loved him and showed up for him wherever he went. I could see the fire marshal stepping in at some point tonight.

After having the valet park my car, I headed inside, bypassing the line of waiting patrons. Inside was already packed. As I scanned the crowd, I pulled out my phone to text Rhythm.

Me: Hey, are you here?

R&B: Right where you wanted me.

I smirked to myself as I made my way to the section I'd booked for us. I tapped lightly on the door then opened it to find her standing at the private bar, leaning over the counter, talking to the bartender.

"Got... damn," I muttered as my eyes passed over her.

Tonight, she was dressed in a silky orange top with a few buttons undone, exposing her supple breasts, cut-off jean shorts that stopped right below her ample ass, and orange heels. Her smooth skin glistened with that shimmery shit I loved. Her hair hung freely with a middle part, and gold accessories completed the outfit. Her face was free of makeup, and she looked gorgeous.

She turned her head toward the door and smiled at me. Grabbing her drink, she strutted over to me as I closed the door.

"Hey," she said, looking up at me with innocent eyes.

"Hey, baby."

I slipped an arm around her waist and pulled her into me. Leaning in, I pressed my lips to hers. Much to my surprise, she cupped my face and opened her mouth to receive my tongue. An innocent peck led to her moaning into my mouth as the kiss turned lustful. It wasn't until I grabbed her ass and she erupted in giggles did our lips part.

"I'm sorry. I got a head start on drinks," she said, swiping her lip gloss from my lips.

"You good." I stepped back and looked her over once more. "Damn, you look beautiful."

She blushed. "Thank you."

"Did you have any problems getting in?"

"Nope. Quick and easy."

I nodded as I grabbed her hand. After I ordered myself a drink from the bar, I led her over to the seating area. I took a seat, and when she sat next to me, I pulled her legs into my lap.

"Comfortable?" I asked.

"With you... yes. It's just a little weird sneaking in here."

"We ain't sneaking. We have privacy with not so many eyes on us. I mean, I'm not so much of an asshole that I'd ruin tonight's event by flaunting this in his face."

"Mmm, we kinda are."

"You feel any type of way about that?"

"Nope."

"Good, 'cause I swear I don't give a fuck."

She giggled. "So how long have you been in the music business?"

"Professionally, about twelve years. Personally, I've loved music my whole life. My mama said she used to put headphones on her stomach while she was pregnant, and I would go crazy in there. Ever since I can remember, I've been making beats and shit. I got put out of class so much for drumming beats with my pencils or on anything I could make a sound with."

"I know your mama got on your ass about that."

I chuckled. "She did. She's threatened me more times than I can remember. My grandfather was the one who introduced me to the studio when I was six. Back in the day, he was heavy into music. He had all the equipment and thought he was gonna go big. Then he and Grams had my mother, and he put his dreams aside to make sure they could eat. He didn't regret choosing his family over a career, but he always wondered 'what if,' you know?"

"I get that. Those questions keep you up at night."

"Facts. Anyway, when I told Grams I wanted to pursue music, she encouraged me to go for it. She said there was no reason I shouldn't live out my dreams, unlike my grandfather."

"Can I just say I love your Grams?"

I chuckled. "Me and Grams are gonna have a problem if she doesn't stop feeding my baby all kinds of shit. Koda is on a strict diet. I prepare all of her meals and pack them when she goes over there."

"Prepare? Like you cook for her?"

"Yes. She has her own dog food seasoning and all."

She laughed. "Oh, she's bougie."

"She definitely thinks she's a princess."

"If you're this kind of dog dad, I can only imagine you with kids."

"My kids will absolutely be spoiled, especially if I have a daughter."

"With you taking care of your mom and grandma, I can see your daughter having you wrapped around her finger. All she'll have to do is bat those eyelashes, and you'll be a total sucker."

"I can't disagree there. My mother will be worse."

"Your mom is a sweetheart. And I never would have guessed she had a grown son. She looks so youthful."

"She had me young, which I think is another reason my dad didn't stick around. Nigga felt like he was missing out on life and decided he'd rather be free than be a parent."

"How old were you?"

"Five."

She shook her head. "I'm sorry. No child deserves that."

"You close with your people? I mean, I assume you're close with your father since you told me he'd hunt my ass down if anything happened to you."

She giggled. "I am pretty close with them. It's been hard being away from them for so long. I make a trip home at least one weekend a month. It's been a while though. I suspect my mother will be calling me soon, asking where I am. I just didn't want to bring this embarrassment home with me. She was already against me coming out here, and I don't feel like hearing I told you so."

"I get that. But hey, you've got your bestie out here now."

"I do! I didn't know how much I missed her until she came to stay. It's been like a sleepover every night."

"So, you live together?"

"We do. I moved out of Raheem's a few weeks before we hooked up."

"So it's been over with him that long?"

"Yeah... why?"

"He just makes it seem like you're still at home having problems."

"He talks about me to you?"

"He's only spoken about you twice, and both times were before I knew he was talking about you. The first time was a couple weeks ago when he was in the studio with Lady Lingo, working on a track. The nigga couldn't catch the beat to save his damn life. You must have stressed that man out."

"I packed my shit and left while he was out of town. He came by my hotel, asking me to come home, and I refused." She shook her head. "Can I ask you something, Channing?"

"I may be inclined to answer."

"I just need to know... have you ever seen them be intimate with each other?"

I sighed as I ran my hand over my head. I wasn't a snitch, but shit, she asked.

"I haven't seen him all over her, but the chemistry is there. She's very affectionate with him, and he doesn't seem bothered by it."

I hesitated for a moment, contemplating if I should tell her what he said about things being "like that" with Imani. Technically, 'like that' could mean a lot of different things. I wasn't sure of the extent of his and her relationship, so I decided not to divulge that bit of information. I was sure she had her own suspicions.

I looked over at her, and she simply nodded. For a second, she looked sad. I knew that shit had to be hurtful to hear.

"Well, I guess I dodged a bullet, huh?" she asked, taking a sip of her drink.

"I'd say you did."

She downed the rest of her drink. "To hell with both of them. I don't feel bad about fucking you now."

"You felt bad?"

"Maybe that was the wrong choice of words. I didn't feel bad. I felt like I did it for the wrong reasons."

"And now?"

"Now... I'm thinking about doing it again."

She set her drink on the table and straddled my lap. Her hands came to my face, and she kissed me slow yet passionately. My arms came around her waist with one hand resting on her back and the other planted firmly on her ass.

"Don't start no shit you can't finish," I mumbled between kisses.

"We both know I can finish you," she countered.

Memories of the way she rode my dick that night flooded my mind.

She mounted me, on her knees, and gripped the headboard as she rolled and lifted her hips as I gripped her waist. Her pussy was so wet that I felt like I slipped deeper into the muthafucka with every stroke.

"Shit!" I cursed as my fingers dug into her sides. "Goddamn, baby. Ride that shit."

She smirked as she picked up the pace. Bending my knees, I thrusted upward to meet her. The sound of her ass clapping against my thighs echoed throughout the room.

"Fuck!" she yelled. "It's so good!"

"I know, baby. You riding the fuck outta this dick too."

She positioned herself on her feet and bounced on my shit like she was chasing her orgasm. She'd already cum three times, and the way her pussy was juicing up let me know she was gearing up for a fourth. Reaching between us, I strummed her clit, causing her body to shudder.

Her movements slowed but didn't stop.

"Give it to me," I commanded. "This pussy so fucking juicy. I need all that. Stop fucking playing with me and bust that nut."

She wildly threw her hips, her cries of pleasure filling the room. The faster she rode me, the faster I strummed her clit. The next thing I knew, she bucked against me, and her pussy creamed as she came forcefully.

"Shit! Shit! Shit! Fuck!" she yelled.

Her body shook violently, and her walls clenched around me, pulling my own nut to the forefront. I easily filled the condom as I erupted.

The memory was so vivid that I could see it in my head.

"I see you thinking about it," she said, peering down at me. "You want this pussy to cream like that for you again?"

I grinned. "That's a given. When we leave here, you're mine. Am I clear?"

She smirked. "Crystal."

Rolling off of me, she stood and went to the bar for another drink. I watched her walk away, adjusting myself in the process. Fuck Raheem. If he couldn't take care of what he had, I had no issue picking up his slack. The better nigga would always win. In this case, that nigga would always be me.

Chapter Nineteen

Rhythm

I'd been having the time of my life in the VIP section with Channing. When he asked me to come two weeks ago, I was hesitant. I liked him, but I wasn't sure it was a good idea. Since the night I called him, we'd spoken every day. We'd had a few lunch dates too. He'd brought his grandmother to her last two appointments, and I could honestly say, I enjoyed his company.

He'd taken heed to my advice about taking her out in public and accommodating her. Watching him care for her was softening my heart toward him. He'd told me she had a few irritable moments and moments of forgetfulness. He also admitted that he'd been feeling more confident in caring for her since he'd been doing more research on her condition himself. I was proud of him for that.

I could admit when I first showed up, I was nervous as hell. I prayed I could get into the VIP before Raheem or any of his flunkies saw me. Nique refused to come with me. At first, she thought I was going to appease Raheem. The girl damn near cursed me out. When she learned that I was going because Channing requested to spend time with me, her petty side kicked in.

"Bitch, how are you going to see your new nigga at your old nigga's event?" she asked, cackling.

"First of all, he's not my new nigga."

"Not yet. If you don't come home tonight, I know where you are."

She told me to have fun and that she didn't want to see me sucking face with him in a room with just the three of us all night. Granted, we had been sucking face, but we'd also been dancing and getting to know each other for the last hour.

We talked about our childhoods and our careers. I discovered that before he was a producer, he'd actually tried his hand at rapping. When he pulled up this old ass music video from when he was sixteen that was clearly shot on a cell phone, I fell out laughing.

"Wait, wait! Rewind it back!"

"Hell no. You already laughing too damn hard."

I tried to grab the phone from him, but he held it just out of reach.

"Come on, Channing. Just one more playback."

He kissed his teeth as he handed me the phone. I watched the playback in literal tears because while he sounded okay, the video was terrible.

"You have to send me that!" I declared.

He playfully shoved me as he snatched the phone. "I'm not sending you shit. You seem like you would show it to my grams at her next session."

"Wait, has she seen this?"

"Yes, and we don't need to relive that."

"I'm sure she would get a kick out of it."

"She would never let me live it down as long as she can remember it. She laughed as bad as you did when she saw it. Then she showed it to my mama, and they both laughed."

"Awww, baby! Were your feelings hurt."

He grinned. "Baby? I like that. Don't go spoiling me with affection." He leaned over and pecked my lips. "To answer your question, yes, my feelings were hurt. I realized in that moment, I was more of a behind the scenes type of person versus an in front of the camera person."

"That's okay. The spotlight isn't for everyone. That was one of my issues with Raheem. He wanted me to be glued to his side at events or shows or whatnot. Make no mistake; I was always a very supportive girlfriend. I just didn't want to be in front of the camera. I'm not a celebrity. I have no desire to have the media combing through every inch of my life or people saying I'm a gold digger and shit. I wanted to be private, but not a secret."

"I get that. The media is filled with vultures. Most of the time, they tell half ass truths or spin the narrative to fit some messy ass agenda. People know me, but they don't know my business, and that's the way I like it."

I smiled. I liked that about him. He understood the need to not have everything so public. Some things should be reserved for you and your partner only. I knew a lot of people would ask me why date a celebrity if I didn't want to be in the public eye. In my opinion, celebrities were regular ass people, just with more money than the average Joe.

I wouldn't treat them any differently just because they had money. Shit, it wasn't my money.

After taking the last sip of my drink, I stood from my seat.

"I think I had a little too much to drink. I have to pee."

"I can walk you to the bathroom."

"I'm okay. I promise. I'll be right back."

He didn't listen. Instead, he opened the door and motioned for security. A big, burly man appeared at the door.

"Aye, escort her to the bathroom. She better make it back without a hair outta place."

The man nodded as he motioned for me to come out. As I walked past Channing, he gently gripped my arm, causing me to stop. Cupping my chin, he kissed my lips.

"Don't be too long, okay?"

I blushed as I nodded. He released me, and I grabbed ahold of the big man's arm. He led me down the hall and downstairs to the main floor where the bathrooms were located. The club was much more packed than when I initially arrived. Raheem still hadn't gotten here, and I could hear the anxious comments of people waiting for him to arrive.

I headed into the bathroom to relieve myself. All those drinks were slowly sneaking up on me. Once I was done, I flushed the toilet and left the stall to wash my hands. The bathroom was surprisingly empty, but not for long. The door opened, and I looked up. A frown found its way to my face as that bitch walked in.

Fucking Imani.

When she saw me, she smirked.

"What are you doing here?" she asked.

"I was invited, not that it's any of your business."

"Just tell me... why are you doing this to yourself?"

I didn't respond right away. Instead, I grabbed some paper towels and dried my hands. She stood with her arms crossed as she waited for an answer. Tossing the wet towels in the trash, I turned to her.

"Please... tell me what I'm doing."

"Chasing after a nigga that clearly wants to be elsewhere."

"Let me guess, elsewhere is with you?"

She smirked. "Elsewhere has *been* with me."

"Really? Because every chance I give that man to be in my face, that's where he is. Now, I don't know what he's telling you, but it's been *me* he's begging to come home. That doesn't sound like he wants to be elsewhere to me. I gave that nigga to you, and he's still trying to come back. I guess your pussy ain't enough to keep him, sis."

I brushed past her to walk out of the bathroom, but she grabbed me. I spun around and did what I'd been dying to do every time she gave me that shit eating smirk. I decked that bitch right in her mouth since she wanted to do all that fucking talking.

Her head snapped back, and she stumbled. When she regained her balance, I saw that I had busted her lip. Blood ripped from the wound as she grabbed paper towels to catch it.

"You fucking bitch!" she screamed.

"I got your bitch! Don't ever put your muthafucking hands on me, ho. You thought I was one of those pussy ass bitches. Let that be a lesson to you. Just because I don't do drama doesn't mean I won't bat you in yo' shit. You earned that one. Don't let it happen again."

I left the bathroom, leaving her to tend to her busted lip. Security was waiting for me outside. Grabbing ahold of his arm, I allowed him to lead me back toward the stairs that led to the VIP section. Just as we passed the stage, I felt a tug on my arm.

"You came!" I heard over the music.

I looked back to see Raheem smiling at me. He tried to pull me into a hug, but I held up a hand to stop him.

"Don't touch me."

"What's wrong with you?"

Just as I opened my mouth to speak, the DJ called the attention of the crowd.

"All right, all right, all right! I know y'all have been waiting, and the man of the hour is finally here. Give it up for Prince Cole!"

The crowd went wild. Raheem looked back at me.

"Can you just give me a minute?"

I crossed my arms. "No."

"Baby, please."

"Don't you have fans waiting, Raheem?"

He looked back at the stage, then at me. The next thing I knew, he was pulling me on stage with him. My first instinct was to fight him off, but I had a brand to uphold. I couldn't be plastered all over the internet acting a fool in here. Reluctantly, I allowed him to pull me on stage, but inside, I was fuming.

"How y'all doing tonight!" Raheem yelled into the microphone.

The crowd went wild with cheers. I looked around the club full of people and immediately wished I'd stayed my ass home. My eyes drifted to the second floor and found Channing standing at the balcony with a frown on his face. My face flushed with discomfort, and the moment it did, he started making his way toward the stairs.

"Thank y'all for coming out to celebrate this album release with me. It's been a long time coming, and I'm proud to say this is my best work yet. There are a few people I want to thank for making this album possible. First, I have to thank the Most High. Without Him, I wouldn't be here. Second, shout out to my mother, standing up there in the VIP section. Y'all show my mama some love."

The spotlight drifted to Ms. Cole who stood with a smile on her face. She blew Raheem a kiss and waved at the crowd.

"Without her, I wouldn't be the man I am today. Shout out to my manager, Malcom Essex and my team of engineers and producers. Big shout out the homie Channing Watson. He's somewhere in here. My mans really came through with his legendary skills to produce what I think is my greatest album. Thank you to my fans. Y'all have been loyal and really fucking with me since I hit the scene ten years ago."

He looked at me and squeezed my hand. I looked around for Channing and found him having a heated conversation with ol' dude that escorted me to the bathroom. Imani appeared at the steps with a deep frown on her face.

Raheem cupped my chin and turned my face back to his.

"Last but not least, I wanna thank this woman right here. She's put up with a lot of my shit, and she deserves to be recognized. For all the late-night sessions she stayed up for, the homecooked meals, the love I'm welcomed home with after a hard day's work, the support she's given... background and foreground... she deserves the world, and I'm gonna give it to her."

He leaned in and kissed my cheek. I wanted to spit in his face. How dare he do this here and now!

He kissed my hand and said, "I know I haven't been the best

152

boyfriend lately, and I want my apology to be as loud as my disrespect."

Many of the women in the crowd awed at his declaration. The Rhythm from a few months ago might have bought this act, but this Rhythm was disgusted with him. I wanted so badly to embarrass us both, but I kept my composure and plastered a fake smile on my face.

"You're fucking pushing it," I said through my teeth as I dug my nails into his hand.

He winced as he turned back to the crowd. "How about we get this party started? DJ, drop my shit!"

The DJ dropped the intro to the album as Raheem led me offstage, brushing right past Imani. She didn't like that too much because the next thing we knew, she was grabbing the mic from his hand and storming on stage. The DJ cut the music as she yelled over it.

"I have something to say!"

I snatched away from Raheem as he turned his attention to her with a wide-eyed expression. Channing grabbed my hand and pulled me into the sea of people.

"Let's go," he commanded.

I didn't protest. Raheem was so busy trying to get Imani's attention that he didn't even notice me walking away.

"While Prince Cole here was giving his thank yous, I think he forgot one," Imani said. "I certainly remember being the one to introduce you to Channing. *I* was in the studio with you all those long nights. I absolutely remember all the nights you spent in *my* bed after said studio sessions."

I stopped in my tracks and looked back to find Raheem on stage, wrestling the mic from her. He finally got it from her hands, and they started arguing right there on stage. It went on for a minute or so. The DJ tried to distract the crowd by playing Raheem's music, but everybody was tuned into the disaster on stage.

Imani hauled off and slapped him before storming off stage. I couldn't even say that I felt any type of way about her confession at this point. I think in my heart, I knew the truth all along, but I made excuses for it. That ended tonight. Tonight and this little display was the fucking benediction for real this time.

I turned back to Channing. "Please get me the fuck outta here."

He nodded and grabbed my hand, pulling me through the crowd toward the exit. There was nothing else to see here.

Chapter Twenty

Channing

"Nique, I'm fine," Rhythm assured her friend.

If I hadn't taken her out of the club when I did, I was gon' jump on that stage and beat Raheem's ass. The moment I saw the look of discomfort on Rhythm's face, anger fueled my footsteps. I ran up on that fat fuck of a security guard and let his ass have it. He was stuttering all over himself, trying to explain what happened.

I didn't need an explanation. I could clearly see that she was up there against her will because he wasn't doing his job. I didn't give a damn who Raheem was. He should have never been able to get close enough to Rhythm to pull her on stage and embarrass her like that. Then for Imani's ass to get up there and further embarrass them all? The shit was crazy. She clearly didn't know her role as a side bitch.

I could hear Monique going off on the other end of the phone, and it wasn't even on speaker. She'd called that man everything but a child of God, and I wholeheartedly agreed with her.

"Nique, I promise, I'm okay, boo... Please don't call that man. There is nothing else that needs to be said to him. Fuck him. Fuck her. She deserves that nigga as much as she deserved my fist to her mouth."

My eyes widened at the sound of that. She'd been on the phone with Monique since we walked out of the club, so I hadn't been privy to the news of her hitting Imani. The whole incident on stage had been live streamed. By morning, I was sure every news and gossip blog were going to be talking about it.

"I'm with Channing... Yes, he's taking care of me..."

She snickered, and I could only imagine that Monique had said something out of pocket.

"Bitch, get off my phone. I love you, and I'll see you tomorrow."

She hung up the phone and dropped it into the cup holder.

"You sure you good?" I asked.

"I'm fine."

"So, tell me, Mayweather. How did you end up putting hands on that girl?"

"She came in the bathroom talking shit while I was in there. We exchanged words, and when I tried to walk out, she grabbed me; therefore, she got hit."

I shook my head. "Shit is finna be real tight around the studio. I'm glad I finished the track they were working on."

She shrugged. "I don't wanna talk about them anymore."

"Fair enough."

"Where are we going?"

"To my house."

"Oh! I get to see where the big-time producer lives, huh?"

I chuckled. "It ain't even like that. I live comfortably. No extra shit. It's not a mansion. It's not even a mini mansion, but it's nice. I worked my ass off for it."

"I believe you."

We drove in comfortable silence to my neighborhood. I lived in a subdivision called Haven Heights. Most of the homes were around $500,000. My home was a four-bedroom, three-and-a-half-bath split level. It had a home theater, gym, and game room. I'd also had a pool and a basketball court installed. When I bought it, I bought the lot next door, too, to make room for the extra amenities and my studio. If I didn't feel like leaving my house, I didn't have to.

We pulled into my driveway about twenty minutes later. Rhythm's eyes widened.

"Not a mini mansion, huh?" she said with a giggle. "This is beautiful."

"Thank you."

Shutting off the car, I climbed out and went around to open her door, extending my hand to help her out. We headed inside so I could give her a tour of the place. She absolutely fell in love with my kitchen, stating she loved to cook, and it was a chef's dream.

We ended the tour in my master bedroom. As we walked in, she surveyed the room. This room was what sold me on the house. It was huge and equipped with double walk-in closets, a sitting room that led out to my balcony, and a spacious en suite bathroom.

"So, this is where the magic happens?" Rhythm asked, leaning against the bed.

I stepped into her space and placed my hands on either side of her.

Leaning in close, I said, "Ain't no magic. Straight fuckin'."

She smirked as her hand snaked to the back of my neck. She pulled my head to hers and dropped a sexy, sensual kiss on my lips. Her hands tugged at the hem of my shirt, and she pulled it off and tossed it aside. Our lips never parted as she found my belt buckle and undid it, pulling it from the loops.

I fumbled with the buttons of her shirt, opening them one by one. When I pushed it from her shoulders, I was greeted with a sexy black lace bra. Her nipple piercings were visible, causing me to stoop down and latch onto the hardened buds through the fabric.

She moaned softly as I alternated between one then the other. Her hands continued to mess with my pants, unbuttoning and unzipping them. When she tried to push them and my boxers down, I slapped her hands away.

"Patience, baby," I said, pushing her flat on the bed.

Grabbing her foot, I placed it to my chest and took off one heel then the other. She had the sexiest feet I'd ever seen. They were so soft and well taken care of that I just wanted to suck her pretty ass toes. I reached to unbutton her shorts before slipping them off. A matching pair of lace thongs greeted me, causing me to lick my lips.

"Damn."

The way the set did her body justice was a fucking sin and a shame.

"On your knees," I commanded.

She did the sexiest roll over and pushed her ass into the air. Threading my fingers through her hair, I gave a generous tug. She moaned as she followed the pull of my arm to sit upright. I peppered kisses along her collarbone as I unclasped her bra and pulled it from her shoulders.

My hands came around to cup her full breasts, tweaking her nipples in the process. She moaned her pleasure.

"Mmmm..."

"Can I taste you?" I whispered in her ear.

"Yes!"

I pushed her forward, back into the arch she had previously held. My eyes marveled at the sight of her ass eating up that thong. Gently, I massaged her cheeks before giving them a generous smack, eliciting a moan from her. Hooking my fingers in the bands of the thin fabric, I pulled them down and off.

Before me, her pussy was already secreting its juices. She trembled as I ran my finger through her slit, stopping to massage her clit.

"Wet ass pussy..." I mumbled, positioning myself behind her.

Without warning, I sucked her clit between my lips, causing her to cry out.

"Shit!"

Spreading her plump cheeks, I took my time devouring the sweetness of her pussy. I could hear the sharpness of the breaths she drew as I circled and sucked her sensitive pearl. She was so damn wet that my beard was saturated in her juices in no time.

Her moans multiplied as I slid my middle and ring fingers into her wet canal. Locating her G-spot, I stroked my fingers against it, causing her to squirt just a little.

"Oooo shit!" she cried out, throwing her hips back at me.

The slow assault on her pussy had her trembling everywhere. When I felt her walls clench around my fingers, I knew I had her.

"Give it to me, mama," I coached between slurps of her clit. "Don't hold back. Bust that shit for me."

As if her pussy needed my permission, she squirted against my hand. Her top half collapsed against the bed, and she lay there panting. I pulled my fingers away and stood to my full height. After fully undressing, I walked around to my nightstand and opened the drawer to retrieve a condom.

She looked over at me with lust in her eyes and a drunken smile on her face.

I smirked as I rolled on the condom. "Why are you looking at me like that?"

"Because I've fantasized about this dick on more than one occasion."

"Before or after you fucked me?"

"Both."

I circled the bed, stroking my fully erect piece until I was standing behind her.

"So why deny yourself the type of pleasure I can give both of us?" I slapped her ass. "Should I give you this shit?"

"Yes..." she whispered. She backed up against me until my dick rested between her ass cheeks.

"Why?"

"Because I want it." She lifted her hips, and my dick settled at her soaking wet entrance. She pushed back against me, causing me to slide in with a single thrust of her hips. "Fuck! I want it so bad!"

I stood there, watching her get herself off while her ass clapped against my thighs. The ripple effect was almost mesmerizing.

"Oooo shit!" She cried out in pleasure as she picked up her pace.

I slapped her ass, and she moaned louder. Gripping her hips, I met her stroke for stroke. Her walls were just as tight as they had been the last time I was inside her. She had that vice grip that could make a nigga tap out if he didn't pace himself.

"Oooo, Channing... fuck me!"

She gasped as I sank deeper into her. Repeatedly, she fought for the breath that every stroke stole. Her fists clenched the covers, bunching them together. When she buried her face in them to muffle her screams, I wrapped her silky tresses around my fist and pulled her head back up.

"Don't be quiet now, mama. Let me hear how good this dick is to you."

"So fucking good!"

"Are you gonna deny yourself this good dick again?"

"No... fuck no!"

"You done with that nigga, you hear me?"

"Yes! Fuck! I'm gonna cum! I'm cumming!"

Again, she squirted against me. That shit was so damn sexy that it caused me to join her. Pulling out of her, I snatched off the condom and shot my load all over her back.

"Fuck!" I yelled, emptying the last of my seed.

She collapsed to the bed, panting heavily as her body continued to tremble in orgasmic aftershock. My knees felt weak as I stumbled over to the trash can to dispose of the condom. I headed into the bathroom to get a warm towel to clean us both up with and to start the shower.

She moaned as I swiped at the mess we'd made of her. I tossed the towel into the laundry hamper and rolled her over onto her back. She looked up at me, completely spent.

"How about a shower?" I asked.

She didn't answer. All she could do was nod. Scooping her up bridal style, I carried her into my bathroom. I hoped she was up for another round because I wasn't done with her pretty ass yet. We had a lot of wasted time to make up for, and tonight was as good of a night as any to do just that.

Chapter Twenty-One

Rhythm

The sound of my phone going off woke me from my slumber. Last night started off sweet, then it went to shit. Then it went to hell before Channing took me to heaven. The way he handled me had me thinking, *Raheem who? Fuck that nigga.*

It really was fuck him.

I could kick my own ass for being so down over him for weeks. I should have gone with my first mind when pictures of him and Imani first began appearing online. But no, I wanted to believe my man was faithful. I wanted to believe him when he said that there was nothing going on between him and that bitch.

I couldn't even be mad at her, because she really didn't owe me shit, but him? I gave up way too much to be here at his urging for him to shit on me like this. He owed me his loyalty and respect because he'd always had mine.

I rolled over in the king-sized bed, void of Channing's presence, and sat up, reaching for my phone. Picking it up, I saw that it was my mother calling me. I heaved a heavy sigh, knowing that she was probably calling about Raheem. I'd been lying to them for months now that everything was okay. Today, I'd have to come clean.

"Hello?" I answered.

"Hey, baby."

"Hey, Mama."

"Hey, puddin'," came my dad's voice.

"Hey, Daddy."

"I need to see your face. Answer this FaceTime call."

He didn't give me a chance to protest before the call came through. I covered myself with the sheet and answered the call. There sat my parents in my childhood living room with worried looks on their faces. Tamera and Timothy Baker played about a lot of things, but not about being parents. It didn't matter that I was good and grown.

"How are y'all?" I asked.

"We're doing just fine," he answered. "I just need to know if and when I need to book my flight to come kick that nigga's ass."

"Timothy!" my mother scolded. "You promised me we were going to ease into this."

"I ain't easing into nothing when it comes to my baby, Tamera. Where are you, Rhythm?"

"At a friend's house, Daddy."

"Good. Can you stay there until we can come move you out?"

I sighed. "Daddy, I haven't lived with Raheem for two months now."

"What!" he and my mother exclaimed.

"You know Nique moved out here. We share an apartment."

"Okay, that's fine. But you mean to tell me this been going on for two months and you haven't said anything?"

I could hear the frustration in his voice.

"It's been going on longer than that," I admitted. "I didn't have concrete proof, but I got fed up, and I left. Why don't I just explain from the beginning?"

"Please do."

He and my mother listened attentively as I gave them a rundown of the events that led to last night. I could see the anger brewing in my father's eyes. If there was one thing he hated, it was people fucking with me or my mama.

"See, now I gotta bust a cap in his ass," he said when I finished.

I rolled my eyes. "Daddy, that's unnecessary. Karma will hit him harder than I ever can."

"Oh, I can hit him just as hard."

"Timothy, stop it!" my mother warned him. "Are you sure you're okay, baby?"

"I'm fine. I wasn't perfect, but I was good to Raheem. My only regret is not leaving sooner. I love the arrangement Nique and I have. I've really missed her, and she's made getting through this bearable."

"You two were always inseparable," my mother agreed. "I can't believe both of you moved to California." She shook her head and sighed. "At least, now, you have each other. Plus, Rhyon and Emerald are there."

"Who's this friend you spent the night with?" my father asked.

As if on cue, Channing walked through the door with a tray of breakfast food that made my mouth water. I was so distracted by the fact that he was only wearing boxers and socks that I didn't answer my father. My eyes drifted to his dick print, and I inadvertently licked my lips, causing him to grin.

"Rhythm?" my father called.

I cut my eyes back to the camera. "Huh?"

"Who is this friend?"

"Um... his name is Channing."

"He? You with another nigga? Put him on the phone."

"Daddy!"

"Put him on the phone, Rhythm."

I sighed as I looked up to see Channing pulling on a shirt. He didn't look the least bit bothered as he came over and took a seat beside me.

"Mr. and Mrs. Baker. My name is Channing Watson. It's nice to meet you."

My mother's eyes widened, and my father's brows furrowed.

"Who are you?" my father asked.

My mother slapped his shoulder. "Timothy. Be nice."

"I am being nice."

"Then change your tone. Apologize."

My father sighed. "I apologize. When it comes to my baby girl, I'm very protective."

Channing chuckled. "I completely understand, sir. This is precious cargo."

He leaned in and kissed my cheek, causing me to blush.

"How long have you two known each other?" my father asked.

"Daddy, you're in my business."

"You came outta me. You are my business."

My mother scoffed. "She came out of me."

"Well, I came in—"

"Daddy! Oh my God. Please stop. Channing and I are just friends right now. We've been getting to know each other. His grandmother is one of my clients. It was him that got me out of the club last night."

My father's face softened. "Well... thank you for taking care of my baby. I hate that she's all the way across the country and I can't get to her as quick. Do me a favor."

"What's that?" Channing asked.

"If opportunity presents itself, beat his ass."

"You're done," my mother said, pushing him away from her. "Go find you something to do, Timothy. Just on here embarrassing us. I'm so sorry, Channing."

Channing chuckled. "It's okay, Mrs. Baker. If I had a daughter, I'd be the same way, no question about it. You two have nothing to worry about. Your daughter is safe with me. If it came to it, I'd throw hands behind her."

"Good to know!" my father yelled in the background.

My mother shook her head. "I'm gonna let you go. Call me later so we can talk."

I knew that meant that she was about to get in my business, too, but at least she'd be quiet about it.

"Yes, ma'am," I said.

"I love you, baby."

"I love you. I love you, Daddy."

"I love you too, puddin'."

My mother blew me a kiss before we disconnected the call. I placed the phone on the dresser and turned to Channing.

"Sooo... those were my parents."

"So they were. Your pops is a trip."

"My father is a damn mess."

"He doesn't play about you, though."

"Never."

I turned to fully face him. I couldn't help but smile as I looked at him. Cupping his face, I kissed him sweetly.

"What was that for?" he asked.

"For not taking offense to my father's attitude... and for being you. For future reference, you can't walk in front of me damn near naked when I'm on the phone. You completely distracted me. My mother is going to ask if I slept with you."

He chuckled. "Mine is going to ask the same thing when we show up for Sunday dinner together."

"Sunday dinner!"

"You down to go?"

I thought for a moment. Would it be weird having dinner with his mom and grandmother now? Seeing them at work was one thing, but outside of work was another. I was actively breaking my own policy about not getting personally involved with clients or their family members.

I mean, I didn't know he was Mrs. James's grandson when I met him. When I found out, it was too late. Now that I did, I was choosing to break policy. But as I looked at him, I couldn't help but want to spend time with him and get to know him better.

I found myself nodding. "Sure, I'm down."

He smiled. "I'll let my mom know we're having a guest."

He stood from the bed and moved to grab the tray of food from the dresser. When he placed it over my lap, I licked my lips. I was starving. I hadn't eaten a thing since about six yesterday, and all that fucking we did last night had worked up an appetite.

* * *

After breakfast and a round with Channing immediately following, we showered, and he gave me something to put on. We stopped by my apartment so I could change into something presentable. The moment Nique heard the door unlock, she was on my ass. While Channing waited in the living room, she followed me into my bedroom. First, she wanted details on what happened after the club. Once she had them, she had some tea of her own to spill.

Apparently, after I left the club, Raheem and Imani got into it again backstage, and it was all on video. As I dressed, she showed me the footage. They were in the back of the club arguing about how much she loved him and how he played her by trying to get back with me behind her back.

I had to laugh because, according to Channing, he'd talked about making things right with me in her face. The bitch had to be delusional, and that was coming from *me*. She cursed that man for everything but a child of God, and then she put her hands on him. Security had to restrain her and carry her out of the room. All I could do was shake my head. I didn't feel bad for either of them. Karma was a bitch, and I had a feeling she wasn't done with Raheem.

After all the gossip with Nique, I changed into a pair of fitted jeans, a graphic tee, and my favorite pair of Vans. I'd pulled my hair up into a messy bun then added a pair of white-gold hoops and a few matching pieces to complete my outfit. Grabbing my purse, I headed back out front to Channing.

"I'm ready," I said.

He stood from the couch and reached for my hand. After saying bye to Nique, we headed down to his car and made our way to his mom's. The ride only took about twenty minutes or so before we were pulling into another subdivision called Pivotal Point and up to a beautiful one-story brick home. The yard was well kept with flowers lining the driveway and surrounding the area in front of the porch.

"This is beautiful," I said as we came to a stop.

"Thank you. This was my first big purchase once I started making good money. I wanted my mother and grandmother to have someplace safe to rest their heads and not have to worry about anything."

I smiled. "I love how you take care of them. When I first met your mother, she spoke so highly of you. Now I see why."

A hint of pride showed in his eyes. I knew he did nothing for them for recognition, but I was sure it made him feel good to know she bragged on him a little. We climbed out of the car and headed up the front steps. Channing used his key to get into the house. It was just as beautiful inside as it was outside. The smell coming from the kitchen was divine and had my stomach growling like I hadn't eaten breakfast.

Koda came running around the corner and jumped straight into Channing's arms.

"Hey, my pretty girl," he said, scratching behind her ears as she rested her head on his shoulder.

It was the cutest thing and a tad bit funny. Every big man I'd ever seen with a pet was always so sensitive toward them. I could tell she loved him immensely, and he loved her, too.

"Mama! Grams!" he called, standing to his feet. "Where y'all at!"

"Boy, don't come in here doing all that damn yelling!" Ms. Watson said, coming around the corner.

When her eyes landed on me, she froze.

"Dr. Baker! What are you doing here? Not that you aren't welcomed."

"Good afternoon, Ms. Watson. Channing invited me to dinner. I hope that's okay."

"You're the guest... ooooh.... oh!"

It was like it finally hit her. She smiled as she came over to hug me.

"Welcome to our home."

Mrs. James came around the corner with a smile on her face.

"I thought that was you!" she said, coming to hug me.

"Damn, Grams," Channing said, pretending to be offended. "You just bypass your only grandchild?"

She swatted his arm. "Hush up, boy." Cupping his face, she pulled his head to her lips and kissed his forehead. "Better?"

He grinned. "Much better."

"What are you doing here, baby?" she asked me.

"Channing invited me to dinner."

"Oh! Did you two run into each other this morning?"

"Something like that, Grams," Channing answered. "How are you feeling?"

"I feel good today. Now that my favorite person is here, I'm sure it'll be a great day." She looped her arm through mine. "Come on, baby. Come sit with an old woman. You can tell me what you're doing with my fast ass grandson."

I couldn't help but to laugh as I followed her. She insisted that Channing was fast but had no idea that I had no problem being the person he was being fast with. She led me into the den, and I helped her onto the couch before taking a seat beside her.

"So, you and Channing?" she asked, jumping right into it. "I told my grandson he needed someone like you."

I blushed. "He's a good man. He put a few things in perspective for me and helped me see things clearly."

She smiled. "He's a good boy. You let me know if I have to get on him about you."

169

I giggled. "Yes, ma'am."

I sat talking to his grandmother for a little while before Channing joined us. He came right in and pulled me to my feet before claiming my seat and pulling me onto his lap.

"Fresh ass," Mrs. James said.

"Grams, how do you expect to get these great grandchildren if I'm not being fresh?"

"Get you a wife. Don't worry. My girl here is wife material." She patted my leg reassuringly. "You do want children, don't you, Dr. Baker?"

Even though we'd had this conversation before, I answered.

"Yes, ma'am."

"See, problem solved."

Channing chuckled as he shook his head. There would be no babies anytime soon, but I had to admit, if it ever got there, our children would be beautiful, and I knew they would be loved.

"Dr. Baker, would you come here, please?" Ms. Watson called.

"Yes, ma'am!"

Channing kissed my cheek before allowing me to leave his lap. I headed into the kitchen where I found his mother pulling a delicious-looking pan of mac and cheese from the oven.

"Yes?"

She motioned to the empty seat at the kitchen island. "Have a seat, dear."

I slowly sat and waited to see what she wanted. She put the dish down and turned to the stove to turn the eye on low before turning back to me.

"Dr. Baker—"

"Rhythm," I corrected.

"Rhythm... you really like my son?"

I blushed. "I do like him. It was unexpected, but I've grown to know him better over the last couple of weeks."

"You and this Prince Cole character... I assume that's done?"

My eyes widened.

"I saw the footage from last night," she explained.

"Yes, ma'am. That's been done for a while now."

"Were you aware that Channing was his producer?"

"Not at first."

"I'm only asking because I don't want things to get messy with my son. He's worked very hard to get where he is. Industry beef has a tendency to turn deadly sometimes. I don't want my son caught up in that. I like you, Rhythm. You're a beautiful girl with a good head on your shoulders. I think you two would be great together.... but he's my only child. I couldn't bear it if I had to bury him if things took a turn if your affiliation is discovered."

I nodded. "I understand your concern. Believe me, I do. The last thing I want is drama between the two of them."

"Just... be careful with him... for my sake."

I nodded. I didn't want any drama between Raheem and Channing, but in all honesty, it might be inevitable. They worked together. I was sure our budding romance wasn't going to be a secret. Channing didn't strike me as the type of man to back down if he was pressed about anything he was doing or had done. If Raheem stepped to him on some hot shit, there was bound to be a problem.

Ms. Watson called everybody into the kitchen for dinner. By the time we sat at the table, the little apprehension I felt in the air had left. We enjoyed a great meal and good conversation. Ms. Watson and Mrs. James told me a few embarrassing stories from Channing's childhood to go along with what I already knew about him.

I'd spent half the night doubled over in laughter, at his expense, while he frowned at them telling his business. His mother promised me she had a million stories to share about him, and I was looking forward to hearing them.

"I don't know how I like the three of you teaming up against me," he jested as he drove me home. "I'm greatly outnumbered."

"Don't worry. Nique will gladly fill you in on some of my most embarrassing moments. I mean, shit, you've already witnessed one."

"Nah, that was a lesson. If it didn't give you what you needed, it taught you what you should know."

"What I know is, I will never let another man play in my face like that." I looked over at him as he pulled into a parking space. "Where do you see this going?"

He shut off the car and remained quiet for a moment. I wasn't sure if that was a good or bad thing until he spoke again.

"I feel like we have great chemistry, and I want to explore that. I love being with you and around you. Moms and Grams already adore you, so that's a plus. I told myself that the next woman I get romantically involved with would be my wife, so make no mistake that I'm going to be intentional. I don't care what you had going on with that nigga. You just let me know if you wanna give this shit a shot, and we can move from there."

I thought about his proposal. Sure, I was freshly single as of two months ago, but in all honesty, I'd been in a one-sided ass relationship for a long time. Why should there be a time frame for me to move on from something that no longer served me good?

I looked at him and nodded. "I'm open to seeing where things go."

"Okay then."

He beckoned me to him. Unhooking my seat belt, I climbed across the seat to straddle him. Our lips connected in the most sensual of kisses. His hands didn't stray from my waist. Instead, he held me close to him in an intimate manner. I wasn't sure how this became more than just fucking, but I couldn't complain.

Chapter Twenty-Two

Channing

I'd been listening to these niggas talk about Raheem's disaster of an album release all fucking day, and I was over that shit. It had been four days. Everybody that came into the studio wanted to discuss what took place over the weekend. They were pulling up videos and reading comments out loud and shit.

Fans were eating him up.

They called him stupid for cheating on Rhythm with Imani. Imani was beautiful, but she couldn't hold a candle to Rhythm. The niggas in the room shared the same sentiment.

"Did you see how bad shorty was? I'd keep her in the house my-damn-self."

"Hell yeah. A woman that fine needs to be at home. Ain't nothing but niggas lurking for space and opportunity to take yo' bitch."

"Y'all see how she disappeared, right? I guarantee somebody took her home that night. You know women and their get-back game be strong."

173

"Damn, I would have loved to be a fly on the wall, watching her thick ass."

"Can y'all shut the fuck up!" I finally snapped. "Goddamn. Y'all are way too invested in this shit. Give it a fuckin' rest."

They all looked at me like I was crazy.

"Damn, man," Theo said. "We're just joking around."

"That's y'all problem. Too much talking and not enough working."

The sound of my phone going off alerted me of an incoming call. Pulling it out, I saw it was Rhythm.

"I gotta take this. When I get back, I expect y'all to have this conversation wrapped up."

I stood from my seat and left the room. Walking a little ways down the hall, I answered the call.

"Hey, baby."

"Hey, you. Are we still on for lunch?"

"We are."

"I miss you."

"I miss you too, love."

"You sound frustrated."

"I am. All anybody wants to talk about is Saturday night."

"Can you blame them? It was a shit show."

"I mean, I get that. But then they started talking about you, and I was ready to take a fucking head off."

She giggled. "Please don't fight anybody on my behalf. I promised your mother there wouldn't be any drama."

"It's bound to be drama, baby."

"I know, I know." She sighed heavily. "He's been calling me from his mother's phone today."

I frowned. "For what?"

"Trying to explain shit. At first, I answered because I thought it was her. I have no beef with his mother. She's a sweet lady, and she's always been good to me. When I answered and heard his voice, I

174

hung up. He called five times in the span of thirty minutes before I had to block the number."

"Block his ass every time. I'd really hate to have to act a fool in here. He knew what he was doing. Ain't shit to explain."

"Exactly. Anyway, I'll see you at lunch. I want hibachi."

"I got you. I'll see you in about an hour."

"Okay."

We disconnected the call, and I turned to head back into the studio. Much to my surprise, there stood Nate, one of Theo's home-boys that sometimes sat in on sessions with us. The look on his face told me he'd been listening to my conversation.

"You got something you wanna say?" I asked.

He shook his head. "Nah. Nah, man. You got it. I was just going to the bathroom."

He brushed past me and darted around the corner. I just knew he was going to run his mouth, but honestly, I didn't care. Who was gon' check me about shit? I headed back into the studio. For the next forty-five minutes, we actually got some work done. Every so often, Nate and Theo looked over at me but didn't say anything. The two of them had been on their phones, and if I had to guess, I'd say they were talking to each other about what Nate overheard.

By the time we got ready to break for lunch, I was over the day. I grabbed my shit and dipped out of the studio. I took the elevator down to the parking garage where my car was and prepared to make the short trip to pick up my lady. Things between us were going well, even though it had only been a few days since we agreed to see where things would go.

She'd spent the last two nights at my place, and I had to admit, I enjoyed having her there. It wasn't just because I could wake up at three in the morning and slide in that pussy if I wanted to. I genuinely enjoyed her company. She was a chill female that didn't require much.

All she wanted was quality time. She'd lay up on me, and we'd talk or watch movies. At night, she damn near lived in my skin because she slept right up under me. I didn't complain because I found I loved that shit. There was something about her that was different than the women I kept around for sex.

Honestly, I think it was largely due to her being part of the care-giving team for my grams. I got to see a softness in her that I didn't look for in other women. She went above and beyond for one of the women I loved, and for that, she could get parts of me that no other woman could ever say they had.

Rhythm was waiting outside when I pulled into the parking lot. She smiled as I rolled up to the curb and stood back as I got out to let her in.

"Hey, baby," I said, pulling her in for a hug.

"Hey."

I cupped her chin and kissed her, giving her ass a generous squeeze. She giggled as she swatted my hand away.

"We are right in front of the glass!" she said dramatically.

"So. I'm sure everybody in there done grabbed a lil ass before."

For good measure, I grabbed her ass and lifted her into the air. I'd driven my truck today, so it was as good of an excuse as any to put her inside. She laughed as I placed her in the passenger seat. I pecked her lips before closing the door and heading around to the driver's side. Once inside, I headed to the hibachi spot she'd told me she loved.

We pulled into the parking lot about ten minutes later, and I got out to help her. Hand in hand, we headed inside. Surprisingly, it wasn't packed. We were able to get a table right away. Once seated and our orders were placed, she turned to me.

"How was it after we got off the phone?"

"It was straight. I made it clear that when I got back, we were going to work. Nobody said anything else about it. At least not to me. I'm sure one of them overheard our conversation, though. I turned to go back inside, and he was standing there."

"Did you say something?"

"Nah. Ain't shit to really say. I'm not hiding anything. I could never be ashamed of you, love."

She smiled. "So... my dad called this morning."

I grinned. "What did he have to say this time?"

"He was just calling to check on me and make sure Raheem wasn't causing me any trouble. He asked about you."

"Oh, really?"

"He wanted to make sure he didn't have to bust a cap in your ass either."

"While I'd never give him a reason, I need Pops to know that if push came to shove, I'm not going out easily."

"You have to ignore that man and his ignorance at times. I think he will like you. He and my mama are supposed to come out here for a visit in two weeks. He said they needed to lay eyes on me."

"Maybe we could do dinner or something? Does your pops like basketball?"

"He's sickening about it. I bought him a season's pass for the Carolina Rippers for his birthday last year, and he dragged my mama to every home game. She was so sick of that man."

I chuckled. "Mama being a hater. She just doesn't understand the love of the game. It's a home game coming up. Maybe I could take you all to it. I have floor seats."

"Look, you're gonna be his best friend after that. I'm not even gonna tell him. I'll let you surprise him."

She looked at me with a smile on her face and grabbed my hand. Cupping my chin, she pulled my face to hers and softly kissed my lips. Our faces lingered close to each other as we gazed into each other's eyes.

"What was that for?" I asked.

"For being peace every time I'm with you. I needed that. My thoughts were so jumbled for the longest. I was torn between choosing me and choosing the man I loved. I don't feel like I'd have to do that with you."

"You wouldn't. I'll always make sure you choose you. If you aren't happy with yourself, we can't be happy together."

"You're right." She fingered my beard and smirked. "I bet I can make this grow."

I laughed out loud. "You wild, man! Don't come for my beard."

"I'll just cum on it then."

"Don't get your ass bent over something in this restaurant."

She giggled as our cook approached the table with his cart. We watched as he did all the flips and tricks with his utensils as he cooked and plated our food. The service was good, and the food was even better. By the time we got ready to leave, we were stuffed.

Hand in hand, we walked out of the restaurant and back to my truck. I helped her in then climbed in myself and headed back to The Baker Method. As I drove, my phone vibrated in my cup holder. I looked to see that it was none other than Raheem sending me a text.

At first, I ignored it. Then he called me. Rhythm looked over at me then back to the phone.

"Are you gonna answer?" she asked.

I sighed and answered the phone on speaker.

"Hello?"

"You busy?" he asked, sounding distraught.

"What's up?"

"I fucked up, Channing. You told me to get my shit together with my lady, and I was trying, man. I really was."

"Raheem, I'm really not the person to talk to about this shit."

"But—"

"For real. You just gotta take that L. Ain't no coming back from that."

"Nah, she loves me. I just gotta give her some time. Imani didn't mean shit to me."

"It didn't look that way. She wouldn't have called you out in front of all those people if it was nothing. Frankly, I've had to hear enough about that shit at work the last four days. I'm not trying to hear it again. I gotta go."

I didn't give him a chance to protest before I was hanging up in his ear. I looked over at Rhythm who was stifling a laugh.

"What's funny?"

"The fact that he called you about me and I'm sitting here with you."

I shook my head. It was ironic that he was seeking advice from me about her, still not knowing the parameters of my relationship with his ex. I was just counting down the moments until somebody went running their mouth to him about us. The feeling in my gut told me that it was going to be soon.

My grandfather always said if you give a nigga a rib, they will tell everything. Nate couldn't wait to tell Theo what he heard, and I was sure that when I walked out of the session, he'd told everybody else too. The thing was, I didn't give a fuck.

Nobody was gonna check me about a *single* woman.

Chapter Twenty-Three

Rhythm

"What are you cooking?" Nique asked, looking over my shoulder.

She'd just gotten in from work and had made a beeline for the kitchen.

"Rice, fried pork chops, and cabbage with sausage and bacon."

She moaned. "Oooo. That just screams southern comfort. I like L.A., but they have nothing on a good ol' country meal."

"Facts. It'll be done in a little bit."

"I'm surprised to see you here. You and Channing have been spending a lot of time together."

I smiled. "We have."

"I feel a little neglected, bitch."

I turned to her to find a playful grin on her face. I wanted to make sure she wasn't serious. The last thing I wanted her to feel was neglected, especially since she moved to be closer to me.

"I'm playing, girl," she said, slapping my arm. "I know you been over there letting that man blow your back out. I appreciate you taking it to his house 'cause I need my beauty sleep. You know your ass gets loud."

I laughed. "Shut up, Nique!"

"You know I'm right! We shared a suite in college, remember. I had to listen to you and Carter through those paper-thin ass walls. I love you, but I've never aspired to know what you sound like when you cum."

"Oh, whatever! I know what you sound like too. You're just as loud."

She rolled her eyes. "Anyway! How are things with you and him?"

"Good, actually. I mean, he told me there was more to him than dick, and there is. I feel relaxed with him, Nique. There is nothing but peace when we are together."

"I love that for you. You see ol' girl has been wildin' on Twitter, right?"

I rolled my eyes. "I saw that shit."

Imani was still on one from Raheem's album release. All week long, she'd been sharing screenshots of text messages, pictures, and videos of them to her page and calling him out. According to the messages, they'd been messing around for at least a year now.

She had pictures of him at her house and his, pictures of them in his car, gifts he'd bought her, and all types of shit. That didn't bother me as much as the picture of the ultrasound she posted. She'd been pregnant six months ago and lost it. When I saw that, I could admit I felt hurt and anger. Part of me wanted to unblock him just so I could curse him the fuck out.

All his skeletons were coming out of the closet, and I was realizing more and more that the man I fell in love with was a fraud. He had no respect for me or our relationship. He begged me to be with him. He'd begged me to move here, only to mistreat me when I did.

I felt stupid.

"You okay?" Nique asked, breaking me out of my thoughts.

"I'm fine," I answered quietly.

I was thankful the doorbell sounded so she wouldn't ask me anything else. I turned back to the pot while she went to answer. A few seconds later, I heard the door open.

"Oh, hell no!" she yelled.

I sprinted around the corner to see Raheem and Ms. Cole standing at the door.

"Monique, Rhythm," his mother said with a soft smile. "Do you mind if we come in?"

Nique shook her head. "Ms. Cole, you know I love you, but this bastard ain't welcomed in our home."

"Watch your mouth, Nique," Raheem warned her.

Nique mushed his head. "Or what? My name ain't Imani, nigga."

"Monique, please," Ms. Cole pleaded. She looked at me. "Baby, I just want to apologize on behalf of my son. You know he was raised to respect women—"

"Mama Cole, it's not your place to apologize for him. Raheem is a grown man and knew what he was doing. He knew he was wrong every time he laid down with that girl. There is nothing he needs to say to me."

"Rhythm, I'm sorry!" he said, grabbing the knob as Nique went to close the door. "I love you. I fucked up and let this music go to my head. Imani didn't mean anything to me, baby. She's not who I wanna be with. I asked you to move here because I wanted to build a life with you, Rhy."

I scoffed. "You are such a liar. If you wanted to build a life with me, you would have never found yourself in bed with the next bitch. You don't get to do this. You can't come over here with your mother, trying to plead your case, Raheem. You did that shit. You've *been* doing that, and it's just now coming to the light. Your little girlfriend has exposed way more than I could ever forgive you for. You got her pregnant, Raheem! You were out here fucking that girl raw and coming home to me. You sat up in my face telling me lies and making me feel like I was tripping, when really, you are just an ain't shit ass nigga."

"I ain't shit? I took care of you. I put you in that car you drive. I laced you in the diamonds and expensive shit you like to wear now. I cut the check for that nice ass clinic you own, and I was generous enough to put it all in your name."

I clapped dramatically. "Kudos to you! Do you want it back?" I asked, pulling the current jewelry from various places on me. I threw it at him then grabbed my car keys and threw those too. "You want it all back, since you wanna throw in my face what you've done for me? I never asked you for anything, Raheem! I was never with you for your damn money! I liked you when you didn't have a pot to piss in or a window to throw it out of. If that's how you wanna act, take it all back."

"He's not taking anything back," Ms. Cole said, cutting her eyes at Raheem.

She stooped to pick up my keys and handed them to me. When I refused to take them, she placed them on the table beside the door. She grabbed my hands and squeezed them.

"I'm so sorry that my son hurt you."

"Again, it's not for you to apologize for, Ms. Cole. Honestly, I don't wish any harm to him. I just want him to leave me alone. There will never be a me with him again. The sooner he accepts that, the better. He needs to move on because I sure have."

Raheem frowned. "So you with another nigga already, Rhythm?"

"Who I'm entertaining is none of your concern just like *I'm* none of your concern. Go worry about your side chick continuing to air out your dirty laundry. Ms. Cole, I'm sorry, but please take your son off my doorstep."

This time, it was me that grabbed the door and shut it in their faces. I could hear Raheem on the other side yelling obscenities like he wasn't the one who played in my face and cheated on me.

"You better get the hell outta here before you add jailbird to your resume!" Nique yelled at the door.

I shook my head as I walked back into the kitchen to tend to my food. Nique followed me and grabbed a bottle of wine from the fridge. She popped it open and poured us both a full glass. When she handed it to me, I gulped the whole thing down.

"I need liquor," I said, placing the glass on the counter.

"Shit, I got that, too."

She went under the sink and grabbed the bottle of Henny to pour an additional glass for me. I took a big gulp of it, allowing the liquid to burn my chest.

"That fucking asshole!" I yelled. "How dare he bring his mama over here to try to apologize!"

Nique shook her head. "Niggas are never short on audacity, boo. I can't believe she even agreed to come here in the first place. I know she has to be embarrassed. They have been dragging her on Twitter, too."

"She doesn't deserve that. I mean, yeah, she raised him, but that woman is a good mother. She can't control what her raggedy, grown ass son does. Wait 'til I tell Channing about this shit."

Nique snorted. "Wait 'til Raheem finds out Channing is who you are moving on with. Shit is gonna hit the fan. You ready for that?"

"At this point, Nique, I don't care. I didn't cheat on him. I was a single woman when we were intimate. I was single when I left the club with him. Ain't nothing Raheem can say, but it's messy."

Nique shrugged her shoulders. "True. I guess we'll just have to see how it plays out."

"I guess we do."

I prayed that Raheem got the hint. I'd been telling him it was over since I left the house. I made that shit very clear. Now that his dirt was coming out, he couldn't possibly think there would ever be another us. I was embarrassed enough by him. I refused to be a clown and go back to him again.

Chapter Twenty-Four

Channing

I looked down at my phone and frowned for the umpteenth time. Raheem had been blowing my phone up all damn day. I didn't know who told this man we were friends, but he had the game all fucked up. We didn't hang out. We didn't get together to smoke or drink and shit. I definitely wasn't his listening ear. I was his producer for one project, and that was it.

I pressed the ignore button then tossed the phone on the table beside me and refocused my attention back on Stella Solar. She was in the studio today, recording her second single. Her first had gotten mad play on the radio, and the label decided it was time to push her a little more. Listening to her belt her original piece was an experience.

As she came to a close, I stood and clapped for her.

"That's what the fuck I'm talking about!" I declared.

She grinned and covered her face in excitement.

"You are gonna be a star, baby. Come on out here and listen to this playback."

She eagerly pulled off the headphones and hung them up before coming out of the booth and taking a seat next to me. Her smile was bright as she listened to her vocals echoing through the speakers.

"I don't even have anything to say," I told her. "That was a perfect take."

"Really? You mean that?"

"You were made for this, love."

She buried her hands in her face and began to cry. "You've literally changed my life, Mr. Watson. If it wasn't for you, I'd still be waiting tables at the diner."

"I just gave you a chance to take a chance on yourself. *You* are the talent, Stella. You've got what it takes to have a long-lasting career. Big things are coming for you."

She nodded as she wiped her tears. "I wish my father could be here to witness this. This was his dream for both of us."

"Then you sing for him every time you sing. Make every note worth it."

She smiled. "I will."

"Good. You got anything else in your arsenal today? We could knock out another track."

"Yes! Just let me grab my song book."

She rushed back into the booth just as the door to the studio opened.

"This is a closed session," I said without looking up.

"Boss... you may wanna go to the parking garage."

I looked up to see James, the head of security, standing there with a worried look on his face.

"What's up?"

"Um... the guys have Price Cole detained, and the police are on the way."

"Detained? What's that gotta do with me?"

He looked around the room at the rest of the engineers. A few guilty looks presented on their faces, and it told me everything I needed to know. Nate had run his mouth, and somebody in this room ran back to Raheem. James motioned for me to follow him. I sighed as I grabbed my phone and keys.

"I'll be right back," I stated as I walked out of the room. As soon as I closed the door, I turned to James. "How bad is it?"

"He fucked up your car pretty bad. He was trying to get into the building, but the guys got to him in time."

I nodded. I could feel the anger brewing in my chest as we took the elevator down to the parking level where my car was. This man had lost his fucking mind. When we stepped off the elevator, I saw Raheem struggling to get away from the guards that held him. I smoothly walked over to where they stood, my eyes assessing the damage to my car. All four tires were flat. He'd busted out every single window and taken a steel bat to the frame.

Bitch shit.

"You fuckin' my girl, nigga?" he asked, seething in anger.

I crossed my hands at my waist. "Nah, I'm fuckin' mine."

He tried to get at me, but security held him back.

"Let him go," I said. "He's got some shit he wants to get off his chest, and I'm in the mood to hear him out this time."

The guards looked at each other then back at me.

"Let. Him. Go."

Slowly, they released Raheem. Just as I anticipated, he swung at me. I stepped back just in time for him to miss, and I caught him in a headlock. I had a good thirty pounds and a couple of inches on him, so he wasn't getting out of my grasp.

"Don't you ever in yo' muthafucking life swing at me, nigga," I said in a low tone in his ear.

Releasing him, I shoved him away from me.

"How you gon' fuck my bitch!" he yelled.

"One, I knew nothing of your involvement when I initially met her. Two, she was a single woman when I met her. You were too busy up Imani's ass, so why the hell does it matter to you? Were you thinking about her when you basically admitted to me that you were fucking your labelmate? You couldn't even be loyal to your woman, so what kind of loyalty should either of us have toward you?"

"That ain't yo' fuckin' business!"

"You made it my business by opening yo' mouth. You were out here making babies and shit and had the muthafucking audacity to be moping about a female *you* were cheating on because *she* decided she deserved better. That better wasn't me at the time, but it is now. I'm having the time of my life with the woman that *used* to be yours."

He tried to swing at me again, and this time, I let him have it. My fist connected with his face, and his body hit the ground.

"Didn't I tell you not to fucking swing at me!" I yelled, towering over him. "Don't make me beat your ass in this parking lot. You might be used to them country ass whuppings, but you don't know nothing about this Cali shit. Fuck around and get yo' muthafuckin' top blown off and sent back to South Carolina in a body bag."

I stepped back as the police rolled into the parking level with their lights on. They got out of the car and walked over to us.

"What seems to be the problem?" asked the one named Officer Penn.

"The problem is this grown ass man throwing a hissy fit. Look at my damn car."

He looked around me at the damage.

"Did anybody witness this man in the act?"

The guards nodded and told him it was all on video. While Officer Penn followed James to the security office, Raheem was placed in cuffs and into the back of the crusader. I stepped off to the side to call Martin's Auto Shop to come get my car. Raheem was gonna pay for my shit, whether he knew it or not. It was coming right off the top of those royalty payments.

He was more than likely going to get off with a slap on the wrist. The most he'd get was community service and a hefty fine. That was fine for the country, but he was coming up off my check.

While I waited for the officer to return, my phone rang. I pulled it from my pocket, looking to see that it was Rhythm. I sighed as I stepped away and answered it.

"Hey, love."

"Hey, baby... is everything okay? You sound upset."

"I *am* upset. I'm about to fuck Raheem up."

"What happened?"

"Well, he now knows about you and me. He decided to grow some balls today and call himself confronting me, but not before taking a bat to my car. My tires are slashed, my windows are busted, and my shit is all dented up."

"What!"

"Yeah. He was big mad. Now he's sitting in the back of a police car."

"Channing... I'm so sorry. This is all my fault—"

"No, it's not. I'm just as much in this shit as you are. Ain't no blame game."

She sighed heavily. "I hate this happened. I'll pay for your car—"

"You'll do no such thing. He's gonna pay for it, and that's it."

"Can I at least pick you up for our lunch date? I just need to lay eyes on you, and I don't wanna cancel."

I sighed. "Okay. I'll meet you downstairs."

"Okay."

I could hear the worry in her voice as we disconnected the call, and I knew she was going to think about this shit all day. I almost wished I hadn't told her, but it was bound to make the news. She would ask me, and I'd still have to tell her what happened.

Once the officer confirmed that Raheem had indeed vandalized my car, he was formally read his rights and taken down to the station. I had the guard wait with my car while I headed back into the building and up to the studio. He'd fucked up my day, but I wouldn't take that out on Stella Solar. When I walked back into the studio, nobody looked me in the eye but her.

"Is everything okay?" she asked.

"It will be," I said, looking around the room. "Let's knock this out."

We were able to make leeway in her second recording before it was time to wrap it up for the day. She left out with a smile, leaving the rest of us alone. I stood to gather my things so I could dip out for lunch. Everybody else left out while Theo hung behind.

"Yo," he said, leaning against the wall. "You really dealing with Cole's ol' lady?"

I chuckled. "Since when do we discuss personal shit with each other?"

"I mean, people been talking."

"By people, you mean Nate's ass."

"It ain't just Nate. People have been seeing you two out together. That's some messy shit, Channing."

"Look, I didn't know he even had a girl, just like damn near everybody else. Wasn't shit as messy as him parading around with Imani's ass, knowing he had a girl. Not that I owe you or anybody else an explanation, but they were already broken up when I met her, Theo. I didn't even know they were affiliated until his listening party. By then, it was too late. I'm not concerned with her being his ex because he wasn't concerned with her being his woman when he had her."

He shrugged. "I mean, I guess I can see that point."

"It ain't a point for you or anybody else to see. We grown. Y'all don't need to do that gossiping shit either. Let this be the first and last time you address me about anything I'm doing outside of this music. Don't let finding yourself in my business find you an ass whupping."

"I didn't mean any harm, man. I'd just hate to see this shit overshadow your talent."

"One thing about me, Theo. I've never concerned myself with other people's opinions. Y'all know me at work. Outside of this building, I have shit going on that none of you know about, and I'm gonna keep it that way. Now, if you'll excuse me, my lady is waiting on me to take her to lunch."

I didn't say anything else as I left the studio.

Chapter Twenty-Five

Rhythm

"You better be careful out here, Rhythm," Nique warned me as I drove to pick Channing up. "I can see that fool trying to confront you, too, at some point."

"I promise, I'll be aware of my surroundings. If I have to get a restraining order, I will."

"Good. All I know is he better not show up here again. I've got a gun and bullets with his name on it."

"I don't think it will go that far, Nique. He's just mad without being justified. He's making things worse for himself."

"Right. If him and ol' girl keep acting out, both of them are gonna get dropped from that label."

"Well, that's on them. Karma is a bitch."

I couldn't believe that Raheem showed his ass the way he did. At this point, we'd been broken up for almost three months now. I'd made it clear that there was no us, and we were never getting back together. I'd made it a point to return the money and the gifts he'd purchased me after our breakup because I wouldn't have that shit lingering over my head.

Nique told me I was crazy to give the money back, and maybe I was, but I didn't want anything tying me to that man any longer. My car and my business were both in my name, so he could never take that from me. Everything else was disposable.

I said goodbye to Nique as I pulled up in front of Channing's work building. It was around twelve, and he was waiting outside. A deep frown had embedded itself on his face. I could tell that he was livid, and he had every right to be. I was sure he wanted to know exactly who told Raheem about us. Then again, knowing him, he didn't care who told him. It was probably the car that had him pissed.

When he looked up to see me, his face softened a bit. He stood and came to the driver's side and opened the door.

Immediately, I cupped his face and kissed him softly. He seemed like he needed a little love, and I was happy to give it to him. When I pulled away, I unhooked my seat belt and climbed across to the passenger seat so he could drive. The moment my ass was in the air, he smacked it.

I squealed as I looked back at him. "Ouch!"

He grinned as he climbed in. "How long do you have until your next appointment?" he asked.

"Actually, my last appointment got canceled. I'm done for the day."

"Great minds think alike. I'm done with this shit for the day, too. How about we head to my place, and we can cook lunch together?"

"I'm down for that."

I strapped myself in and relaxed into the seat. He pulled into traffic, and we made our way to his home. For most of the ride, he held my hand. Every so often, he kissed my knuckles or the back of my hand, all while keeping his eyes on the road. I could tell he was in deep thought.

I still felt bad that Raheem had fucked up his car. It wasn't a cheap car either. He drove a custom black-on-black Aston Martin

DB12. Between the base price of the car plus the customizations, it was worth well over a half million. That was a lot of money gone to waste now.

I couldn't make up for his loss, but I wanted to at least make him feel better. Unbuckling my seat belt, I climbed to my knees and leaned over the armrest. The way he was sitting with the seat back gave me the perfect angle.

"What are you doing?" he asked as I undid his pants.

"Just drive and don't make us wreck."

I pulled his dick from his pants and spit on the head, using it to lube him up. He hissed as I took him in my mouth to the back of my throat.

"Fuck!"

His hand wrapped around my ponytail, and he gripped it tightly as my head and hand bobbed up and down his shaft. My mouth was so wet that he slid in and out with ease.

"Goddamn, baby... Suck that shit."

He reached over and smacked my ass, exciting me. I knew once we reached his house, the seat of my panties would be ruined. As if that was his goal, he slipped his hand into the back of my scrub pants then between the elastic of my panties and cupped my pussy from behind. His fingers teased my clit, causing a moan to spill from my lips.

I was already slick with desire when his fingers entered my wet center. I was thankful that I had tinted windows or else someone riding beside us would see the show we were putting on. As his fingers stroked my middle, I sucked his dick with all my might.

My hands and jaws worked overtime to please him. I knew sucking him off wouldn't make up for the damage done to his property, but it would at least relax him. I felt the car come to a stop and the sound of his garage door opening. We slowly rolled inside, and the car shut off.

Again, I felt his hand on the back of my head. He held it in place as he thrusted his big, beautiful dick into my mouth repeatedly.

"I'm 'bout to nut," he warned me. "You gon' catch that shit?"

I didn't answer. Instead, I sucked and jacked him faster. When his balls drew up, I knew he was about to cum. I took him deep into the back of my mouth, and he shot his load down my throat as I exploded all over his fingers.

"Shiiiit!" he yelled, yanking my mouth away.

He eased his fingers out of me, and I sat up. Reaching over, he gently grabbed me by my throat and placed those saturated fingers to my lips.

"Open."

I smirked as I opened my mouth. He slipped his fingers in and slowly moved them in and out.

"That's my nasty girl," he praised. "Savor that good pussy."

Once I'd sucked his fingers clean, he crashed his lips into mine, devouring the taste of me on my tongue.

"Lunch can wait," he said, opening his door. "I need you."

I smirked as I wiped the corners of my mouth. Who was I to deny his needs?

After a rendezvous right there in the garage, Channing and I headed inside for a quick shower and to put something on our stomachs. He'd given me a pair of his boxers, socks, and a shirt to change into so I could be comfortable. Currently, we were in the kitchen making a quick lunch of beef and chicken tacos.

While he cooked the meat, I cut up the vegetables. R&B music blared through his surround sound. I danced to the smooth sounds of Jagged Edge and Ashanti's "Put A Little Umph In It." I felt Channing's hands on my hips and his pelvis against my ass as he danced back against me. The hardness of his dick caused me to giggle.

"Why is your dick always hard?"

"That's what you do to me, woman. My shit ain't ever bricked up this much. He loves your ass."

I laughed loudly as I turned in his arms. He bent down and pecked my lips.

"How are you feeling?" I asked, massaging his temples.

"I'm still mad as fuck about my car, but you being here is keeping me from going to put a foot in his ass."

"You ever think we're being messy?"

"From the outside looking in, it looks messy. The fact of the matter is, you were single, and we didn't know the degrees of separation between us. If you're asking if I regret anything, I don't. I like you, Rhythm. I care about you, and I want to be with you. Fuck whoever has something to say about that."

I swallowed hard. "I like being with you, Channing. It feels... easy... no pressure to be anybody but myself."

"I wouldn't want you if you were anything less."

I smiled softly as I wrapped my arms around him and rested my head against his chest. Being in his arms gave me so much comfort. There was no doubt or second guessing myself. There was no impending feeling that I was making the wrong decision by being with him.

We finished prepping our tacos and fixed ourselves a plate. Settled in the living room, Channing turned on a movie to watch while we ate. We were watching *A Thin Line Between Love and Hate* and hard down having a debate about who was wrong.

"What do you mean she was wrong!" I exclaimed.

"Did you not see how she went cuckoo for fucking coco puffs? She's acting like Raheem's ass."

I laughed. "First of all, my girl told that man to leave her alone, and he continued to pursue her. She warned him she couldn't be hurt again, and what does he do? He tells her he loves her and plays in her face until his friend gives him a chance. Then he couldn't be bothered with her."

"Now, I can admit he was foul for that. But she took shit to a whole other level."

"He *drove* her crazy. I stand ten toes down behind that."

He chuckled. "Remind me to never turn you into Brandy."

I giggled. "I wouldn't take it that far. I'm too pretty for jail. I'm not built for a hard life or prison walls."

"I hear you, love. Still... I'd leave before I ever hurt you. My mama ain't finna whup my grown ass."

"Ms. Watson looks like she'd swing a mean belt."

"Believe it or not, she's never physically hit me as punishment. Now, she has taken all my shit and taken my door off the hinges before."

"What the hell did you do?"

"I was smoking weed in the house with a few of my friends. It was the first and only time I got caught."

"Now you knew better than that."

"I did. I was just following the wrong people. After she took everything but my clothes and took the door, she banned them from ever coming in the house again. Not only that, she called all of their parents. Moms really fucked up my street cred by snitching."

I laughed. "Oh, please!"

"For real! I had to threaten a few people to get back right."

I rolled my eyes as I placed my plate on the coffee table. I maneuvered myself onto his lap and wrapped my arms around him, resting my head next to his. Something about this man made me want to be in his damn skin. He had me in height and weight, and when he held me, I just wanted to melt.

His hands massaged my back before moving down to grip and massage my ass.

"You are being a stage five clinger right now," he joked.

I giggled. "I know. Physical touch is my love language. I can never get enough of it. I have months of making up to do for it."

"So you're using me?"

"I'll let you use me later," I promised, smirking against his ear.

I placed a soft kiss on his neck before relaxing again. For the longest time, I didn't move, and he didn't make me. I sat there, wrapped up in him until my eyes began to drift close.

* * *

I ended up leaving Channing's place around ten. The day we thought we'd have to chill ended up being anything but that after a while. He got a call from his lawyer, telling him that Raheem had made bail, and he'd be going to court a few weeks from now. His arrest made headlines on social media, and the record label had to put out yet another statement on his behalf.

Fans were speculating about what caused him to act out like that. Many of the comments mentioned Imani and me; however, none of them mentioned Channing. We knew he was released when he got on Twitter making subliminal tweets.

"Pussy ass niggas always be plotting."

"The same muthafucka that smiles in your face will stab you in the back."

"Hos be crying and cappin' like they ain't for everybody, too."

I couldn't, for the life of me, understand how he had the audacity to be mad in a situation he started. It had to be his ego and pride because nothing else made sense to me. I wondered how long he was going to drag this shit out. I didn't have the energy to devote to him or this situation anymore.

"Drive safe and let me know when you make it home," Channing said, pulling me into his arms. "Keep your location on and share it with me."

"I will."

Cupping my face, he kissed me softly, then opened my door. I climbed in and strapped myself in as he opened the garage. I backed out and down the driveway. With a blow of my horn, I pulled onto the street.

I turned on some music to vibe to while I drove. As I bobbed my head to "BPW" by Jazmine Sullivan, I noticed the bright lights in my rearview.

"Fucking asshole," I mumbled, speeding up.

To my surprise, the car sped up too. I switched lanes, and so did they.

"What the hell!"

I decided to make a left turn to see if they were really following me or being an asshole. The car followed. I made three additional left turns, and they followed those too. I knew it had to be Raheem. I was livid at this point. Reaching into my armrest, I pulled out my gun and loaded the clip.

My father had gifted it to me when I first decided to move out here. He told me that if I were ever in trouble and needed to protect myself, shoot first and ask questions later. Because of him, I had killer aim. I wouldn't miss. I would hate to have to shoot Raheem, but if he was going to act crazy, I could stoop to his level.

I pulled into the empty parking lot of a grocery store and threw my car in park. The car tailing me pulled in behind me, and the door opened. I flung my door open and got out with my gun raised. My eyes met Raheem's angry face.

"Why the fuck are you following me!" I yelled.

"What the fuck are you doing with that nigga, Rhythm? My fucking producer?"

"It wouldn't matter if he was your damn brother. It's not *you!*"

"When did you start fucking with him? Huh? You had me introducing you and shit at my listening party, and you knew who he was?"

"Did I ask you to introduce me to anybody? No."

"That ain't the point!"

"No, Raheem. You wanna know what the point is? The point that has been made repeatedly to you? You. Aren't. My. Man! I never cheated on you. I didn't fuck anybody you knew behind your back. Channing was a one-night stand that happened to go past one night. I'm not sorry about that, and I don't regret it. You know what I don't get, Raheem? You lied and cheated on me. You got your side bitch pregnant, and you're upset because *I* moved on."

"You moved on with him, somebody I work with."

"*You* moved on with somebody you work with. What's the difference? Imani has been to the home *we* shared together. Before she started acting funny with me, I've fed that bitch at my table. You've flaunted your whore in my face so many times, and I knew nothing of what you were doing with her."

His jaw clenched as he remained silent because he knew I was right. I lowered my gun.

"Just tell me why? Why couldn't you just tell me you didn't want to be with me anymore?"

"Because I did want to be with you. You just... You enjoyed the fruits of my labor but acted like you wanted me to be the same nigga you knew in high school. I grew into the person I needed to be to change my circumstances." He laughed as he raised his hands. "I love this shit! This is the life I was meant to have. I was on my grind and working my ass off to get here.

"I needed more than you were willing to give, too, baby. Why would you agree to move out here if you knew you couldn't keep up? Imani understood this lifestyle. I didn't have to beg her to be with me the way I wanted you to. I've had a thing for you since we were kids, Rhythm. I wanted you so fucking bad, and I had nothing to offer you back then. When I finally got you, I thought we would be on some turning up, lavish living, taking trips around the world type of shit.

"I just knew that once I got you out here, you'd see how good we could have it, and you didn't. I love you, but you've been fucking boring me. I thought Imani might have lit a fire under your ass to finally get with the program."

I scoffed. "Bastard. You must be smoking that good shit for that to be the kind of logic that makes sense in your head. You should have left me where the fuck you found me. I blame myself for thinking I'd get an adult version of the boy I crushed on in high school. That's my bad. I won't ever make that mistake again. Leave me the fuck alone, Raheem. And while you're at it, leave my man alone, too. Neither of us owe you a drop of loyalty. You come at us again, and I'll have my father pay your ass a visit, and you already know how he's coming."

I backed away from him and went to climb in my car.

"And if you follow me again, I'm shooting your black ass."

I got into the car and slammed the door. Putting the car in drive, I sped out of the parking lot, leaving him behind yelling obscenities. As I sped down the road, I called Channing to tell him what happened.

"Hey, you home already?"

"No. I had a little detour."

"Detour?"

"Raheem. He followed me from your house."

"Son of a bitch! Did he touch you?"

"No. I had my gun. I'm guessing since he's blocked on everything, he tracked my car. Channing, I'm so sick of him. Why can't he just leave me the fuck alone?"

I began to cry. This whole thing was frustrating and overwhelming. He was doing the most for a nigga that couldn't be faithful to me.

"Calm down, love," Channing said softly. "I want you to get home safe. I'm coming to get your car on my lunch break tomorrow and have my guy at the mechanic shop take that damn tracker off. Ain't no reason for him to be on you like that. If he knows what's good for him, he'll lay his ass low."

"I almost want to let my daddy get at him."

"Me and Pops can always pull up on his punk ass."

I sniffled. "Karma will get him. I believe that. Just stay on the phone with me until I make it in the house, okay? I left him in the grocery store parking lot, but who's to say he won't show up at the apartment?"

"Do you need me to come there?"

"No. I'm gonna call security and have them wait to escort me up."

"Are you sure?"

"I'm sure."

He sighed reluctantly. I said a silent prayer that this didn't turn into a thing with Raheem. Enough was fucking enough.

Chapter Twenty-Six

Channing

After the bullshit Rhythm and I both had to deal with from Raheem's ass, I figured we both needed a mental break. When she told me he followed her from my house, it took everything in me not to pull up on him and beat his ass. I took her truck to my mechanic and had him take the tracking device off her car and replace it with a new one.

That was a week ago.

Since then, Raheem had been radio silent. Word was the label was talking about releasing him from his contract if he caused any more bad publicity. While he was one of their money makers, they took extreme pride in their image, and his antics were ruining that. The CEO called me personally to apologize for him fucking up my car and ensured me that he would cover the costs of repairs.

To escape the madness surrounding us, I told Rhythm to pack an overnight bag and be ready for me to pick her up after work today. I was taking her to my beach house in Malibu. It had been a while since I'd been there, and now was as good a reason as any to make the trip. I canceled my sessions for today so I could spend a little time with my mom and Grams before we left out.

I'd taken them out for lunch and to do a little shopping. Grams was having a good day, and I prayed she had a good weekend. Just to be on the safe side, I had slid Raven a few extra bands to spend the weekend with them, just so it wouldn't be too much on my mother. Grams typically liked her and didn't give her much trouble unless she was upset.

"You drive safe and let me know when you get there," Mom said as I prepared to leave her house.

I chuckled. "Ma, I'm only going an hour away."

"So. I still wanna know you made it safe. Don't sass me, boy." She pulled me in for a hug and kissed my cheek. "I love you."

"I love you too, Mama."

I felt a slap to my arm and turned to see Grams pointing her finger at me.

"You be careful with my girl," she warned me. "Get her there and back in one piece. Don't be out here driving like a bat outta hell."

"Grams, I don't even drive that fast."

"Shit me."

I laughed and pulled her in for a hug. "I hear you, woman. Don't you give Raven and my mama a hard time this weekend. It's gon' be me and you if you be mean to my mama."

I playfully jabbed at her, and she returned the sentiment.

"I'll be on my best behavior." She kissed my cheek. "I love you."

"I love you too, Grams. Come on, Koda."

She trotted behind me, her tail busy wagging as we left the house. I opened the back door, and she hopped in, making herself comfortable. I closed the door and climbed in, then we were on the road to Rhythm's. The drive took a little longer because of the after-work traffic, but we still made good time. I parked, and we headed up to her floor. I knocked on the door, and a few seconds later, Monique opened it with a smile.

"Hey," she said, stepping back to let me in.

"Hey, Nique."

She stooped to give Koda some love. "Hey, pretty girl! How are you!"

I chuckled. "Damn, you gave her a better greeting than me."

She rolled her eyes. "Whatever. You aren't *my* man, and how could I not be happy to see this cute face?"

She continued to love on Koda as I made my way back to Rhythm's room. I found her struggling to close her suitcase. I shook my head.

"Baby, I said an overnight bag. Why do you have a whole suitcase?"

"First of all, mind your business. Second, come help me please!"

I rolled my eyes as I walked over and held the suitcase down so she could fully zip it.

"Thank you."

"You're welcome, but you realize we come back on Sunday, right?"

"Are you judging me?"

"I am, because why do you need so many clothes?"

She scoffed. "You know women need options. You haven't given me an itinerary so—"

"I didn't give you an itinerary because we are just relaxing and enjoying time away from all the bullshit we've been dealing with. Besides..." I pulled her into my arms. "Clothes won't be needed for what I have planned for you."

"Oh, really now?"

"Damn right."

I lifted her from the floor and placed her in the center of the bed, resting my body on top of hers. She cupped my face and pressed her lips to mine. The kiss we shared was sweet and sensual, all while being filled with lust.

"You think we have time for a quickie?" I jested.

"For Nique to talk shit? After you stayed over here the other week and we woke her up, she said we can't be fucking in here."

I laughed. "Not your friend being a cockblocker."

She giggled. "Once you get me to Malibu, you can have your way with me, and I can be as loud as I need to be."

"Bet. Let's get going."

I pushed myself up and off her before helping her to her feet. As she walked in front of me, I slapped her ass. That shit was looking so right in the biker shorts she wore that I just had to. She giggled as she grabbed her purse and headed for the door. I grabbed her heavy ass suitcase and rolled it out to the front room.

"You should be ashamed, Rhythm," Nique said, shaking her head as I placed her suitcase next to the door.

"I'm not." She pulled her in for a hug.

"Let me know when y'all make it. Have fun and I love you."

"I love you, too."

"Sir, drive safely with my best friend. I know she's your woman now and all, but she's my sister, and I need her back in one piece... even if you have stolen our nights together."

She gave me a playful smack to the arm, but I knew she was happy for her girl. We'd had a conversation the other week when I spent the night. Rhythm had fallen asleep after a session, and I'd gotten up to go get some water. I was standing there quenching my thirst when Nique came into the kitchen.

"Is my girl still alive?" she jested.

I chuckled. "My bad. She was kind of loud."

She rolled her eyes as she grabbed a bottle of water. "It wasn't just her."

"Don't even play with me like that, now."

"I'm just saying!" She giggled and took a sip of her water. "You really like her, Channing?"

"I do. I don't know what it is about her. We've just had a vibe since we met. I fuck with her."

"Good. She likes you, and I need to make sure you're good for her. Raheem... he almost made her forget that she was a bad bitch and could have any nigga she wanted. She lost herself for a minute. He had her

feeling like she needed to change who she was to fit his lifestyle, and I hated that shit. With you, she's just free to be herself. I like you for her. Now, I don't like hearing y'all fucking like animals, but I like you."

I chuckled. *"Thanks, Nique. I promise, we'll keep it down."*

"No, no. Y'all take that to your house. Over here making me feel bad 'cause I ain't getting none."

She rolled her eyes as she headed back to her room.

"I promise, I will return her to you safe and sound."

"You better."

She and Rhythm shared another embrace before we finally left the apartment.

An hour and some change later, we were pulling up to my beach house. Rhythm's eyes widened as the car came to a stop.

"This is yours?" she asked.

"Yes. Sometimes, I just need to get away for a little while. It's been a minute since I've been here, though. With Gram's diagnosis, I try to stay close to home in case my mom needs me. Come on, I'll show you around."

We filed out of the car, then I grabbed our things. After putting in the code to the front door, I led her up to the house. The exterior was covered in weathered cedar shingles that complemented the nature surrounding the property. A spacious, wraparound porch offered a dope ass view of the beach and the ocean. I'd gone with comfortable, overstuffed chairs and a porch swing for the outside décor because I came here to relax and nothing else.

Inside, the house had an open floor plan, with the living room, dining area, and kitchen flowing seamlessly together. The living room house a cozy, oversized sofa and several armchairs.

The kitchen was a chef's dream, with top-of-the-line stainless steel appliances, granite countertops, and a large island with bar seating. Upstairs were four bedrooms and three bathrooms. The master suite was equipped with a king-sized bed, a private balcony overlooking the ocean, and an en suite bathroom with a large soaker tub and separate shower.

Outside, there was a private path that led directly to the beach, and a huge deck with hot tub, a built-in barbecue, and fire pit.

"This is beautiful," Rhythm said as we stood on the deck overlooking the ocean. "You're gonna have to drag me out of here."

"You're welcome to come anytime you want. I'm sure you and Nique would have a nice little girls' trip."

"We would. I can see us out here drunk as hell, twerking to some ratchet shit."

She bent over and shook her ass on me, laughing as she did. She stood upright and wrapped her arms around my waist.

"Thank you for this. You have no idea how bad I needed it."

"I do."

She pecked my lips several times before squeezing me tightly. I picked her up, and she wrapped her legs around my waist. I'd never been one to like that clingy shit, but I didn't mind it with her. I honestly didn't think there was much I minded when it came to her. I mean, her ex fucked up my car, and here I was spending the weekend with her at my beach house.

Shit, maybe I was the crazy one.

We got settled, and Rhythm wanted to take a walk along the beach before the sun set. When we finally got back in the house, I ordered us some food to be delivered. We took a shower and got comfortable while we waited. Koda had run along the beach to her heart's content. When we got back inside, I fed her, and she was currently knocked the fuck out in the sunroom.

Instead of watching TV, she decided she wanted to play a game. She pulled out this card game called A Deeper Love: Couple's Edition from her purse, and I knew we were about to have several real conversations.

Right out the gate, shit got deep when she pulled the first card.

We were about ten cards in, and it didn't surprise me that we shared a lot of the same viewpoints. We just had that vibe.

"How do you define love, and how do you express love in our relationship?"

"I see they went straight for the jugular," I jested. "How do I define love? Love, for me, is caring about someone more than you care for yourself. It's going the extra mile to make them happy or ensure their safety. It's showing up for them the same way they show up for you.

"I'm a giver; that's the way I express my love. It's not necessarily monetary, but if I'm dealing with a woman and I love her, I devote a lot of personal time to one-on-one things with her. It can be cooking, trips, dinner, movie nights... it doesn't matter. Anything where I can spend quality time with her."

Rhythm smiled. "Sounds like that's your love language."

"I guess it is. I spend a lot of time with family, and I want my lady to consider herself family."

"I like that. Your turn."

I plucked a card and read it to myself before reading it aloud. "What do you believe is the role of honesty in our relationship, and how can we create an environment that encourages open and truthful communication?"

She thought for a moment. "For me, honesty is right there next to trust. If we don't have either, we won't make it. I think creating a space where we can be truthful isn't as hard as people make it out to be. You should be able to be vulnerable with your partner. You should be able to bring anything to them without it feeling like a personal attack or accusation. Unless you are guilty, my feelings about anything shouldn't offend you if we are just having a conversation."

I nodded. "I can agree with that part. You gotta know *who* you are dealing with, though. Past relationships and trauma can be a mutha-fucka on the mental. It isn't an excuse, but it does explain a lot."

"I guess I can agree with that. What was your last relationship like?"

I chuckled. "I've been single for years, but we just grew apart in my last relationship. There wasn't any bad blood or anything. We just realized we were moving in two different directions and let each other go."

"That was mature. I can respect that more than just holding on to someone because you love them. I'll never do that shit again." She looked at me, her fingers playing with my beard. "So, I take it you've been enjoying the single life, huh? Are there any women that will be coming out of the woodwork on me?"

"Nah, baby. They've been put on notice. You never have to worry about me embarrassing you like that."

She giggled. "I don't know. I know the type of dick you give me. You might have created a stalker and not even know it."

I chuckled. "I doubt that. Make no mistake, I'm respectful, but don't make me disrespect you. My mouth can get reckless."

"Somehow, that doesn't surprise me. I can see you mouthing off to your teachers in school."

"Nah, I was a good student, actually. I may have clowned around a little bit, but I didn't test limits like that. Shey Watson ain't play that. She would have come up to that school and showed her ass on me."

"I love your mom. She's the sweetest."

I kissed my teeth. "She's a'ight." I chuckled. "Nah, for real, she is sweet. That woman is my backbone. She and Grams have always been my biggest cheerleaders. Living out my dreams makes them happy. They can have the world from me if it's within reach."

She smiled and kissed my cheek. "They've always said you were a good boy."

She moved to straddle my lap. My hands gripped her thighs as she peered down at me with a smirk.

"What?"

"You wanna be my good boy, baby?" she asked, seductively wrapping her fingers around my neck.

"Is that even a question?" I asked, pulling her shirt over her head.

She was wearing nothing but one of my shirts and a thong. With the shirt gone, her pierced nipples taunted and beckoned me to them. I sucked one between my lips and flicked my tongue over the hardened bud. Pulling her thong aside, I slipped my fingers into her wetness. I loved how she was always so ready for me.

Slouching down on the couch, I rested my head against the back.

"Get your fine ass up here and take your seat."

She smirked as she moved to stand over me. She cupped the back of my head and placed her knee next to my head. Her free hand slipped between her thighs, and she stroked her clit as she lowered herself onto my mouth.

"Good boy..." She panted heavily as she rode my face. "Good... fuckin'... boy."

If this was how we were ending our first night away, I had no qualms about that. Once I drained this pussy of its juices, she was getting this dick until she couldn't take it anymore. Who needed the beach when I could crash into her waves?

It was Saturday.

Rhythm and I had spent the majority of the morning lounging around. I'd cooked us breakfast while she went for a walk on the beach with Koda. When the food was done, I'd stepped out onto the back patio to call them in. I found her sitting on a blanket with Koda in her lap, soaking up all the love Rhythm was giving her. Koda's head rested on Rhythm's shoulder as she stroked her back and talked to her.

I smiled. My girl loved attention. Most people were afraid of her because of her breed, but Koda was the sweetest dog. She'd taken to Rhythm pretty quickly, and the two were building a beautiful bond.

All the women I loved most seemed to love her, and I couldn't have asked for anything more.

It was now around seven, and we were prepared to go to Sunset Terrace, a rooftop bar and lounge, for dinner. I'd dressed comfortably in a brown polo style shirt with black trimmings, black slacks, and black loafers with gold jewelry to accessorize.

After spraying on my favorite cologne, I sat on the bed and waited for Rhythm to emerge from the bathroom. I checked in on my mama and Grams, and they were okay. Moms made sure to tell me to send pictures of us, and I promised I would.

The bathroom door finally opened, and my lady stepped out. The moment my eyes settled on her, my dick bricked in my pants. She was dressed in a tube-top like shirt that carried traces of orange, gold, and a few other colors in the pattern. It was held together with a gold accent piece. The long skirt she wore was orange with a three link, gold waist chain. Gold jewelry and heels completed the outfit.

"You know you look too damn good," I said, standing.

"Thank you, baby."

She did a slow spin, and the sight of her ass in the skirt made me want to bend her over this bed once more before we left. She switched over to me and planted a kiss on my lips.

"Are you ready to eat?" she asked.

I smirked. "Eat what?"

"Food, fool!"

I chuckled. "I'm starving."

Hand in hand, we headed out to my truck and made our way to the restaurant. It wasn't a long drive. The place was located on the strip, not too far from the boardwalk. We valeted the car and headed inside. I gave the hostess my name, and we were led up to the rooftop where our table was set up.

I'd gone the extra mile to have the space blocked off with privacy partitions. I'd also had fresh flowers and her favorite wine waiting for us.

"Thank you," I said to the hostess as she placed our menus on the table. A young man appeared around the partition and approached the table.

"You're welcome. This is your server, Adam."

"It's a pleasure to serve you tonight. Can I get you started with our famous dinner rolls? Perhaps some water?"

I nodded as I pulled out Rhythm's chair for her to sit down. "Both are fine."

"I'll be right back."

He left the table. I claimed my own seat, and she reached for my hands.

"This is beautiful, Channing," she said softly. "Thank you for a relaxing weekend."

I kissed her knuckles. "It was no problem. We both needed this, and I love spending uninterrupted time with you."

She smiled. "How are you feeling about this... us?"

"Confident. I know shit won't be perfect, but I think as long as we acknowledge what we want and need from each other, we'll be okay. How do you feel?"

"I think we are in a good space. We have more in common than I would have thought we did. Honestly, I was thinking this was going to be a one-night stand until somebody had me on the counter in the bathroom with his fingers in my pussy. I can't believe you walked out and left me like that!"

I chuckled. "Have I not made up for that? I mean, you get my mouth or my dick every time I see you. I don't hear you complaining."

"I'm not complaining at all, love."

She smiled, and I swore the surrounding lights got brighter. Her smile had been one of my favorite features of hers since the day I damn near knocked her down coming out of the bathroom.

We'd come quite a long way from then to now. It hadn't been a smooth sailing journey, but I think the worst was over when it came to Raheem. He wanted to be Prince Cole so badly that I didn't think he'd do anything else to fuck up his brand. With him out of sight and out of mind, things could only go up from here.

Adam returned with our water and bread, and we placed our orders. While we waited, we stood at the railing of the rooftop, sipping wine and looking out at the sunset. She giggled as I peppered the side of her face with kisses. She loved that cutesy shit, and I couldn't lie, I loved cutesy shit with her.

Our dinner arrived about twenty minutes later, and we sat to enjoy our meal. Sunset Terrace had a bomb ass menu when it came to food. I ate here every time I came to town. Rhythm and I ordered quite a bit of food so she could sample a few different things.

She fell in love with it all, making me promise to bring her back again. I had no problem with that. I loved to eat, and I loved that she was a woman that appreciated a good meal.

After dinner, I paid the bill, and we took a stroll down the boardwalk. The area had a few rides, and vendors were out selling a little of everything. Hand in hand, we walked the boardwalk, stopping ever so often for her to look at things. If she even looked like she wanted it, I bought it for her.

"You really didn't have to buy me anything, Channing," she stated as we copped a seat at the end of the pier.

"I didn't mind at all."

She crossed her legs and snuggled up next to me.

"This was a great getaway," she said softly.

"It was."

"Next time, I need a full week like this."

"I can make that happen. Wherever you wanna go, let me know, and I'll make something shake. And I don't wanna hear any lip about it."

She playfully scoffed. "You can at least let me pay for something. I'd feel bad about you funding an entire trip—"

"Did I ask you for anything?"

"No."

"All right then. Let your man handle shit."

She sighed. "I can see we are gonna fight. I don't ask for much."

"Which is why you deserve the world." I cupped her chin and

tilted her head up so her eyes met mine. "You never have to go in your wallet with me, and I'll never throw anything I do for you back in your face. I ain't built like that."

She smiled softly. "Thank you," she whispered.

She cupped my face and kissed me passionately. I could tell that meant a lot to her. Since their breakup, Raheem had thrown what he'd done for her back in her face on several occasions. I wasn't the type of nigga to do extravagant shit if it wasn't from my heart.

I gave of my own free will and expected nothing in return. As my woman, she was right next to my mother and grandmother. They were extensions of me. I loved them with my soul, and if it was God's will, I'd love her too.

Chapter Twenty-Seven

Rhythm

I sat nervously in Channing's truck as we waited outside the airport. Today, my parents were flying in, and I couldn't wait to see them. Next to the weekend Channing and I spent at his place in Malibu, this would be the highlight of the last couple months of my life.

I missed Timothy and Tamera Baker so much. When things first began going downhill with Raheem, I'd seriously considered moving back home. While I knew I was always welcomed, I didn't just wanna run to Mommy and Daddy anytime I had a problem.

They would try to fix things for me, and it wasn't their burden to bear. I'd created a life here, and my business was here. So I sucked it up and stuck things out. Still, having them come to see me was just as good as going back home.

"Would you stop shaking your leg?" Channing asked, wrapping his large hand around my thigh.

"I can't! I haven't seen my parents in months, baby."

"I know, but you have no reason to be nervous. They know everything that's happened. They came all the way out here just to see you. Loosen up."

I sighed. "I'm just anxious. What's taking them so long? Their flight got in thirty minutes ago!"

"You know LAX. The shuttle's probably busted or something. That's a long ass walk from the gate."

"You're right. I guess—there they are!"

I pointed out my parents as they came through the double doors. I didn't wait for Channing to open my door before I was out of my seat belt and bolting from the truck. When my father saw me, he abandoned his bags and ran toward me. I felt like a little girl again as he scooped me up in his big, strong arms and spun me around.

"There's my baby girl!" He smothered my cheeks with kisses. "Damn, I missed you puddin'!"

"I missed you too, Daddy."

"Let me get a look at you."

He placed me on my feet and took a step back. A smile found its way to his face as he looked me over.

"You look good, baby. Still as beautiful as ever, just like your mother."

"Damnit, Timothy!" my mother fussed, pushing him out of the way. "Stop hogging her. Hey, my baby!"

"Hey, Mommy!"

She pulled me into her arms and rocked me side to side. I was all smiles. I never knew how badly I needed a hug from my mama.

"Look at you!" she exclaimed, spinning me around. "You're about as thick as me now!"

She didn't mean that in a bad way. Tamera Baker was thick as hell and fine as wine. She didn't look a day over thirty-five, and my daddy couldn't keep his hands off her. I'd seen him rubbing on her booty more times than I cared to.

"I've *been* trying to get as thick as you, Ma."

"Mmm hmm. I bet that man has something to do with that."

"Mommy!"

She laughed. Thankfully, my father had gone to retrieve his forgotten luggage. Channing walked over with a smile.

"Mrs. Baker, it's nice to finally meet you in person."

He'd been present for several of our FaceTime calls over the last couple of weeks. My mother already adored him, and my father seemed to like him too. He said he'd have to meet him in person to make a final verdict.

"It's nice to meet you, Channing."

My mother pulled him into a warm hug. When he pulled back, he looked between us.

"You stole her entire face," he stated. "I knew you looked alike on camera, but in person is crazy."

Me and my mom giggled.

"I've been asked several times if she was my older sister," I stated.

My mother flipped her hair. "What can I say? Black don't crack."

"You should see his mother," I said. "She doesn't look old enough to have a grown son."

Channing chuckled. "She doesn't, and I've threatened more people than I care to admit about hitting on my mama. By the way, she is insisting that you and Mr. Baker join us for dinner tonight."

My mother smiled. "That would be lovely."

"Channing, my boy!"

My father came over with open arms to embrace Channing. I'd never seen him nervous, but I could tell that hugging my dad caused him a little hesitation. They shared a quick embrace before he reclaimed his spot at my side.

"How are you, Mr. Baker?" he asked.

"I'm good, now that I've laid eyes on my baby. Where's that nigga at? He's gon' have to see me before we leave Cali."

"Daddy, please," I pleaded. "There is no reason you need to see Raheem."

"Him following you after dark is plenty reason. I just wanna talk. Fist to face."

"Mommy, get your husband."

"Timothy, calm your old ass down. I don't have any money to bail you outta jail out here."

"So you gon' let me sit in jail?"

"I didn't help your ass get there, did I?"

Channing and I laughed at their banter. My mother talked shit, but she'd be the first one down to bail my father out.

"Children, children!" I said, waving my hands in their faces. "Nobody is going to jail because nobody is pulling up on him. Can we go?"

My father kissed his teeth. "Lead the way."

Channing grabbed my mother's luggage, lagging behind as he and my father talked lowly. I just knew my dad was pumping him for information. There was really nothing to tell. Raheem hadn't so much as whispered to either of us.

He hadn't been seen publicly aside from court where he was ordered to pay a hefty fine for vandalism, pay for all the repairs of Channing's car, and received a year's probation. He deleted his Twitter rants and had gone radio silent.

The only indication that he was even alive was the package that showed up on my doorstep with the rest of my belongings. Much to my surprise, nothing was damaged. It was all neatly packed and sealed in perfect condition. Even if he was on my shit list, I appreciated my things being returned.

We stopped by my parents' hotel so they could drop off their luggage. I offered for them to stay with me and Nique. She and I were used to sharing a bed, so it wouldn't have been a problem. My father declined, saying they needed their privacy. I didn't argue with him because I knew what that meant. The last thing I wanted to hear were my parents fucking, especially not in my bed.

When we left the hotel, we headed for the Watson residence. After a six-hour flight through three different time zones, I was sure my parents were hungry. I was a little nervous about them meeting Channing's mom and grandmother, but it was better now than later. I was sure this man was going to be

217

around for a while. The family might as well get used to each other.

* * *

My mother and Ms. Watson were acting like they'd known each other their entire lives. From the moment we stepped through the door, they instantly bonded over the decor of Ms. Watson's home. My mother was an interior design fanatic. She was always dragging my father to Home Goods, Marshalls, or some other store to see what she could find for our home.

He complained, but he was right there swiping his bank card to make it happen. Currently, we were in the kitchen, sipping wine and talking while she finished dinner. Channing and my dad were outside doing only God knows what. As soon as I could sneak away, I was going to be nosy.

"Rhythm?"

The sound of my mother calling my name broke my thoughts. "Ma'am?"

"You okay?"

"Yes. I just went somewhere in my head."

She smirked. "You must be thinking about Channing."

"Don't they make a lovely couple?" Ms. Watson asked. "I can already tell that my son is smitten with her."

I blushed. The truth was, I was smitten with him too.

"I wasn't thinking about him," I said. "Well, not completely. I just zoned out for a moment."

"How is business going?" my mother asked.

"Great. We're getting new clients every week."

She smiled. "I'm so proud of you, baby. The work you do is beautiful."

"It really is," Ms. Watson agreed. "I may be biased because you're my mother's therapist, but you really have a gift, Rhythm. You treat clients like family, and that makes a difference."

Rhythm's Blues

"Thank you. I do like to think of them as family. I want to take care of them like I'd want someone to take care of my parents."

My mother lovingly rubbed my back. "She's always been a nurturer. Once time when she was little, I caught her breastfeeding her dolls—"

"Mama!" I shrieked.

Ms. Watson and Grams burst into laughter.

"What! It was the cutest thing watching your little flat chested self trying to make that baby doll latch on."

I palmed my face. "I'm glad Channing and Daddy are outside. That's so embarrassing, Ma."

Ms. Watson giggled. "Don't be embarrassed, baby. When Channing was younger, he used to love following his grandfather around before he passed away. When I tell you, he acted every bit of a middle-aged man at the age of five! He walked like him. He spoke like him. My father even dressed him like him. Hold on, I have pictures!"

She left the kitchen, returning shortly with a photo album. She flipped through until she found what she was looking for. I couldn't help but laugh at a younger Channing cheesing like hell as he stood next to his grandfather. They were dressed in matching outfits consisting of a white button-up, brown slacks with suspenders attached, loafers, and a brown fedora.

"He is too precious!" my mother exclaimed. "Look at those cheeks!"

Grams smiled softly as she looked at the picture. "Those were my two men. After Channing's father left, he clung to my husband. It broke his heart when he lost his grandfather just two years later."

She looked so sad for a moment, and my heart broke for her. I knew how much she'd loved him. She'd told me all about their younger days many times during therapy. What broke me was her saying she was dreading the moment when she wouldn't remember him at all. It was sad to have a lifetime of memories slowly fade away.

"I think I'm gonna go lie down for a little while," she said softly.

"You sure, Mama?" Ms. Watson asked.

"I'm sure."

She left the kitchen with us looking after her. Part of me wanted to go after her, but I decided to let her have some time alone. Ms. Watson's face mimicked her mother's sadness. I pulled her into my arms and hugged her tightly. My mother didn't hesitate to follow suit. For the longest time, we held her until her small cries turned to sniffles.

"I'm sorry," she said, wiping her face. "I know this disease is hard for her, but it's hard for me, too."

"You have nothing to apologize for," my mother said. "I know we've only just met, but if you need someone to talk to or vent to, my door is always open. We can exchange numbers before we leave tonight."

Ms. Watson smiled. "I'd like that."

I smiled too. Maybe I'd just introduced my mother to her new bestie.

"I'm gonna go check on Channing and Daddy," I said, standing. "They have been together too long, and I feel like they may get into trouble."

Both my mother and his laughed as I headed out the back door. The backyard was pretty big, housing a pool, a grilling area, and a pool house. Since I didn't see them anywhere outside, I figured they were in the pool house. I made my way over and found the door slightly ajar. As I went to open it, I heard them talking.

"Tell me the truth," my father said. "Baby girl isn't gonna tell me because she knows what I will do to that boy. Is he still fucking with her?"

"As far as I know, no, sir. There was the incident of him following her home from my place a little while ago, but he's been quiet since then."

"She told me about that. I almost hopped on a plane that night."

Channing chuckled. "Trust me. I wanted to pull up on him myself. I don't play the games he's playing. I don't know how y'all do it in the Carolinas, but here, you are asking to catch hands or a bullet if you do that."

"I know that's right." My father took a sip of his beer. "You really like my daughter? I mean, you ain't on no conquest type of shit?"

"I mean this in the most humble way possible, Mr. Baker. Getting pussy has never been an issue for me. Between groupies, industry hos, and these women out here willing to sleep with men for nothing, there isn't a shortage. I care very much for your daughter. From the moment I met her, something about her drew me in. She's special. She's one of these people you don't let go of when you finally get them."

My father nodded. "I'm glad to hear that and glad you recognize that. Those two women are my heart and soul. I'd do hard time behind them."

"I respect that. Just know that as long as she's here, she's in good hands."

My father extended his hand to Channing. They shook before he pulled him into a fatherly embrace. I swiped a tear from the corner of my eye and gathered myself before I entered the room.

"Knock, knock! What are y'all doing?"

"Talking like men," my father answered.

"About?"

"You see how nosy she is?"

"Daddy!"

He chuckled. "Did you need something?"

"I can't check on two of my favorite people?" I threw my arms around him and kissed his cheek repeatedly. "I've missed you, old man."

"I've missed you too. What do you have planned for us?"

I looked at Channing and nodded. Now was as good a time as any for his surprise.

He cleared his throat. "Well, a little birdie told me you like basketball."

"I'm an avid fan."

"I have a season pass for the L.A. Bombers. They are floor seats, and I can even get you in to meet a few players."

My father grinned. "Shit, you don't have to convince me. What time should we be ready?"

I shook my head. "I'll just let you break the news to your wife."

He waved me off. "She'll be okay. She'll let me drag her anywhere as long as I bargain with her."

Channing and I laughed. It was a sad but true fact.

We finally headed back inside to dinner. The rest of the night went by pretty smooth. Grams rejoined us after her nap and seemed to be in better spirits. The four of them took turns embarrassing Channing and me with childhood stories. At one point, we just gave up and waited to see what they would tell next.

By the time we made it back to his house, I was exhausted and had fallen asleep. It wasn't until he lightly shook me did I wake up.

"We're home," he said.

I slowly opened my eyes and found him standing in the passenger doorway looking at me.

"I just wanna climb in bed," I mumbled.

He chuckled. "Do I need to carry the big baby in the house?"

I smirked. "If you're offering."

He shook his head as he reached for me and lifted me out of the truck. I wrapped my arms and legs around him and allowed myself to be carried inside. He took me upstairs and undressed me. Much to my surprise, he put me in the shower, then bathed us both before dressing me for bed. When he slid into bed, he immediately reached for me, pulling me into his chest and draping my leg across his.

I couldn't help but to laugh.

"What's funny?" he asked.

"You've grown accustomed to me sleeping in your skin."

He chuckled. "Take your silly ass to sleep, woman."

I snuggled up closer to him and raised my head for a kiss. He obliged me with the sweetest, most sensual press of his lips. I rested my head against his chest and closed my eyes. In no time, I was falling fast asleep, listening to the sound of his heartbeat.

* * *

It was Saturday, and we had a full day ahead of us.

The day started with me, Channing, and my parents going out to breakfast with Nique. She demanded she get some time with them while they were here. They loved her like a second child, so of course, they were down.

From there, my mother wanted to visit Rhyon since she hadn't seen her in forever. Luckily, she and Emerald were home, so we spent some time with them. Being in their home brought back memories of all the time we spent together as kids. There we were, going down memory lane, doing dances from our younger years and spilling secrets about shit we'd done that we wouldn't get in trouble for now that we were grown.

Or so we thought.

My mom ended up FaceTiming my aunt Halle and cluing her in on our antics. They fussed, and all we could do was laugh.

After leaving Rhyon and Emerald's, we'd dropped my parents off at their hotel to get ready for the game. Currently, we were sitting courtside in the massive arena. My father and Channing were talking stats, while my mama, Nique, and I sipped on mixed drinks and vibed to the music.

"I'm trying to catch a baller," Nique said, scanning the players who were practicing their shots. "I can totally be on *Basketball Wives.*"

"You don't even like reality TV," I reminded her.

"But I would like those reality TV checks."

My mother shook her head. "You don't need to be on TV acting ratchet, Monique."

"I wouldn't act ratchet, Auntie Tam."

"Baby, people have a way of bringing the worst out of you, especially for likes and views."

"You're right about that."

She continued watching the players and sipping her drink seductively. One of them happened to look in our direction and tapped the arm of his teammate. He pointed at us then waved. Nique was all smiles as she waved back. Channing instantly slapped her hand down.

"Neither of those two," he said firmly. "Trust me, I'm doing you a favor."

She huffed. "I thought it would be a while before I got big brother vibes from you."

He chuckled. "I'm just looking out for you. You're my lady's best friend. I can't let you end up with no busta. She'd never forgive me. I don't want no smoke."

I blushed as he leaned in to kiss me. I slipped my arm through his and rested my head against his shoulder.

"Y'all are adorable," Nique declared. "One day, this will be me."

I rolled my eyes, but I really hoped she found happiness.

The jumbotron camera began scanning the area for unsuspecting attendees. I'd always seen these moments online, but this was a different experience. Thankfully, the camera didn't zoom in on us. The game was just about to start when an unexpected presence made their way in front of us. I looked up to see Imani glaring at me.

"Move around, Imani," Channing warned her. "This ain't the time or the place."

She giggled. "I wasn't even going to say anything to her. I stopped to speak to you."

"Spoke."

Nique snickered next to me as I tried hard not to laugh. He was so blunt, and the shit was funny as hell. Imani threw her a dirty look.

"Something funny?" she asked.

"Don't make me embarrass you, baby," Nique said. "You've done a good job of that yourself."

Imani started toward her, causing all of us to stand up, but not so quick as to draw attention to ourselves.

"Didn't I say this ain't the time or place?" Channing said lowly. "Take your messy ass to your seat."

She scoffed. "You're calling me messy, but you're sitting here with your client's ex?"

I laughed. "You weren't even worried about him being my man when you were messing around with him. Why are you so concerned with who I'm with now? You keep talking, and you are gonna get that ass whupping I owe you."

"Bi—"

"Don't even think about finishing that statement," Channing said, stepping in front of me. "Move. Around…. Now. You're already on probation with your label. Don't let this be the thing that gets you dropped."

Imani kissed her teeth. "Just so you know, our work relationship is done."

"I'm sure I'll manage just fine."

She glared from him to me before storming off. We reclaimed our seats, and I exhaled a frustrated breath.

"She was about to get jumped," my mother stated, breaking the tension. Nique and I looked at her and burst into laughter.

Channing and my father shook their heads.

"Mrs. Baker, I thought you were the calm one," Channing said.

"About my baby, we can take it there. If that little girl had said one more word, y'all were gonna be bailing us out of jail."

"I know that's right, Auntie Tam," Nique chimed in. "As cute as I look tonight, I would have been mad as hell if I had to fight."

"Well, it's over now," Channing said. "We're gonna enjoy the rest of the night and block out all negativity."

He cupped my chin and pecked my lips before lacing his fingers through mine. He leaned over and whispered in my ear.

"I like your aggressive side. You gon' have to show me that when we get home."

225

He pulled back and focused on the game playing in front of us like he hadn't just turned me on in front of my parents. I felt eyes on me and looked to see Nique and my mother smirking at me. They looked at each other.

"Mmm hmm."

I rolled my eyes and ignored them.

For the duration of the game, things went smoothly. Channing and my father were invested, although they both checked in with me and my mother to make sure we were good. My mother, Nique, and I spent most of our time people watching and listening to my best friend point out the cute players.

She almost fainted when the ball rolled under her chair, and the player she'd been eyeballing all night came to retrieve it. Not only did he smile and wink at her, he held up the game to give her his number. She immediately looked to Channing for his approval before she handed over her phone. That same player came over after they won the game and invited us to an after-party.

While I initially thought to decline because my parents were here, my father insisted we go out and have a good time because he needed some time alone with my mother since this was their last night in town. I didn't protest. Channing called for them a car, and we ensured they got in safely before he, Nique, and I headed to the lounge where the party was being held.

While I thought our good day was going to go to shit with Imani's ass, we ended the night on a good note. We had good food, good drinks, and just all-around good vibes with the people we linked with. After all that, my man took me back to his place and gave me some good dick that put me right to sleep.

Chapter Twenty-Eight

Channing

L ife was funny.

When I first met Rhythm at her office, there was nothing that could have ever prepared me to be in the space we were in now. What I thought would end up as a friend with bene-fits type of deal, had quickly migrated into a full-blown relationship. Though we'd never officially asked to be each other's, she was mine, and I was hers—point, blank, period.

A couple of weeks had passed since Rhythm's parents visited. My baby was sad to see them go, but I promised her I would fly them out whenever they were ready to come back. I could say that I enjoyed the time we spent with her people. Her parents were funny as hell, and her dad was that guy. He didn't play about his baby, and he said it gave him comfort that I didn't either.

I was glad he could see I cared for her. I was also glad that he came to me like a man and not some nigga on the street about her. I believed that respect was earned, not given. I wouldn't give my respect just because somebody felt like they deserved it, no matter who they were.

Over the last couple of weeks, she'd introduced me to a number of her family members via FaceTime. Much like her parents, they were all warm and welcoming. They made her promise to visit soon so we could get a face-to-face introduction. I'd never been down south, and I wasn't sure what to expect. Rhythm assured me that at least with her family, I'd be shown some southern hospitality.

It was Friday night.

Tonight, we were going to a banquet my baby had been invited to. It was a charity event, and all proceeds were being donated to research efforts in Alzheimer's and dementia. With Grams being so close to my heart, I had to go. I already had a check made out to do my part.

I stood in front of the mirror in my five-piece black-on-black suit with the matching black loafers. My hair was freshly cut, and my beard was freshly lined up. I honestly hated wearing suits, but for special occasions, I'd make an exception.

"Baby! We're gonna be late!" I yelled into the bathroom.

"I'm coming!"

She'd been in the bathroom for a good forty-five minutes now. I wasn't sure what she was doing, but when she opened the bathroom door, it all made sense. She stepped out in a strapless black sequin gown that touched the floor and hugged her every curve. Her naturally curly hair was bone straight and hung with a middle part. White-gold diamond jewelry adorned her neck, wrists, and arms. Her face held a light beat of makeup.

She was perfect... flawless.

"Damn," I mumbled.

She smirked. "I know. I look good, don't I?"

She did a little twirl for me then struck a pose.

"You look gorgeous. I can already see me giving out a few dirty looks tonight."

She giggled as she walked over and slid her arms around my waist. "I'm all yours. You have nothing to worry about."

"I'm never worried, love." I pecked her lips. "Come on and get your pictures so we can head out."

She eagerly went to fetch her phone so she could snap a few pictures. I noticed a while ago that she loved to capture intimate moments. I rarely saw her post them online, but every so often, she would sit and flip through her photo album and smile at the memories. She told me everything didn't have to be shared with the world. Some things were fine being meant just for you.

I could understand that. I wasn't big on social media. While I had it, it was rare that I posted anything that wasn't business related. I couldn't stand people who posted everything online and then complained about everybody being in their business.

After snapping her pictures, we finally headed out of the house, hopped in my truck and made our way to the event venue. Cars were already lined up, waiting to be valet parked. After about ten minutes, we finally handed over my keys and headed inside. The space was immaculate and grand. It was clear that the elite of the elite were in the building tonight.

After dropping our checks in the donation box, Rhythm and I headed into the event space. It was packed, but we had a table with Nique and the baller she met named Anthony Diego. I liked him for her. He was a good guy that wasn't in any trouble. Anytime I heard anything about him, it was for his avid community service. His story was well known and one he didn't mind sharing. He grew up in the system and worked hard to make good grades so he could get a basketball scholarship to pay for his degree in social work. I had mad respect for him.

"It's about time you two got here," Nique said, standing to greet us with hugs.

"Somebody here took almost an hour in the bathroom," I said.

"Don't come for my friend! It was worth it because she looks damn good."

She twirled Rhythm around, who was smiling from ear to ear.

Anthony chuckled. "She took forever, too. I guess birds of a feather flock together."

Nique scoffed, causing him to laugh and lean over to kiss her cheek. He then extended his hand to shake mine. Rhythm and I took our seats, and she moved hers a little closer so she could rest in the cusp of my arm. For a while, we sat talking with Nique and Anthony and people watching.

People began taking their seats so the speeches could begin. While several people took the stage, dinner was served. I was pleasantly surprised that the food was actually good. I just knew we'd be leaving here and going to get a burger tonight.

Eva Langford, the president of the organization responsible for tonight's event, took the stage once more. Everyone looked confused, like this wasn't a part of the plans. The room quieted down as she spoke into the mic.

"I know her," Rhythm said quietly. "She's the one that sent me the invite."

"I know this wasn't on the program tonight and it was intentional. There is a very special person here tonight that I would like to shine a light on. I've had the pleasure of meeting this beautiful young lady. She's such a light, and the work she does is filled with so much love and exceptional care. As many of you know, my father was diagnosed with Alzheimer's a year ago. His condition has progressed, and it's been very hard on him and the family.

"A friend of mine recommended this young lady to me, and I can honestly say that since my father has been in the care of her and her team, it's made all the difference in the world in how we accommodate him. She always stresses that he may have the disease, but the disease doesn't have to have him. Because of what my family has learned from her, my father's quality of life has improved. I am so grateful to her. I know that the same way she's touched my family's life, she's touched so many others.

"I've had the pleasure of speaking with her staff and many families of her clients. They all say such wonderful things about her, and I know them to be true. Whether it's Alzheimer's, dementia, or whatever, she always gives one hundred percent of herself. Tonight, I'd like to recognize and present Dr. Rhythm Baker of The Baker Method with the Occupational Therapy Award of Merit."

Beside me, Rhythm gasped. "Oh my God!"

"Ms. Baker, if you're here, please come up and accept your award."

The crowd erupted with applause.

"Congratulations, love," I said, kissing her cheek.

I stood and helped a shocked Rhythm from her seat. She nervously made her way up to the stage.

"That's my bestie!" Nique yelled.

My baby was a little teary-eyed as she hugged Eva and accepted her award. I stood with my phone, ensuring that I captured this moment for her to watch later.

"Wow... I um... I wasn't expecting this. Thank you so much for this honor. I love what I do. I know dealing with a loved one who's no longer the version you remember can be difficult. I know it can be frustrating, and you may want to give up. It takes hard work and dedication to be a caregiver. At The Baker Method, we strive to alleviate some of that pressure.

"We care about not only your loved ones, but you, too. It's been an honor to work with so many families to improve their quality of life. We may not have a cure for dementia or Alzheimer's, but there is so much we can do to ensure that our loved ones live the rest of their days as happy and healthy as possible. I thank you for this award and the recognition. I promise to continue to do my part in this fight. Thank you."

Again, she hugged Eva before returning to her seat. Nique, Anthony, and I greeted her with hugs and congrats. She absolutely deserved that award.

"I'm so proud of you, baby," I said, cupping her face.

"Thank you."

Eva spoke into the microphone again. "We also have a few people who wanted to sing your praises, Ms. Baker."

As we took our seats, she motioned to the back, and a screen dropped from the ceiling. The lights dimmed, and soon, a video began to play. On screen were testimonials from several families Rhythm had serviced over the years. She couldn't contain her tears as each person had nothing but beautiful things to say about her. When my mother and Grams popped on the screen, she cried harder. I was surprised my mom hadn't mentioned this to me, but she probably thought I'd ruin the surprise.

By the end of the video, Rhythm's makeup was beginning to run. She excused herself to the bathroom with Nique to gather herself, leaving Anthony and me alone.

"Did you know about this?" he asked.

"Nah, I didn't. But she deserves it."

"I saw the pride in your face when she was up there, man. You look like you're in love."

I grinned. "Shit, maybe I am."

I thought about it. Maybe it was too soon. Maybe she didn't feel the same way, but everything in my heart was telling me that wasn't the case. We connected and vibed too well for it not to be something deeper. I wouldn't push it. I wouldn't force it to be said. When the time was right and the moment was perfect, it would happen.

If I believed in nothing else, I believed in fate. Grams always told me that what was for me would always be for me. She was it. She was mine, and there was no way I was ever letting up off her.

Chapter Twenty-Nine

Rhythm

Today had been the longest day.

For some reason, I had back-to-back clients. I missed my lunch break, and I barely had time to pee. By the time we closed down for the day, I was exhausted and mentally drained. All I wanted to do was eat, shower, and lay up under my man so he could baby me.

I smiled to myself as I thought about him.

That man had lit up my life since the moment I met him. It had only been a couple of months, yet I knew we had something special. He was everything I could ever want and then some.

The sound of my phone ringing broke me from my thoughts. I looked down to see Channing calling. I smiled at his contact picture. It was a picture of us from the time we spent in Malibu. We looked so happy. Well, I looked happy. He looked like he wanted to devour me.

I swiped the button to answer.

"Hey, baby."

"Hey, love. You off?"

"Yes, finally. I'm gathering my things now. I'm so damn tired, and I'm starving. I haven't eaten since breakfast."

"Come on over. I'm cooking. How about I run you a bubble bath? Maybe light some candles... put on some music."

I giggled. "That sounds wonderful."

"Well bring your fine ass on over here so I can cater to you."

"I'm on my way. I..."

I paused, hesitating in what I really wanted to say.

"You what?" he asked.

"Nothing. I'll see you soon."

"Okay. Drive safe."

"I will."

We disconnected the call, and I sat back in my chair.

"I love you..." I mumbled.

I hadn't been able to bring myself to say those words to him yet. It didn't feel real, but it was what I felt. I'd spent so much time with this man over the last couple of months. I'd gotten to know him and the people closest to him. I got to see him beyond what people saw of him in the studio, and I loved every part of him.

So many times, I found myself ready to utter those three words, but I hadn't. I didn't know if he was there yet. Sure, he cared for me. He showed it in every way. But did he love me? *Could* he love me?

I sighed as I stood from the chair and grabbed my bag. As I left my office, I fell in line with the rest of the staff preparing to leave the building. We said our goodbyes, and I locked the door before heading to my car. As I rounded the corner, I stopped dead in my tracks at the sight of a man standing next to my car.

Raheem.

After the night he followed me home, I hadn't spoken to him at all, so I was a little weary of him being here now. Reaching into my purse, I grabbed my pepper spray and made my way toward him.

"What are you doing here?" I asked.

He raised his hands in surrender. "I just wanted to talk."

"About?"

He pushed off from the car and stepped closer to me. "I need to apologize to you."

"Oh, really?" I crossed my arms. "I'm listening."

"I'm sorry for the pain I've caused you. I was in a fucked-up frame of mind, and I was wrong. I did and said shit to you that you never deserved, especially not from a nigga telling you he loved you. I'm ashamed that I wanted you for as long as I did and mistreated you when I got you. You have always been one of the sweetest people I know. Even when I didn't have shit, you never treated me any different. I fucked up royally with Imani. I disrespected you too many times on so many levels. You were a great girlfriend, Rhythm. You should have left me a long time ago, and I should have let you go."

"You're right about that. I would have respected you more if you'd just told me you didn't want to be with me."

"I did want to be with you. My actions say otherwise, but it's true. I loved you. Hell, I still love you. No woman has ever wanted just me. You were a rare find, and I fumbled that ball. You deserve all the happiness in the world. I'll forever hate myself for not being that for you."

"No need for that. Because of you, I'm right where I need to be."

He chuckled. "Watson being good to you?"

"He is."

"Good. You gotta admit, you being with him was messy."

I shrugged. "Maybe it was. It wasn't intentional, but I don't regret meeting him. He sees me... He hears me."

He nodded. "I'm happy for you."

I raised an eyebrow, causing him to laugh.

"I'm serious. He's a good dude. He's not out here in these streets. Other than the shit with me, every time I heard his name, nothing but good things were said about him. You deserve someone who loves you the way he seems to."

"I do." I shifted my weight from one foot to the other. "Is that all?"

He nodded. "Yeah... yeah, I guess so."

"Good. I'll see you around."

Again, he nodded. He shoved his hand into his pocket and walked away with his head down. Just as I was climbing into my car, he called my name.

"Rhythm?"

"What?"

"Happiness looks good on you. I wish you two the best."

I hesitated for a moment, contemplating if I wanted to respond. After a moment, I declined a response and climbed into my car. It wasn't that I wished bad upon him. I just had nothing left to say. Our relationship had run its course, and I was done. If I never spoke to him again, I'd be perfectly fine with that.

Without another word, I cranked up and headed for my man.

* * *

I pulled into Channing's driveway about thirty minutes later. Traffic had been hell and put me behind my normal arrival time. I'd let Channing know when I was about ten minutes away. Grabbing my things, I got out of the car and headed up the front steps then inside.

The heavenly smell of whatever Channing was cooking caused my mouth to water. I placed my things down as Koda came running around the corner to me. I smiled as I stooped to greet her.

"Hi, baby!"

She put her paws on my shoulders and rested her head against mine.

"My sweet girl. Did you miss me?"

Koda had become like my child. She was always so happy to see me or Channing. Every time I came over, she greeted me with so much love, and my heart couldn't take it.

"Let's go see daddy. Come on."

I stood and followed her into the kitchen where I found my man putting a pan in the oven. Closing the door, he stood upright and looked at me. A smile spread across his face.

"Hey, baby," he said, sauntering over to me.

"Hey, babe."

He pulled me into his arms and lifted me onto the countertop. Finding his way between my legs, he cupped my face and kissed me softly.

"I missed you, mama."

"I missed you, too. You won't believe who showed up at my job today."

"Who?"

"Raheem."

He frowned. "The fuck he want?"

I sighed before running him the story of Raheem's surprise visit.

"He said he wanted to apologize for everything. That he was wrong, and I deserved to be happy. He actually wished us the best."

"You believe him?"

I shrugged. "It doesn't matter. That chapter is closed, and I don't need to reread it ever again." I cupped his face and pecked his lips. "All the man I need is right here."

"You damn right."

I giggled, and a smile finally spread across his lips.

"Your bath is ready. Why don't you get undressed and soak?"

"Thank you, baby."

We shared another kiss before he lifted me from the counter and placed me back on my feet. I headed upstairs to his bedroom. As soon as I entered, soft R&B music began playing from the speaker in the bathroom. I stripped down and walked into the en suite.

Candles were lit all around the room. The tub was filled with bubbles, with rose petals scattered about. Next to the tub was an ice bucket with a bottle of my favorite wine and a big glass because he knew how I felt about my wine.

I dipped a toe in to test the water, before sliding my whole body in and releasing a relaxed sigh. After pouring a nice serving of wine, I rested my back against the tub. Closing my eyes, I let the smooth sounds of Patti Labelle's "If Only You Knew" lull me into a Zen state.

I was so relaxed that I didn't even hear Channing come in until he placed a kiss on my forehead. I looked up to see him standing over me with a plate of food. He placed it on the counter and left the bathroom, returning shortly with a stool. Placing it next to the tub, he grabbed the plate and took a seat.

"How are you feeling?" he asked.

"Much better. I needed this."

I peered at the plate of macaroni, mashed potatoes, and pot roast in his hands.

"Is that for me?"

"Of course it is."

He forked a helping of macaroni and blew on it before placing it to my lips.

"Open."

I didn't hesitate to open my mouth and accept the offer. The flavors danced on my pallet, causing me to moan at the goodness. I loved when he cooked for me. It was like someone's grandmother entered his spirit, and he cooked with the guidance of his ancestors.

"Good?" he asked.

"Amazing. You could have been a chef in another life."

He chuckled. "I like to cook, but there are very few people I'd cook for. I'd hate to have to tell a muthafucka about themselves if they get disrespectful about my shit."

I giggled. "You are always ready to tell somebody off."

"If you don't let people know that they got you fucked up, who else will?"

I rolled my eyes. "I guess. How was your day?"

"It was decent. I had a meeting."

"Oh? What for?"

He grinned, and I gathered that it must have been big news.

"I've decided to open my own record label."

My eyes widened. "Baby! That's great news! I'm so proud of you!"

"Thank you."

"What's it called?"

"Capo Music."

"Why didn't you tell me about this?"

"I really didn't tell anybody. I've been going back and forth with it for a while now. Sure, I was happy with artists and their labels seeking me out for my services, but I feel like I have much more to offer. I know a lot of people, and I've learned a lot in this industry. It's time to move on to bigger and better things."

I smiled. "I love that for you. I know you are gonna be great. We have to celebrate."

He smirked. "The sooner you get out of this tub, the sooner we can."

I gave him a sly smile. "I hear you."

He continued to feed me and tell me all about his vision for his label. Hearing the excitement in his voice told me that he had put a lot of thought into this. I had no doubt that he was going to be one of the biggest things to come out of L.A.

After I finished eating, he left me to take my shower, while he went to eat and take Koda for a walk. By the time I was out of the shower and moisturizing my skin, he came back into the room. Taking the shea butter cream from my hands, he picked up where I left off, continuing my routine. I lay across the bed on my stomach with my head resting against my arms, and he massaged the cream into my skin. A smirk found its way to my face as he caressed my ass cheeks.

"What are you doing, sir?"

I felt the bed dip under his weight. His arm slid under me, and he pulled me up into an arch. I felt the tip of his dick sliding up and down my slit.

"Baby... oooo, shit!"

In one swift movement, he entered me and filled me to the hilt. His strokes were long and hard. My ass clapped loudly against his thighs as he held me in place and fucked me like it would be the last time.

"Oooo, shit... oooo, fuck! Don't stop!"

He slapped my ass hard then smoothed the sting over with his hand.

"Goddamn, that's a beautiful sight!" he declared, slapping it again. "Your pussy is so pretty with my dick in you, love."

"It's your pussy, baby."

"All mine?"

"All yours!"

His hand crept around my neck, and he pulled me upright and against his chest.

"Say it again," he demanded.

"It's all yours, daddy... all yours!"

His other hand came around to strum my clit as he thrusted his hips upward. My teeth sank into my bottom lip as I basked in the feeling of him filling me repeatedly. Him kissing and sucking on my neck only heightened my arousal. He pushed me forward and gripped my hips as he pounded me from behind.

"Throw that shit back," he commanded.

My hips had a mind of their own as I rode him with perfect synchronicity. My pussy was juicing up so bad that I could feel my essence dripping down my thighs. No other man had ever gotten me as wet as he could. None of them had ever handled me the way he did. My body responded to him in ways beyond my control, and I loved it. When he took ownership of her, she always fully submitted.

"I'm gonna cum.... fuck! I'm cumming!"

"Bust that shit."

My orgasm hit full force. As I was cumming, he pulled out, and the next thing I felt was his mouth on my pussy as he flicked and sucked my clit.

"Ch-Channing!"

"I know you got one more in you, love. Make my pussy spit for me."

He didn't have to tell me twice. My body erupted, and I collapsed against the bed. As I lay there panting, he flipped me over onto my back and climbed between my legs. With one hand resting beside my head, the other snaked to the back of my neck. He pulled me upright and planted the sexiest kiss on my lips. My hands clipped his face as I opened my mouth to receive his tongue. I didn't fight him for dominance. I completely gave him control. For what seemed like forever, our lips remained intertwined. When we finally came up for air, I looked deep into his eyes.

"I love you," I whispered.

He smiled. "I love you, too. Is that what you wanted to tell me earlier?"

"I... yes. I just didn't know how to say it. I love you, and I'm in love with you."

His smile widened. "I'ma have to let my mama know she was right. Now I owe her a pamper day."

I scoffed and slapped his chest. "You made a bet with your mother!"

"Technically, she made a bet with me. I didn't ask for anything, babe."

I rolled my eyes. "Me and your mother need to have a talk. I can't believe she's out here making bets at my expense."

He chuckled. "Cut my girl some slack. She helped me come to terms with my own love for you."

He cupped my chin and stared deep into my eyes.

"I love you, Rhythm. Meeting you was by chance, but loving you is by far the best thing I've experienced. You're it for me, baby."

Tears filled my eyes.

Loving him was the best decision that had ever been made for me too. It was unexpected, but my mama always told me great things happened when you *least* expected it.

Epilogue: One Year Later

Channing

I looked down at the speech in my hands for what seemed like the millionth time. I'd written and rewritten it until it felt right. After being in the industry for so many years, I was finally taking the biggest step of my career. Tonight was the grand opening of Capo Music.

While I'd purchased the building and had it completely renovated, I took my time in selecting engineers and my roster of artists. Some were new and unheard of, some came from being independent, and a few had been in the game for a long time. Either way, I appreciated them for trusting me with their careers.

"Baby, I know you aren't reading that speech again."

I looked back to find my beautiful wife standing at the bottom of the stairs with her hands on her hips. Damn, she looked good. Tonight, she was sporting a sexy little black dress that stopped right above her knees and black stilettos. Her hair was pulled into a sleek, low ponytail, and she was laced in diamonds.

I licked my lips as she approached me. I was one lucky man. We'd gotten married three months ago in a lavish ceremony on the beach. I'd flown her family out and put them up in hotels so they could be a part of our special day. It didn't take me years to know what I wanted with her.

While our union might not have a fairy-tale beginning, we'd shared many fairy-tale moments, our wedding being one of them. Seeing her walk down the aisle with her father stirred up so many emotions in me. I'd never been against getting married, but to actually *get* married hit different. I cried at the altar then took her to consummate halfway through our reception.

"I just wanna make sure I said all I needed to say, baby," I defended.

She shook her head. "You crossed your T's and dotted your I's. I know this because I've read every version of this speech." She cupped my face and softly kissed me. "You're gonna do great, understood?"

"I hear you," I said, pulling her into my chest. "You're looking like tonight might be the night I get my son."

She giggled. I'd been trying to get her pregnant for what seemed like forever now.

"Tonight might be your lucky night," she replied.

"Then let's get the hell outta here so we can get back. Go on and walk up ahead of me and give me a little inspiration."

She laughed but obliged me by adding a little extra sway in her hips as we walked out the door.

Twenty minutes later, we were pulling up at headquarters. I parked in the back of the building, and we entered through the private entrance. Hand in hand, we made our way to the area where I was supposed to meet my publicist, Keri. She was a mogul in the industry, so snagging her had been a must.

She stood on the balcony that overlooked the entrance, talking on the phone. When she saw us, she smiled and ended the call.

"There you are! Congratulations!" She hugged us both before jumping right into business mode. "You have quite the crowd. Every news outlet in the area is here. Every major blog is asking for interviews. There is also quite the gathering of people hoping to give you their demos. The doors haven't even opened, and you're in high demand. How are you feeling?"

"Nervous," Rhythm answered. "He's gone over that speech fifty times tonight alone."

"It has not been fifty," I defended.

"It's close enough, Keri."

She laughed. "I'm sure you'll do great. I'm gonna head down and talk them up before you come give your speech."

"Are my mother and grandmother here yet?"

"Yes. They got here about fifteen minutes ago."

"Is Grams good?"

"She's calm. Her nurse is prepared to make an exit if she gets overwhelmed."

I nodded. Over the last year, Gram's dementia had gotten worse. Her moments of clarity were very few and far between. Her aggression had gotten worse as well. The day she attacked my mother because she didn't know who she was, was the day we realized that we couldn't do this with just me and my mama anymore.

It broke our hearts to put her in an assisted living facility, but that was what it came to. We made it a point to visit her at least three times a week. Most times, she didn't know who we were, and the visits didn't last long. By the grace of God, she'd been having clarity for the last day.

When I went to see her yesterday, I told her all about Capo Music. She asked me if she could come tonight, and I couldn't say no. She was a major factor in me being where I was. Dementia or not, I wanted her here.

"I'm gonna go join everybody," Rhythm said, squeezing my hand.

I was sure she was going to be an extra set of hands in case Grams needed her. Even though she wasn't her client anymore, she still played a major role in her care.

"Okay, baby."

Epilogue: One Year Later

She cupped my face and kissed me sweetly. "I love you. You're gonna do great."

"I love you too."

"Get ready," Keri said. "It's almost time!"

She patted my shoulder before she and Rhythm headed downstairs. I looked over the balcony at all the people waiting for me to make an appearance. I said a silent prayer, thanking God for His grace and mercy. The thing I'd contemplated for the longest was finally coming full circle.

* * *

Rhythm

"Is he nervous?" Ms. Watson asked from beside me.

"You know your son. He'll say he's not, but he is. I've been telling him it's okay to be nervous. This is a monumental moment for him."

"It is."

Keri had taken center stage and was talking to the crowd. There were so many people here and still more waiting to come inside. Aside from me, his mother, and Grams, Nique was here with her baller bae, my parents flew in, and of course, Emerald and Rhyon were here. I knew it was nothing but God that gave Grams clarity to spend this night with him.

I smiled at the thought of everyone showing up to support my husband.

I was still getting used to calling him that.

Never did I imagine a one-night stand turning into this. His proposal was beautiful. Not only had he asked my father's permission, but he flew my parents out to be a part of the moment. I was shocked the morning I woke up and found both of them sitting in his kitchen eating breakfast.

He'd flown them in the night before and had a car bring them to the house. I was so happy to see them that I'd cried. He told me he wanted to take us out for dinner and send me and my mother shopping for something to wear, courtesy of him. I didn't even think anything of it when Nique came along. We spent hours shopping and being pampered while he and my father hung out with Nique's man.

That night, we all got dressed to go eat. Turns out, he'd rented out the entire restaurant for our dinner party. When we walked in, there were rose petals leading into the dining area which was flooded with even more roses and a huge marry me sign. I started crying, and it lasted all the way through his speech and putting the ring on my finger. It was a moment with him that was added to all the other moments with him I wouldn't forget.

"And now, without further ado, I present the man of the hour. The owner, founder, and CEO of Capo Music, Channing Watson!"

The crowd erupted with cheers and applause as my man made his way down the stairs to the podium. I beamed with pride as he took center stage. The crowd quieted down as he took the mic.

"Good evening. Now, if you know me, you know I don't do too many speeches, so we are gonna keep this short and sweet."

Chuckles and murmurs of agreement went up from the crowd.

"I appreciate everyone for coming out to support the grand opening of Capo Music. Unbeknownst to many, this had been a dream of mine for a very long time, so tonight is special for me. To Keri, thank you for taking me on as a client. I know you'll have big shit poppin' for us. To my engineers, thank you for bringing your talents to the new mainstage. To my artists, thank you for trusting me with your careers. We're finna touch major money over here.

"To my mother and grandmother... thank you for loving me unconditionally. Thank you for believing in me, praying for me, and keeping me on the straight and narrow. Everything I am is owed to the both of you. I love you, and I thank God every day that he blessed me with two beautiful, strong black women to teach me everything I needed to know about being a man."

Ms. Watson and Grams both blew him kisses. His eyes settled on me, and he smiled.

Epilogue: One Year Later

"To my beautiful wife... damn I'm lucky to have you."

I couldn't help but to grin and blush.

"God broke the mold when He made you. Thank you for allowing me to love you. Y'all have no idea the work this woman puts in behind the scenes. You may not see her at the forefront day in and day out, but know she is always right by my side with everything I do. Many of the artists under Capo, she helped me discover. The details you find in this building are all her. Background or forefront, Mrs. Watson is a big part of Capo Music. I appreciate you, baby. I adore you, and I love you with my soul."

I mouthed, "I love you too," and blew him a kiss.

"All right, I think I've taken up enough of your time. I'm sure you're all anxious to party and do a tour, so I won't hold you up. Welcome to Capo Music."

The crowd clapped and cheered as he descended the stairs and came over to us. I waited patiently as he greeted everyone before coming to me. My smile widened as he pulled me into his arms.

"Congratulations, baby," I said, cupping his face. "I'm so proud of you."

"Thank you, love. Y'all ready for the tour?"

Everyone agreed. The crowd had already broken off into groups to follow the guides giving the tours. For the next thirty minutes, Channing showed our family the ins and outs of his new venture. The smile never left his face, and I couldn't wait to get him home to give him a whole other reason to smile.

We finally migrated into the venue portion of the building where the party was. He said it didn't make sense to pay for a venue space to host events or album releases when he could have his own. The building he bought was huge, so why not take advantage of the space.

Currently, we were on the dance floor, vibing to music from one of his up-and-coming artists. We were in our own world when someone approached us. Looking up, I was surprised to see Raheem. I hadn't spoken to him since he apologized to me in the parking lot at work. When Channing and I got married, fans never let him live that shit down. They were tagging him in pictures and videos. People asked him about it in interviews, and he always elected not to comment. I wasn't sure if it was the label or if he was over it, but I appreciated it.

Channing wrapped a protective arm around me and pulled me into his side. Raheem raised his hands in mock surrender.

"I just wanted to congratulate you," he said. "I know you're bringing the competition."

"Ain't no competition. It's enough room for all of us to eat."

"I respect that." He swallowed hard. "I um... I know I spoke to Rhythm, but I don't think I ever apologized to you back then, Channing. I was on some other shit, and my ego was bruised. I sincerely apologize for the way I acted. Rhythm is and has always been a good woman. She deserves the world. I couldn't give her what she needed, but I see that you can. I'm happy for you both." He extended his hand. "Man to man, I'm sorry."

Channing looked down at his hand for a moment before shaking it.

"Thank you."

"Maybe I can get you on my next album?"

"You pushing it."

Raheem chuckled. "I'm joking. Even though we make magic, I completely understand. Y'all have a good night. Congratulations again."

He nodded before disappearing into the crowd. I looked up at Channing.

"Well... I wasn't expecting that," I said.

"Me either. I wonder who let that nigga in. I should fire their ass."

I playfully slapped his chest. "Don't. Everything's good. You got me, and I'm not going anywhere."

"Damn right you ain't."

He pulled me into his arms and kissed my lips. A smirk spread across his face.

"Mrs. Watson?"

"Yes, Mr. Watson?"

"I do believe my office hasn't been broken in yet. What do you say we dip outta here for a little bit?"

I smirked. "I knew that was coming, and I'm ready for you."

"Oh, really?"

I leaned in and whispered in his ear. "I'm not wearing any panties."

He chuckled. "Easy access. Bring your ass on."

I didn't hesitate to follow as he grabbed my hand and led me out of the venue space. Honestly, I wouldn't hesitate to follow this man anywhere. He made me the happiest I'd ever been. To go from crying and fretting over a nigga that was too busy doing him to think about me, to having a man that didn't play about me in any capacity was a blessing.

My connection to this man was the most natural thing I'd ever experienced. I wasn't forced to be or act like anyone other than myself. My identity wasn't wrapped up in his career, and neither was my image. Yet and still, at the end of the day, I was his woman and his wife. He was as loyal to me as I was to him. He saw me for what I brought to the table whether I was in the background or the forefront.

That was the difference between him and Raheem.

He understood that support from any end was *still* support, and he appreciated it. I was showered with love and affection. My heart was safe and well taken care of, and I was immensely respected. My days of having the blues over a man were long gone. These days, I sang love songs at the top of my lungs because I felt every word, and it was all because of him.

The End

Afterword

Thank you for reading *Rhythm's Blues*. I hope you enjoyed Rhythm and Channing's story as much as I enjoyed writing it! Feel free to connect with me on Facebook, Twitter, and Instagram! Don't forget to sign up for my mailing list for sneak peeks, giveaways, and more!

Much love,
    Kimberly Brown

Facebook: https://www.facebook.com/authorkimberlybrown

Facebook Readers Group:
https://www.facebook.com/groups/kimberlyscozycorner

Instagram: https://www.instagram.com/authorkimberlybrown

Twitter: https://twitter.com/AuthorKBrown

Website: https://www.authorkimberlybrown.com

Also by Kimberly Brown

Series:

All For Love Series:

Pretty Caged Bird

Tame Me

With Everything in Me

Against All Odds Series:

Beyond Measures: An Urban Romance

More Than Words

After All Is Said And Done

The Jareau Family Series

Where Love Blooms: A Jareau Family Novel (Book 1)

Deep In My Soul: A Jareau Family Novel (Book 2)

Signed, Sealed, Delivered: A Jareau Family Wedding

The Burial of a Player: A Jareau Family Novel (Book 3)

I Commit To You: A Jareau Family Wedding

Strip Me Bare: A Jareau Family Novel (Book 4)

From This Day Forth: A Jareau Family Wedding(Book 3)

Nothing Like You: A Jareau Family Novel (Book 5)

Love Me Like You Do: A Jareau Family Wedding (Book 4)

Not Finished Loving You

Hold Me While You Wait

The Perfection of a Moment

Courage To Love Again

<u>Mailing List Exclusives:</u>

If I Fall For You: A Valentine's Day Short

BLP

Visit bit.ly/readBLP to join our mailing list for sneak peeks and release day links!

Let's connect on social media!
Facebook - B. Love Publications
Twitter - @blovepub
Instagram - @blovepublications

We hate errors, but we are human! If the B. Love team leaves any grammatical errors behind, do us a kindness and send them to us directly in an email to blovepublications@gmail.com
with ERRORS as the subject line.

As always, if you enjoyed this book, please leave a review on Amazon/Goodreads, recommend it on social media and/or to a friend, and mark it as READ on your Goodreads profile.

By the Book with B Podcast: bit.ly/bythebookwithb

Printed in Great Britain
by Amazon